Beach Haven

T. I. LOWE

Tyndale House Publishers, Inc.
Carol Stream, Illinois

Visit Tyndale online at www.tyndale.com.

Visit T. I. Lowe at www.tilowe.com.

TYNDALE and Tyndale's quill logo are registered trademarks of Tyndale House Publishers, Inc.

Beach Haven

Designed by Faceout Studio, Jeff Miller

Edited by Kathryn S. Olson

Published in association with the literary agency of Browne & Miller Literary Associates, LLC, 52 Village Place, Hinsdale, IL 60521.

For information about special discounts for bulk purchases, please contact Tyndale House Publishers at csresponse@tyndale.com, or call 1-800-323-9400.

ISBN 978-1-4964-4040-2

Printed in the United States of America

25 24 23 22 21 20 19
7 6 5 4 3 2 1

To my daughter, Lydia Lu.
Dare to be different.

"For I know the plans I have for you," says the LORD. *"They are plans for good and not for disaster, to give you a future and a hope."*

JEREMIAH 29:11

BEACH HAVEN

1

Weaving through a jungle of the most outlandish antiques he'd ever come across, Lincoln Cole was dumbfounded and intrigued all at once. Surrounded by unusually dressed pieces of furniture, he did a three-sixty and scratched at the scruff on his cheek. The scruff indicated he was more than a few days past needing a shave, but the rebellion that had taken root in him since the injury he sustained in Syria had overruled grooming protocol that morning. Waking up from the recurring nightmare often left him too raw to focus on such mundane things. At least he had managed a shower and a fresh change of clothes.

Whimsical feminine humming somehow found its way to him as he suppressed the limp wanting to reside in his left leg while hobbling another few steps forward. Although it was a sunny day in late September, his leg was telling him the pleasant weather wouldn't last for very long.

Nothing good ever lasts long . . .

Lincoln huffed in frustration over his own thoughts and stood semihidden in a section of old desks. He cast his gaze upward and blinked a few times. Various tables and chairs were suspended from the ceiling. A few had been converted into light fixtures, while the rest of them looked like they were being held hostage by thick cables.

"Good morning," a cheery voice came from behind him. "Welcome to Bless This Mess."

Keeping his focus on the ceiling, Lincoln spoke the first thing to flicker through his mind. "Is that even safe?" He pointed to the pieces of furniture that appeared to be floating above their heads.

"Oh yes. Code inspectors have deemed my mess safe."

The woman's teasing voice finally had Lincoln turning in her direction. Peering at him from the other side of a wooden hutch that had been transformed into a bath vanity was a sprite of a woman with the wildest head of golden-red curls he'd ever seen. The tips were lighter as if the sun had reached down and stolen the color. She closely resembled the mosaic fairy he'd seen on the outside of the building.

Clearing his throat, he offered a curt "Good."

A smile began to blossom across the lively woman's face as she smoothed some kind of flowy blouse with her petite hand, causing a gaudy collection of bracelets to clang against one another. Lincoln assessed her as he'd been trained to do in the military. He measured her no bigger than a minute and figured he could apprehend her with one hand tied behind his back, but he considered those big green eyes of hers and cataloged them as her secret weapon. They sparkled, but that wasn't what set off the warning bells. No, those eyes were watching him way too closely and had already seen way more than they should. Assessment complete, he began to slowly back away.

"I have the perfect piece for you." She held an index finger in the air, halting his attempted retreat. She skipped off in the opposite direction, sending the spirals of soft red-and-blonde hair into a dance. "I'm Opal, by the way," she said quickly over her shoulder.

She disappeared from sight, but he could hear the banging and clattering from his two o'clock, giving away her location. "I didn't come here for furniture."

"Oh, that's okay. This piece was meant for you, nonetheless, so I insist on you taking it." Her grunts came from the back and sounded like she was struggling with something.

Sighing, Lincoln looked heavenward at the craziness on the ceiling one last time before walking through the maze to find her. He stopped cold in his tracks when he found her sitting on a soldier's footlocker.

"I found this on a junking trip last year." Opal smoothed her tiny hand over the thick gray cushion that had been fitted on the top. It reminded Lincoln of a military-issue wool coat. "For some reason, I just knew it needed to be transformed into a bench seat. Possibly for an entry piece where someone can sit and remove or put on their shoes. Or maybe at the foot of a bed." She swung her feet back and forth, looking like a little kid. Flip-flops peeked from the edges of her fraying bell-bottom jeans each time her legs swayed forward.

Not letting himself get caught in the confusing inquiry of where she found such an odd pair of jeans, Lincoln crossed his arms and regarded the piece suspiciously. "Why'd you make it so tall?" His eyes dropped to the thick wooden spindles she'd used for the legs. They were painted a neutral gray to coordinate with the creamy beige used on the trunk. It was obvious she'd put a lot of thought into the piece, even restenciling the ID number along the front side in the same gray as the legs.

"I had a feeling the owner would need the extra leg

space. What are you, six-four?" She gave him a swift once-over.

Six-five. "Close enough."

She smirked like she had a secret. "If you're not here for furniture, then what are you here for?"

Lincoln moved his eyes away from the peculiar woman and swept them over the menagerie of furniture pieces while rubbing a hand through his long brown hair. Haircuts were another ritual he'd allowed to die several months ago, right along with his military career.

After giving her question some thought, Lincoln answered honestly, "I'm not sure." He turned and began moving through the rows as quick as his achy leg would carry him.

"You forgot your bench!" Opal called from behind him. "And you didn't even introduce yourself!"

Her petitions did nothing to slow his already-sluggish getaway. He didn't stop until he was piled back into his Jeep and heading down the beachfront road.

"Smooth, Cole. Real smooth." He groaned and released one tight-fisted pound against the steering wheel. Between the throb in his knee and the unsettling encounter with the store's owner, all he wanted to do was go back to his beach cottage and hide from the feeling that he didn't fit anywhere anymore. The doctors had done the best they could with his knee, putting enough hardware in his leg for him to be considered part cyborg, but no bolt or pin could put his destroyed life back together.

The promise he'd made to meet his buddy Carter for a late breakfast trumped the desire to hide. No matter how many vicissitudes had occurred in his life, Lincoln Cole still remained a man of his word. So instead of doing what his bones ached to do, Lincoln pulled up at Driftwood

Diner and made his way inside, where he found Carter was already perched on a stool at the counter.

"You eating without me?" Lincoln gave Carter a manly slap on the shoulder while inspecting an untouched plate of delicious-looking fare—biscuits and gravy, bacon, French toast, and eggs.

Carter stood and gave him a bear hug. Lincoln cringed at the contact. The Cole family was not an affectionate bunch. Handshakes from the men and hugs from the women that were so brief they could hardly constitute as hugs were what he was used to receiving. Carter and his family were the complete opposite, offering long embraces and draping arms over each other's shoulders without thought.

Carter finally released him and gestured for him to have a seat. "I was beginning to think you ditched me. Good to see you, man."

"Sorry. This bum knee won't let me get anything done fast. It's good to see you too." Lincoln stifled a grunt as he settled on the stool beside Carter. Moving in and unpacking the last few days had stiffened his leg considerably, making him feel more like a decrepit old geezer than the thirty-three-year-old he was. He pulled in a deep breath, stealing the enticing aroma of fried bacon and rich, robust coffee. "This place looks like it's ready to collapse, but it sure does smell good."

"The dilapidated shack is part of the charm, but wait until you taste the food." Carter waved over a tall blonde. "Josie, you think you could bring my buddy Lincoln one of your Hungry Sailor's Specials?"

"You got it." She offered Lincoln a welcoming smile. "What can I get you to drink?"

Lincoln motioned to Carter's cup. "Coffee would be great, please."

Once the waitress disappeared into the kitchen, Lincoln angled himself on the stool to keep a better eye on the perimeter of the dining area. The place was busy considering it was well past Labor Day, but most of the clientele looked to be made up of fishermen. The telltale signs of fishing bibs and hats gave them away. He noticed a few tables in the back corner occupied by young mothers chatting it up over coffee while their little ones either slept in their carriers or made a gaum in their high chairs.

"You settled in at the cottage all right?" Carter asked as he studied his plate, looking as starved as Lincoln but being polite enough to wait.

"Yeah. It's peaceful for sure." And peace was exactly what he was looking for.

The blonde waitress was back in a flash and placed several plates before him. The savory scents of breakfast meats and a sweet vanilla perfume wafting from a thick stack of French toast had him turning to face the counter.

"Wow." Lincoln picked up his fork and pointed it in the direction of one of Carter's plates. "Why didn't I get any biscuits and gravy?" he asked the waitress. "And is that shrimp in the gravy?"

"A batch of biscuits just came out the oven. I'll bring you out a serving in a minute. We use shrimp instead of sausage."

"It's genius," Carter commented.

Josie only added a timid smile as she placed a cup beside Lincoln's plate and filled it with aromatic coffee.

"Thank you, ma'am." Lincoln tipped his head before taking a sip. Still unable to shake off the bad night's sleep, it was exactly what he needed.

"You're welcome. I'll go grab you some biscuits and gravy." She backtracked to the kitchen.

Lincoln cut into the thick slices of toast and crammed a bite into his mouth. Before he could start chewing, Carter bowed his head and said grace, thanking God for the food and for Lincoln's safe return from overseas. Lincoln, feeling uneasy, waited to take another bite until his friend wrapped up the prayer.

He wasn't on good terms with God as of late. His gran and paps always said God wanted to answer his prayers and to see him prosper. Lincoln had wholeheartedly believed them until a rocket attack showed him just how naive he'd been.

Lincoln came from a long line of Marines. He was a Cole, and Coles were born to protect their country. His grandfather, great-uncle, uncle, and dad had all been career soldiers, and that was Lincoln's projected path. He'd managed almost two tours until an attack in Syria ended his plans, leaving him broken and uncertain of any future. The need for a little space to heal and overcome the shame of letting his family down was one of the reasons he finally accepted his friend August's advice to take a break from Beaufort, South Carolina, and headed up the coast to Sunset Cove.

"When's August going to grace us with his presence?" Lincoln asked between bites, trying to ignore his dismal thoughts.

Carter sopped up the creamy gravy with a chunk of biscuit and chuckled. "That one has been globe-trotting for so long, I think he sometimes forgets he's supposed to grace us with his appearance now and then."

August was Carter's nephew even though the two guys were fairly close in age and acted more like brothers. Lincoln had met them both at a summer ministry camp in Beaufort years ago when they were all teens, before Lincoln became a soldier and August a world-renowned artist. They had instantly clicked and had remained in touch over the years. August was the type of guy to draw others to him, so it was no surprise when Lincoln formed a close-knit bond with him similar to that he would later find with his military brothers. Carter was also a great friend, but he was now in love and that kept the sucker too preoccupied.

"He's back in the States now, though, right?" Lincoln shoved another bite of sweet toast in and followed it with a strip of bacon.

"Yeah. Wrapping up an inner-city art project in New York," Carter explained around a mouthful of food.

Lincoln chewed thoughtfully while musing over August. The guy was an artistic genius with a penchant for hair dye and piercings, and he could create art out of just about anything. Lincoln was right proud of how his friend had used that incredible talent to share with others through an international art ministry that introduced fine arts to the less fortunate. August had also found his place in the world of art. His paintings hung in galleries from California to New York. "He's really made a name for himself, hasn't he?"

Carter's face lit up with pride. "He sure has. He's gone and gotten famous on us."

Carter Bradford had made a name for himself in his own right. Until recently, he and his fiancée, Dominica, had been members of a praise and worship band that shared their talent at camps and conferences across the United States. Carter was the sound tech guy but knew his way around a piano and could pick about any song on a guitar. Dominica was the bass player. Lincoln didn't know what all was behind their early retirement, but he figured Carter would share it if he wanted to. And if not, Lincoln deduced it was none of his business.

Carter reached over and grabbed the carafe and refilled both their cups with coffee. "August told me he set you up with a job at Bless This Mess. When do you start?" He took another sip of coffee.

Lincoln stared down at his plate. "I'm not working there."

"Why not?" Carter groaned. "August promised Opal you would, and he doesn't make a habit of promising something he can't deliver. Was she upset?"

Lincoln's back tensed up, knowing good and well he'd just made his friend do something he himself wouldn't do. But then again, August had no business making promises on his behalf in the first place. "She had no reason to be upset. I didn't even tell her who I was, so she's fine. That woman doesn't seem to be one for getting upset, anyway." Lincoln shrugged and chomped down on another crispy strip of bacon.

Carter gave him a shrewd look while slowly chewing. "You're selling it a little too hard there, buddy."

"What?" Lincoln shook his head. "Am not." He wiped his mouth with his wadded-up napkin and took a sip of coffee. "Look, I'll have August call her up and explain that his friend changed his mind about the job. No harm, no foul."

"She really needs the help, Linc. Don't leave her hanging."

"She's weird. Why would August even suggest me putting up with her? She some kind of hippie or something?" Lincoln asked just as the waitress placed a piping hot plate full of biscuits and gravy before him.

He was about to dive in when he noticed she wasn't wearing that pleasant smile any longer. "I overheard you, and can I just say that Opal may be weird but she's a good weird. The wisest weird woman you'll ever meet. And I can guarantee you'd have a fun time working with her. No chance of boredom."

Lincoln shifted on the stool, aggravated and a little embarrassed. "I'm not looking for a good time." And he certainly didn't want to deal with Opal's intuitiveness, which he'd noticed even in their brief meeting. He grimaced.

"Clearly," the blonde muttered while walking off.

"Who does she think she is?" Lincoln glared at her retreating back.

"That's Josie. One of Opal's best friends. And you just got on her bad side. I'd leave a fat tip after how you just got caught talking about her friend—or find somewhere else to eat from now on." Carter waved a hand toward Lincoln. "And besides, look at you with all that long hair and your old Converses. *You* look like the hippie." He pushed an elbow into Lincoln's side and tsked. "Even got a rip in the knee of your jeans."

Lincoln suppressed the urge to tuck his shoulder-length hair behind his ear, knowing his friend would call him out on it. And he could razz Carter right back. With shaggy brown hair that the sun had faded quite a bit and wearing his own pair of tattered jeans with a surf logo T-shirt, Carter was a cross between country boy USA and SoCal surfer dude.

He let it go and muttered, "I'm not looking for complication, and that woman screams it."

Carter huffed a laugh. "It's just delivering furniture and helping Opal move stuff around. How's that complicated?"

The way she looked at me was complicated. Lincoln held that comment back and focused on enjoying every bite of breakfast just in case it was the last time he was allowed in. It was a mighty fine meal, so he hoped he wouldn't be banned from the premises.

"Your loss then." Carter shook his head, but after another bite of food, he changed the subject and filled Lincoln in on the fine arts camp he was going to open next summer. The conversation remained on that topic until their plates were clean. After settling the bill, and Lincoln placing a twenty in the tip jar while making sure Josie saw him do it, the guys headed outside.

It was quite a nice, sunny day on the beach with a subtle breeze, but the stunning ocean view wasn't the cause of Lincoln coming to a halt. No, it had everything to do with the redhead sitting on the hood of his Jeep. He eyed her with as much annoyance as possible before sliding his focus to the bench wedged in the back of his vehicle. He knew he should have put the top on.

Crossing his arms, he glared at her. "How'd you manage that?" His head ticked in the direction of the bench. "And just how did you know this was my Jeep?"

Opal didn't make a move to get down as he'd expected. Instead, she lifted her legs from the bumper and crisscrossed them. "Honey, this Southern drawl may come out a little slow, but I ain't. I also move faster than you and saw you climb into this beast before peeling out of my parking lot. How *rude*." Her dainty brows rose on that last word.

Lincoln ignored her reprimand and Carter's snort of laughter. "How'd your tiny self get that bench loaded up?"

She sent him a bored look. "I know how to work a dolly."

In his periphery, Lincoln caught Carter trying to slink away. His hand darted out and fisted in the back of his buddy's T-shirt. "Where do you think you're going?"

Carter yanked free. "Taking the high road. You got your ornery butt into this mess. Now figure out how to get out of it." He tipped his head at the young woman. "Opal."

"See ya later, Carter," she said in that breezy voice that was already raking Lincoln's nerves.

Lincoln watched in disbelief as Carter left him high and dry. He turned back to the peculiar woman, knowing he had no other choice unless he was going to physically remove her, and that wasn't an option. Clenching his fists, he waited for her next move.

2

The giant of a man looked close to having a temper tantrum, but Opal made no move to get out of the line of it. She sat a little taller and readied herself as she watched the snare of his lips coil back even further to spit something out. She didn't have to wait long.

"For not being *slow*, you sure didn't grasp my not wanting the bench when I left it at your store," Lincoln said in a sharp tone. A gust of air sent his long hair into his eyes, and he ran a hand through it to brush it back.

"Oh, I grasped that all right, but it's still meant for you." She offered a smile in response to his frown. "Also, I'd have thought you would be enough of a Southern gentleman not to storm out of a job interview."

His eyes widened, indicating Lincoln knew he'd been caught, but they narrowed just as quickly. He crossed his arms over his broad chest again, reminding Opal of a puffer fish. Prickly, yet still cute somehow. "I'm not working with you."

She barely contained the scoff tickling her throat. Clearing it on a small cough, she decided to tease him a little bit to see if that would soften his attitude. "Why? Does little ole me scare you?"

Lincoln's brown eyes flared, giving away the truth,

before they squinted again. She'd only been in his company for less than thirty minutes total and had already discovered that his eyes gave away his secrets whether he wanted them to or not. And for some odd reason, he *was* afraid of her.

"No. Little ole you is annoying. I don't put up with annoying." He pushed the words out there, apparently wanting them to act as a repellent.

Opal considered letting him get away with it, but the challenge of Lincoln Cole won out in the end. She dropped the flirty act and leveled her gaze at him with some seriousness. "Look, I know your big, grouchy self won't be a day at the beach, but I have furniture that needs to be delivered. I sure could use your help."

"I thought you knew how to work a dolly?" He gave her a condescending smirk.

Someone needs a time-out. Opal gave him a blank stare in return, deciding not to play along with the schoolyard word slinging. She'd run away from enough of that in her youth and certainly wouldn't be taking part in it as an adult. "You know where to find me if you change your mind." Her temper was close to boiling over, so she eased off the hood and headed inside the diner for a much-needed glass of iced tea to help cool off.

"I won't," Lincoln fired back before the screen door banged shut behind her.

Opal took a deep breath and let it out slowly. Most people didn't get under her skin, but that crabby man had come close to getting a slap to his hateful mouth just then.

There were more important things to attend to at the moment, though, so Opal grabbed a to-go cup of iced tea and hurried home. After changing into one of her favorite floral dresses, she headed to Higgins Funeral Home.

It was said that the Knitting Club came over on the *Mayflower* and somehow found the fountain of youth upon landing. For as far back as she could remember, Opal had never heard of one of them passing away until now. Even though they each wore a well-defined road map of wrinkles and age spots on their faces, they were a spunky bunch who seemed to outlive every resident of Sunset Cove. Opal and her two closest friends, Josie and Sophia, admired many aspects of the Knitting Club, such as their loyalty to each other and their dedication to spending quality time together, but the younger women shied away from the older women's fondness for gossip and being busybodies.

The day had finally arrived to reveal that at least one of the old ladies had an expiration date. Too bad it belonged to Miss Liza Pierson, who had been Opal's beloved Sunday school teacher from preschool all the way up until high school graduation. Miss Liza had said she'd grown so attached to those in Opal's generation that she simply had to move up each year with them. She must have been truthful about it too, because after graduation Miss Liza went back to solely teaching preschoolers.

Opal found herself standing in line behind the clan of knitting survivors for the viewing. In the small coastal town a viewing might as well be deemed a public event, complete with refreshments set up in the front waiting area. *Everyone* turned out, allegedly to pay their respects, but Opal suspected it was more on the lines of nosiness or maybe just the obligation to pay homage to the tradition.

"They ruined the arrangement we ordered," Ethel Matthews, Sunset Cove's postmaster and the orneriest member of the Knitting Club, complained. The ever-present scent of Pond's cold cream emanated from Ethel and was the only pleasant thing about her. She clucked her tongue and pointed her walking cane at one of the gaudiest funeral wreaths Opal had ever seen. White-and-pink silk flowers formed an artificial pillow with a satin ribbon crossing it as a sash. It read, *Jesus called*, and had a cell phone attached to it.

"Oh, so you didn't actually order such a thing?" Opal asked, relieved that the old ladies had better taste than that. The line inched closer to the casket.

Ethel's sister Bertie tsked on the other side of Opal. "We most certainly did not order that! We told them to use a *real* phone. One with a cord and a rotary dial. Poor Liza never even owned a cellular telephone."

"Ain't that right! Liza wouldn't have known how to answer that contraption if Jesus did call," added Madge, the most wrinkled member of the Knitting Club. She reminded Opal of a pug dog.

Opal motioned toward the pale-gray casket with a beautiful spray of wildflowers draped on top. "Well, Jesus obviously left Miss Liza a voice mail." That comment earned her several harsh scoffs and a firm pinch on the back of the arm from Ethel Matthews. Flinching away from Ethel's claws, she rubbed her stinging skin and huffed. "I'm just saying."

"Maybe it's best you don't say anything at all, smarty-pants," Bertie said in a tizzy as each member of the Knitting Club pushed past Opal. She even got a walker stomped on top of her foot. Luckily, she'd traded her flip-flops for a pair of Keds.

The tiniest, oldest, and certainly the most eccentric member of the group, Dalma Jean Burgess, eased by Opal while munching on a cookie. While all the other members were dressed in their Sunday best dress suits, Dalma wore a pair of high-waisted wool trousers and a plain white T-shirt. Her outfit was completed with suspenders and a newsboy cap. Mischief lit her cloudy-blue eyes as she leaned toward Opal and whispered, "I thought that was funny. Think I'm going to delete my voice mail so he can't leave me a message for a little while longer." She winked and cut in front of Opal with the rest of the old ladies.

Trying to suppress a grin, Opal focused on paying respects to Miss Liza. On her way out, she caught a glimpse of an Italian beauty sashaying through the door in a tailored black pantsuit and oversize sunglasses. Locks of shiny brown hair were perfectly styled in long, loose curls. Even if Sophia Grace Prescott hadn't been in the spotlight of the celebrity world due to her NFL star husband, the woman would have drawn attention with her presence alone.

"You know how to make an entrance, Mrs. Priss." Opal wrapped her arms around Sophia, catching a whiff of expensive perfume, and hugged tightly.

"Hi, chick. Where's Josie?" Sophia leaned back and pulled her sunglasses off, flashing teal-blue eyes fringed with thick eyelashes.

"She had to work but should be swinging by here soon. We're still meeting at my house tonight, right?"

"Yes. Momma is going to watch Collin."

"Good. Josie and I are so glad you were able to get away and come home for this."

"Ty wasn't too happy about me missing his game, but he'll just have to get over it." Sophia spoke with conviction. From the tension slipping in her tone when saying her husband's name, Opal knew there was trouble brewing in their young marriage.

"I'll see you soon then." Opal didn't want any of the Knitting Club members to overhear anything they could cluck about, and Sophia's husky voice tended to carry, so she kept any further comments on Ty to herself and pulled Sophia in for another hug.

• • •

As the day gave way to night, Opal swept the back deck and switched on the string of Edison-style lights over the table she set up for refreshments. Car doors closed from out front, announcing her friends' arrival. Tonight's agenda was to privately celebrate Miss Liza's life and to catch up with each other. Even though Sophia lived several hours away, she was devoted to making it back home almost every month to spend time with Opal and Josie. The three of them had been dubbed the Sand Queens years ago, an identity they embraced as wholeheartedly as they embraced their lifelong friendship with each other.

Moments later, a puffy-eyed Josie walked up the steps with Sophia following behind her.

"Aw, honey, are you okay?" Opal rushed over to Josie.

Josie batted away a tear and shrugged. "It hit me on the way over here that Miss Liza won't be teaching her Sunday school class anymore."

"You really enjoyed assisting her, didn't you?" Opal asked and Josie only nodded. "Are you going to take over teaching?"

Josie wiped her cheek. "Yes. I've been doing most of it anyway this year since her ministroke."

Opal led Josie over to a chair while Sophia grabbed several napkins from inside. Once they had her settled, they scooted chairs close and held her hands. Josie was considered shy by most standards, but her quietness hid a tender heart that only knew how to love—big. It took a while with no one rushing, and once Josie pulled herself together, the women decided the best medicine for a grieving heart had to be something sweet and fattening.

"Well, I can definitely help us out with that." Sophia reached inside a canvas bag and pulled out a plastic container. "Momma made *sfogliatelle*. They were Miss Liza's favorite Italian treat."

"Bless your sweet momma's heart." Opal hopped up and crossed over to the patio door. "I have summer punch and goodies too. Be right back."

"Did you make them?" Josie asked, sounding a little apprehensive, before Opal slid the door shut.

"No, honey. Sorry, but today has been a little hectic." Opal hurried inside and mixed the ginger ale with the frozen pink punch base that consisted of pink lemonade concentrate and pineapple juice. A Sunset Cove get-together wasn't complete without the sweet and tangy beverage, no matter the season. She took the plastic container of cucumber and pimento cheese tea sandwiches out of the fridge. Once she had everything arranged on a tray, she took it outside and presented it to her friends. "Momma made tea sandwiches for us."

Each woman made herself a plate and poured a cup of punch and munched quietly for a spell as the ocean waves set up a melody just beyond the deck railing.

Opal ate a tea sandwich first, saving the *sfogliatelle* for last. She picked up the delicate pastry and studied its golden-brown exterior. "Luciana is such an angel to make these for us." The first bite elicited a moan as the flaky crust gave way to the rich ricotta filling inside. "So, so good."

"Hmm . . ." Josie took another bite of hers and washed it down with punch. "What made your day so hectic, Opal? Everything all right?"

The handsome stranger with his lips pouted out flashed before her eyes. "Oh, nothing really. Everything is just dandy." Opal cringed. Her words sounded fake even to her own ears.

"I served Lincoln Cole breakfast today." Josie refilled each of their cups and gave Opal a measured look. "Was he supposed to start working for you?"

"Supposed to, yes, but no." Opal went for another bite, savoring the subtle hints of orange peel in the filling.

"Tell it straight, Opal," Sophia piped in while checking her phone.

"He basically stormed into the store. Huffed and puffed and acted like he wanted to blow my house down."

Sophia rolled her eyes and snickered. "You just couldn't do it, could you? Always adding flair."

"Lincoln Cole was rude. He refused to work with me. Is that clear enough?" Opal knew it was clear and certainly didn't like the message it conveyed.

Josie frowned. "I'm sorry, Opal."

Opal flicked her wrist to shoo the unpleasant subject away, even though she planned on having a phone conversation with her old friend August about even suggesting it in the first place. "No worries, honey. That's life. I'll figure out something." She directed the conversation to Collin, asking Sophia how the sweet baby boy was doing. As Opal looked through the photos Sophia was showing off on her phone, that ornery man kept weaseling his way into her thoughts. She wondered if she'd see that handsome yet grim face ever again.

• • •

Only a few days slid by before she found out.

Short on help, Opal overdid it in her attempts to deliver the furniture orders on her own. Her brother had helped until going off to college that fall, and she sure was missing him. Sitting stiffly in front of the office computer, her finger had just moved over to hit the Send button for the online help-wanted ad when the door chimed. Leaving it for the time being, she slowly got up from her desk, stretched out her aching back, and began moving toward the front of the shop. Halfway there, she met up with a sulking giant.

He wore a baseball cap low to conceal his eyes. She bit her lip to stop the smile from forming, knowing he was trying to keep his secrets to himself this round and knowing he was going to fail. *Bring it on, big boy.*

Lincoln thrust out his hand, revealing the familiar satchel of seashells. "These were left inside the bench. Thought you'd want them back."

Opal made no move to take them. "You're using the guise of returning the seashells, but we both know you couldn't stay away." She batted her eyelashes, causing his brows to knit together. "It's okay if you wanted to come see me. I don't mind."

"What? No! These were inside the bench . . ." He tried to hand them over again, and again she refused to accept them.

She sighed. Teasing him wasn't any fun if he wasn't going to play along. "They go with the bench."

Lincoln dropped his hand to his side, clutching the tiny bag a bit too aggressively for Opal's liking. "Why?" He spat the word out as if it tasted unpleasant.

"After I complete each piece, I place a shell inside or tuck it away somewhere and make a wish for the next owner."

He blinked slowly and readjusted his hat, but she still had a good view of his face. "What are you, a genie?"

Opal knew he was being insulting, but she chose to giggle anyway. Laughing insults and taunts away had become the armor she used to put up with people who took it upon themselves to express how much her quirkiness bothered them. No matter how many times she was presented with judgmental sneers, the persona suited her and she had no aspiration to change. People like this man before her would just have to deal with it.

Opal leaned a hip against the leopard-print wingback chair beside her, trying to take some tension off her sore back. "No one has ever accused me of that one. My wishes are actually prayers."

"You said you put one shell with each piece?"

"Ye-e-s," she answered slowly.

He lifted the bag. "Then why'd the bench get an entire sack full of shells?"

Opal shrugged. "I sensed the new owner was in need of a lot of prayers."

Lincoln snorted and crossed his arms but didn't let go of the bag of shells. "Well, I had plenty of folks praying for me while I was overseas." He shifted his weight to his right leg. "Fat lot of good it did me." He untwined his arms and shoved the bag into her hand, leaving her no choice but to take it. "I don't need these."

"August said you were hit during a rocket attack." Opal's statement had his stature going rigid, but she was ready to stand her ground.

"He ain't got any business telling *my* business." His statement came out just shy of a snarl.

Opal dismissed his scold and plowed on. "What's the likelihood of someone surviving an attack like that?"

"Slim to none," he answered, anger lacing the three words.

She pointed to his left pant leg, knowing that was the one he favored when walking. "Is there a prosthetic underneath your britches?"

"No!" Lincoln's face turned an impressive shade of red.

Opal let out a low whistle. "What are the odds of them not having to amputate after that kind of damage?"

Lincoln's shoulders deflated, obviously losing steam after being put in his place. "I was told it would be removed during surgery but woke up with it still there."

"Humph." Opal pointed to the door behind him. "You stormed in here earlier and I'm sure you'll exit in the same fashion." She tossed the bag of shells in the air and caught it with ease. "I suppose you're right on not needing these. I'd say plenty of prayers have already been answered on your behalf. You may go ahead and stomp back out now, Mr. Cole." She turned and walked to her office without so much as one glimpse back.

Several punctuated moments passed, making her curious as to why he hadn't left yet. When the bell finally jingled announcing his departure, Opal let out an exasperated sigh. She moved over to her desk and the bubbles dancing along the computer screen caught her attention, reminding her she was still without the much-needed help. She quickly sent the ad before focusing on an old rocking chair begging to be transformed into a plant stand.

"Maybe this will give me the calm I need after that storm," she muttered, picking up a piece of fine-grit sandpaper and getting to work.

She tried envisioning the color that would replace the dingy white, but all she could see was the whirling gold in those livid brown eyes. Shaking her head, she tried again while smoothing a rough patch on the armrest, but the bronzed red of his cheeks took over her thoughts. *Boy, does he have himself some anger issues.*

"Red with gold accents," she declared, finally seeing what the chair would be dressed in once it became a planter. Maybe the heated exchange with that ornery soldier was just what she needed for new inspiration. *The hostile collection,* she mused with a smirk slipping across her lips.

3

Storms had always held an allure for Lincoln in his youth. He used to revel in them barreling in and taking charge of the atmosphere around him, reminding him who was in charge, and that it certainly wasn't him. But those days were long past. Now he dreaded the ache deep in his leg that showed up before a storm and hated knowing he had no power to do anything to stop it. His eyes flicked to the graying skies as he lowered the hammer.

"Storm's a-coming," he mumbled to himself, inflecting his tone to mimic his grandfather's deep Southern drawl. It was what the old man always said when the skies over Beaufort dulled the way the one before Lincoln was doing at the moment. He looked over the storm shutters once more to make sure they covered the cottage windows properly before collecting the other tools and returning them to the small shed behind the house.

He'd only been in Sunset Cove for two weeks and was already thinking the harebrained idea of leaving his hometown was a bit silly. Perhaps after the storm passed, he'd pack up and head on home. He just needed some space to lick his wounds, but no space had been found so far.

On a long sigh, he knew that wasn't an option just yet.

Those last several months he spent in Beaufort flashed before his eyes, emphasizing the fact that he was where he needed to be. They had been the darkest months of his life, and he wasn't even thinking about the injuries or the surgeries or the physical therapy. Those months were filled with misery as he battled some kind of funk he couldn't shake, a battle he came close to losing. Most of those days, he'd lain in bed wondering if there was even a point in ever getting back up. His mother pushing him to make a change was among the reasons for his move. Then the true reason for the abrupt move weighed down on him and had his stomach flinching with embarrassment. Lincoln doubted if he'd ever be ready to go face the mess he had left behind.

He looked out over the abandoned shore and had a nagging feeling that he was about to walk into another type of life storm altogether.

As he limped inside, the shrill tone of his cell phone sounded from where it sat on the weathered kitchen counter. He was renting the place from a friend of the family, and on first glance he knew the aging beach cottage was a good fit.

He grabbed the phone and swiped a finger across the screen before placing it to his ear. "What's up?"

"You battening down the hatches?" Carter asked, his voice a bit muffled.

"Yeah. Just finished putting up the hurricane shutters. I figured you'd be on a surfboard." He leaned over the counter and peered out the small window above the sink, noticing the waves were growing more aggressive by the minute. It used to be their favorite time to be out there on a board in the midst of the chaos.

"No time for that today. I'm finishing up over here at the music studio. You wanna hang out at the firehouse with me and my crowd?" Carter asked on a grunt, sounding hard at it.

"You want me to head over and give you a hand?" Lincoln straightened from the counter, ready to head out.

"Nah. I'm almost done. Pack yourself a bag and head on inland before they shut down the waterway bridge."

"Yeah. Sure."

"Meet you there in about an hour if the traffic isn't too thick."

Lincoln bit back a groan. Traffic was going to be horrendous. "During a tropical storm warning that's close to hurricane strength? *Right.*" Both men chuckled.

"I'll text you directions in a minute. You know how nasty these late-season storms can be, so no dillydallying."

Lincoln snorted, thinking his buddy sounded a little too fatherly. "Yes, sir," he taunted and said a quick goodbye.

Before he could place the phone back down, a voice mail notification caught his attention. The name Jefferson Cole was attached to it, making his heart plummet. Warily, he hit Play and brought the phone back to his ear, prepared for that booming voice to shout out disappointments and harsh reprimands at him. Instead, nothing but a few haughty breaths came from his father's side of the phone. It was a sound of defeat. One that Lincoln recognized all too well. From what his mother's last message informed him, his father wouldn't really be able to say much anyway. In spite of that, the call was just as heavy as if it had been filled with words.

Knowing Beaufort was well out of the storm's projected cone, Lincoln brushed off the voice mail and focused on what needed to be done before the storm made landfall. There was nothing he could do about the storm he had caused back home, anyway.

• • •

Just as he'd expected, it took Lincoln close to two hours to make it inland to the firehouse that was being renovated to become August's home and studio if he ever decided to put down some roots. The building was something to look at, with its redbrick exterior and large bay doors, so he spent a chunk of time exploring the outer perimeter of it as he secured chairs and other items left in the yard.

Carter's gray truck eased up beside Lincoln's Jeep just as a band of rain moved in. Lincoln watched it begin at the far side of the field across the road until it met up with them in the front yard.

"I'd call that perfect timing," Carter yelled as they did a mad dash inside with his two younger nephews on his heels.

The guys took a good part of the next hour to gather sleeping bags, flashlights, and other needed supplies. Each one of them focused on the task at hand until the only thing left to do was to unload the mountain of grocery bags.

Looking around the expansive bottom floor, Lincoln couldn't help but be impressed. August had told him about the renovations, but seeing it in person was an entirely different experience. It remained looking like a firehouse, complete with ladders hung on the wall, a brass pole beside a line of chairs with helmets hanging on hooks behind them. Only thing missing were the fire trucks.

"This is one slamming man cave." Lincoln moved his gaze away from the vintage fire truck photos dressing one of the brick walls and looked over at the kitchenette along the back, where Carter was unloading bags filled with enough junk food to fatten a small army. "You sure you don't want us to move in here with August and you forget about that nonsense of getting married?"

Carter chuckled. "Never been surer of anything in all my life. The wedding can't get here fast enough."

Lincoln sidled up beside him and began adding his loot to the bounty of junk. He tossed a few bags of hot-and-spicy pork rinds and a pack of teriyaki-flavored beef jerky beside a package of Oreos. It was common knowledge that junk food was always a part of the emergency preparedness kits for hurricanes and tropical storms around these parts.

He patiently waited for Carter to peel back the plastic on a plate of homemade blondies before swiping one and taking a bite. "Hmm . . ." It was brown sugar and pecan heaven in a gooey square.

Carter smirked. "My *wife* made those." He took his own bite, looking more than a little smug.

"You ain't married yet," Lincoln mumbled while chewing the sticky goodness. No matter how tasty the treat was, it didn't move one bone in his body to want to take a trip down any aisle. Since his injury, Lincoln didn't even like his own company and wouldn't subject a significant other to his bitterness, especially on those dark days when the pain became unbearable. He needed his space and had no intentions of changing that up.

"I am in my heart." Carter placed a hand against his chest and batted his eyelashes, tease beaming from his dark-blue eyes.

Lincoln couldn't hold back the roar of laughter. His friend's company was good medicine, and Lincoln was in need of a healthy dose of it. Life had been way too heavy in the last few years for his liking. Just thinking about it made swallowing the blondie a little difficult. After he managed to get it down, he asked, "Where is Dominica, anyway?"

"She had a few doctor's appointments back in Maryland and was already planning to visit her parents while she was there before this storm even began brewing. She left yesterday."

"Oh." He didn't find the visit to Maryland odd since that was her home state, but the appointments—and Carter not being there—were. "What's going on and why ain't you with her?"

Carter pulled his hat off and tugged a hand through his hair before putting it back on. "I wanted to go, but I promised Derek I'd help out with the boys during the storm. Dominica insisted I'd be better use to my brother than sitting in a waiting room. Her mom is with her and they plan on a day of pampering afterward that I think will do Dominica some good. She needs a lot of rest." Carter sounded like he was trying to convince himself that he'd made the right decision to stay back.

"Is she okay?"

"Nothing that strong-willed woman can't handle. We're still going through tests to figure it out, but the doctors at Johns Hopkins think she has an autoimmune disease."

Lincoln's chest tightened. "Anything I can do?"

Carter clamped him on the shoulder and cleared his throat. "Just prayer for now would be greatly appreciated."

Lincoln's gut churned. Of course his friend would ask him for something he couldn't handle at the moment. Before he could figure out how to voice that without spilling some of the heavy load he was struggling to carry, a squeal saved him.

"Linc, look at me!" Carter's youngest nephew, Zachary, shouted as he slid down the fireman's pole.

Tucker stood at the bottom and easily caught him but let out a grunt when the rambunctious boy whacked him in the face while trying to squirm out of his arms. "Chill, kid," the teenager reprimanded.

"You're mighty brave for just a tiny kid," Lincoln commented, knowing it would rile the boy up.

"I ain't a tiny kid. I'm five years old." Zachary hurried over and swiped a blondie and a handful of M&M'S.

"Whoa now. Your momma will get ahold of us if you end up with a bellyache before she gets here." Carter pulled Zachary back by the hem of his shirt. "That's enough snacking until supper."

Zachary wiggled free and darted around him to swipe a few more pieces of candy before dodging out of the way. Another effect of storms was turning kids into little balls of spastic energy.

Shaking his head, Lincoln could tell it was going to be one lively night. He tore open a bag of pork rinds, needing something savory to offset the sweet. "So what's for supper?"

Carter peered at him from underneath the brim of his tattered hat. "You're just as bad as Tucker."

"Hey," Tucker garbled out as he grabbed his third blondie while Carter slid the plate out of reach and secured the plastic wrap back over the goodies.

Lincoln knew that wasn't going to keep anyone out of them. "Serious though, supper?" He popped another pork rind into his mouth, enjoying the crunchy spice.

Carter pointed to a rectangular cooler by the side door. "Derek gave me some fish that need frying. He was worried it would go bad before they could use it at the restaurant. I figured we'd set up the propane fryer under the shed out back and get to it in a few, before the rain squalls get heavier."

Lincoln dusted his hands together to get rid of the crumbs. "Sounds like a plan. On the way over here the radio said the weather advisory bumped Lacy up to a category 1 hurricane and is predicted to reach cat 2 by nightfall." He knew a cat 1 was still considered a mild storm, with winds not even reaching one hundred miles an hour, but the warm waters near the coast could send one up to a category 4 if the recipe was just right.

"Yeah. I heard that too." Carter grabbed a roll of paper towels and tucked it under his arm so he could pull a pair of tongs from a drawer. "Derek and Nan planned on riding the storm out at their restaurant, but I finally talked them into staying here with us. They should be here soon. They're gonna stay in the room upstairs. You're welcome to the couch up there."

"Nah. I already told Zachary earlier that I'd camp out with y'all down here." Lincoln motioned toward the cement floor. "Pretty neat floor." Various earth tones swirled in intricate patterns, making it art instead of simply staining.

"Yeah. August popped in for a weekend and did it himself." Carter rummaged around in the cabinet, pulling out a container of seafood breading and handing it over to Lincoln. "You sure your leg can manage the floor?"

"I'm used to roughing it." His leg pulsed in pain, emphasizing the fib he'd just spoken, but he pushed the discomfort off the best he could and followed Carter outside.

● ● ●

And roughing it they did, later that night, with near-about bellyaches. Each guy had eaten his weight in fish and then proceeded to attack the junk food with too much gusto. With rain pounding against the roof and wind howling through it, they were too wound up to properly settle down. All of them, that was, except for Tucker. The teenage boy was nestled inside his sleeping bag snoring in a tone reminiscent of an old hog rooting in mud.

"The kid needs one of those Breathe Right strips," Carter muttered into the darkness.

The power had gone out earlier, as predicted, but Lincoln could still vaguely see and hear the entire goings-on in the firehouse. Every so often, the crack of a tree branch or a harsh gust of wind from outside would catch his attention. It was one of those instincts he was born with that had come in handy as a soldier. Yet lying there, he knew it was useless to him now.

Not much later, Lincoln heard someone get up.

"Carter, I gotta peepee," Zachary whispered loudly.

"Okay, dude. Go ahead," Carter mumbled back.

"I need you to go with me," Zachary said, his voice strained.

Lincoln listened as Carter unzipped his sleeping bag with no protest. He knew his old man would have told him to suck it up and go on by himself. He liked Carter's way of handling things better. It didn't indicate Zachary was weak, in his opinion, though he knew his old man's view would have differed. It showed Carter was there when the little guy needed him, no matter the situation. There was no doubting Carter would make a stand-up dad someday.

Thinking about his father had Lincoln's throat thickening until it was difficult to swallow. When he ran away from Beaufort, he left their relationship in shreds of anger and regret. He was a fixer by nature, but he was pretty sure he'd ruined things past the point of repair.

He heard two sets of feet shuffle back in and then something nudged Lincoln's arm.

"Linc," Carter whispered.

Lincoln rolled over in the direction of Carter's voice. "Yeah?"

"Tucker's snoring awfully loud."

"It's okay. Nothing close to how bad it used to sound in my barracks."

"Yeah, I'm not talking about that. Tucker snoring that loud means he's sleeping deep enough we can have some fun without waking him."

Lincoln was always up for late-night mischief. He unzipped his sleeping bag and sat up. "Whatcha got in mind?"

•   •   •

Morning showed up with all kinds of aches and pains, but Lincoln held in the grunts as best he could while getting up from the floor. The throb began just below his knee and took off in a sprint all the way up to his jaw as soon as he put some weight on his left leg. He grasped the nearby table and took several staggered breaths through his nose until his jaw unlocked. Most days began that way for him anymore. First order of business was to swallow a handful of ibuprofen, so he rummaged around in his duffel bag until finding the bottle.

The doctors had supplied him with plenty of narcotics in the beginning, but only a few months in, it was apparent that he was heading down a slippery slope to becoming too dependent on them. Plus, the man they created was nothing but a dark shadow of his true self. They'd helped to form the darkest days of his life, and it had nothing to do with the explosion flashbacks. Over-the-counter pain meds didn't work near as good, but at least he could function while taking them and keep his demons at bay.

"Hey!" Tucker's muffled yell rang out from the storage closet as a pounding started up on the barricaded door. "Let me out!"

Carter and Zachary joined Lincoln by the door of

the closet. All three had their arms crossed and were grinning. It hadn't taken hardly any effort the night before to pull Tucker and his sleeping bag in there, but it was taking a whole lot more effort not to roar in laughter at the moment. The door shook, but the wedged chair remained in place.

Lincoln glanced over at his cohorts. "Who's gonna let the beast out?"

Biting his bottom lip, Carter scratched the scruff on his cheek. "Perhaps Zachary should." He nodded but stopped when Lincoln and Zachary shook their heads in return.

"Nah. The beast may come out swinging. Can't risk the little guy like that." It was the first time Lincoln could recall the boy not protesting about being called little. Lincoln looked back at Carter. "He's gonna come out in attack mode, so let's think about a plan of action for a minute . . ." He tapped his chin.

Carter scoffed. "Okay, soldier boy . . ." He narrowed his eyes as a menacing grin took over. "I'll be right back." He dashed out the side door and returned in a flash with a large shrimping net.

"I like the way your mind works, *music boy*," Lincoln fired back, sending Zachary into a fit of giggles.

The two men moved over and spread the net in front of the door. Once they had their stance secure, Carter nodded for the little boy to move the chair away from the doorknob. Zachary did and then dashed out the way as Tucker came out like a raging bull only to be stopped in his tracks by the net, tangling himself the more his fists flew all over the place.

"Y'all gonna pay for this," Tucker bellowed as he continued to thrash around with the two men pinning him inside easily.

"You sure are mouthy for someone in your predicament," Carter fired back just as his phone went to singing an old song Lincoln recognized as one of his grandparents' favorites.

"'My Girl,' seriously?" Lincoln teased.

"Dominica's my girl, *seriously*." Carter dropped the net and pulled the phone from his pocket. "Hey."

Tucker untangled himself, and before Lincoln could stop him, the teenage boy kicked his uncle's feet out from under him, sending them both to the floor. As they rolled around, Lincoln scooped up Zachary to keep him out of harm's way.

"They gonna get it from Momma," Zachary whispered as they both watched the wrestling match.

Somehow, Carter managed to pin Tucker down and put the phone back to his ear. Panting, he said, "Sorry, babe. Everything okay?" He suddenly released Tucker and shot to his feet. The normal easy expression on his face transformed into a scowl that looked completely out of place.

Lincoln's body stiffened in response. "What's wrong?"

Carter shook his head, offering nothing, and kept listening. "We'll see if we can get out there to her." He nodded to whatever Dominica was saying. "Okay, babe. Love you." He listened for another second before lowering the phone and fiddling with it a moment or two.

"Well?" Lincoln's voice came out a little sharp with his impatience as he set Zachary down.

"Dominica just saw Opal's store on the news. It was hit pretty hard by the storm."

At the mention of the woman's name, Lincoln's stomach winced with embarrassment. They'd not left things on a good note whatsoever. Just recalling that stern look she'd leveled at him, reminiscent of an ole spinster ready to tear into a petulant child who was irritating her, made Lincoln feel a good bit foolish over his behavior. And now he really felt like a jerk, with the storm throwing attitude at her as well.

Derek bounded down the stairs a few beats later, tugging on a sweatshirt. "Hey, Carter, can you hang out here with the boys for a while? Nan and I need to head over to the restaurant. My manager just arrived and said most of our back deck is floating down the inlet."

"Ah, shoot. Sounds like Lacy went on a rampage last night. Opal's store took a beating too. I was going to go check on her."

Conceding to the fact that he needed to make amends for his folly with the shop owner, Lincoln began looking for his shoes. "I'll go."

"You better grab a coat or something. It's actually chilly out," Carter advised. After a long exhale, he warned, "Just letting you know, her friend Sophia will probably be there too."

Lincoln continued collecting his belongings. "So?"

A snort sounded from behind him. "*So* she probably knows how you treated Opal. You may want to keep out of her way. That one is the feisty member of the Sand Queens."

Lincoln finally glanced over his shoulder, his brow furrowed. "Sand what?"

"Queens. That's what the locals have called those three since they were babies."

"Oh. Okay." Unimpressed, Lincoln went back to rummaging in his duffel bag. He pulled out a zip-up hoodie and shrugged it on. He slung the bag over his shoulder and waved goodbye before heading out the side door.

Sure enough, as he hobbled over to his Jeep that was speckled with leaves and twigs, Lincoln took note of the chill in the air. Another aftereffect to storms late in the season was that they tended to steal the humidity in their paths and leave much cooler temperatures behind. The storms wanted folks to know they'd been there . . . as if the debris and destruction they flung everywhere wasn't enough evidence.

Zipping his hoodie, Lincoln climbed in and begged the throb in his leg to leave him alone long enough to try to make things right with a certain redhead. He sure was feeling awfully remorseful all of a sudden.

● ● ●

It was slow going, dodging downed power lines and trees. Lincoln even had to maneuver the Jeep around an upturned canoe in the middle of an intersection. The closer he got to the coast, the more destruction he found. Several palmetto trees were uprooted and slung in odd places. He noticed one on the roof of the bank. Another was wedged in the spokes of the Ferris wheel. He wondered if he had a beach cottage to go back to but kept his focus on checking on Opal as the main priority.

It was no easy feat to get through town, but Lincoln finally made it to the store and parked in the debris-strewn lot beside it. He gazed out the windshield at the trio of women in the small front yard.

Josie, the tall blonde who towered over the brunette by at least a foot, wore baggy jeans and a tattered long-sleeved T-shirt. Certainly the tomboy resembled nothing close to a queen to him. The other one had to be the feisty Sophia. In her skinny jeans, knee-high boots, and tailored blazer, he could see her as Posh Queen. Oddly enough, those two were hovering around Quirky Queen, who was sitting on her lawn chair throne. The moment they noticed the Jeep, the short one zeroed in on him.

Lincoln didn't understand the firm warning Carter had delivered back at the firehouse about Sophia. She looked even smaller than Opal. The brunette was glaring at him with enough menace, though, that it did kick up his curiosity. "I turned down a job offer. I don't see where that merits you giving me the stink eye," he mumbled, even though she couldn't hear him.

After giving a raised eyebrow in Shorty's direction that he hoped conveyed the message *Bring it*, Lincoln tore his eyes away from her and studied Bless This Mess. Once he got a good look at the building, the idea of heckling Sophia was instantly forgotten.

There it sat, situated on the corner of Front Street, looking quite different from the first time he'd seen it. His first impression, two weeks ago, was that it stuck out like a sore thumb. The left exterior wall was a faded-teal color with the store name written in what reminded him of a faded-black chalkboard font. The other side was dressed in a mosaic mural of ocean waves and sunshine with a fairy in the midst of the swirls. The mural remained, but today it looked beaten down a bit with pieces broken off the top edges of the mural. That wasn't the main problem, though. No roof remained.

"Ah, shoot. All of her junk has to be ruined." Lincoln leaned forward to get a better angle. He glimpsed what appeared to be a chunk of the roof on the street behind the building. He moved his attention back to the redhead sitting there in a floral dress and a bulky cream sweater that looked like something his gran would wear. He wondered why she wasn't sobbing or having some hissy fit over her loss, but there she sat eyeing the building blankly. What was she doing just sitting there like that?

Lincoln took a fortifying breath and braved getting out of the Jeep. As he closed his door, he watched Sophia whisper something to Opal while both women regarded him. Opal nodded once like she really didn't care, and that simple nod had Sophia making a beeline right over to him.

Hands on her hips, manicured fingers tapping against the fancy jeans, she glared up at him. "You have a lot of nerve coming here."

He sent the glare back to the Tasmanian devil. "How's that?"

The chilly breeze whipped her hair around and the prissy thing flicked it away before pointing at him. "You say one thing out of the way to Opal today and I promise you'll regret it."

Lincoln crossed his thick arms, making sure the fabric stretched taut against his bulging biceps, and gave her his best intimidating stare—jaw ticking, lips in a firm line, brows pinched. It was a stare known to intimidate grown men carrying heavy artillery, but it didn't faze Sophia. She sent the look way back up to him before stomping over to Opal.

"What have I gotten myself into?" he mumbled to himself before following in her haughty wake.

In effort to not say anything that could be classified as "out of the way," Lincoln chose to say nothing at all. Instead, he quietly stood just outside the circle they'd made around Opal and got a good look at her. The unruly curls were pulled to the side in a low ponytail, so there was nothing blocking the view of her beautiful face. He noticed her bottom lip kept trembling, the only clue she was battling any emotion. Every so often, she would bite down on it, as if to say, *"Buck up. It's going to be okay."*

Strangely, her resilience in the dismal moment was unnerving. How could such a fragile-looking woman be stronger than he was when faced with such a challenge? He had no clue. Something began to soften inside of him for her, but he quickly chalked it up to pity. Filing it away, he glanced around at other nearby buildings. Most were fine with minimal damage. Bless This Mess seemed to be the only casualty in this battle. Lincoln could relate to that. He was the only one not able to walk away from that last battle he fought overseas.

Josie began to speak, beckoning Lincoln's attention back from the dark thoughts it began to wander toward. "Do you want me to get someone here to help?" she asked while gently placing her hand on Opal's shoulder. "A roofer?"

Opal gave her a faint smile. "No. Daddy is taking care of it."

Josie nodded her head and began walking the soggy perimeter with Lincoln following behind her.

Once they were out of earshot, Lincoln said, "I think we should go ahead and line up some help."

Josie picked up a chunk of mosaic tile lying in a puddle by the wall. "Why?"

"If her dad is anything like her—"

Josie snorted loud enough to hush him. "No worries there. Her dad has this under control." She pointed toward the building. "And you've clearly gotten the wrong impression of Opal. She restored this building once from a plan she'd formed all on her own. She'll do it again."

"Okay . . ." Lincoln sensed it was best to let it go. He was already feeling way too involved in the situation— and the intriguing woman at the center of it—than he wanted to.

4

The day before Hurricane Lacy barreled onto shore and wreaked havoc on Sunset Cove, a few members of the Knitting Club showed up at the store with a plastic baggie filled with Opal's favorite granola cookies and a second-hand account of a Gray Man sighting. Ghost lore was as much a part of low-country culture as fried chicken and collard greens. Sightings of the ghost dressed in a gray suit wandering the coast of Pawleys Island went as far back as the 1800s. According to the legend, if the Gray Man was seen on the shore, locals had been warned of an approaching hurricane and better make preparations.

Opal popped the last bite of a cookie into her mouth and reached to pull down a wind chime as she listened to Bertie Matthews go on and on about the sighting that had taken place earlier in the day.

"The young couple was interviewed on the news and everything. Said he looked like a pirate combing the beach for treasure."

"It's nice and all that the Gray Man is kind enough to warn folks of the approaching storm," Opal commented absently as she placed the wind chime in the wagon with the yard ornament she'd fashioned from soup cans. She was merely humoring the ole gals, wondering why on earth they weren't already hunkered down in the back of Sunset Cove First Baptist Church. "But I think the Weather Channel has it covered. They even gave us an entire week's warning instead of just one day."

Dalma snickered at Opal's comment while the other two gave her a sour face.

"Why do you always gotta be such a smarty-pants?" Ethel yanked the bag of cookies from Opal's hand as she went to pluck another one out, which was unfortunate because Opal was starving. She hadn't had a chance to eat due to hurricane preparations.

"I'm not trying to be smart with you. I'm just looking at it in a practical sense." Opal wiped her hands on the front of her denim overalls before grabbing the handle of the wagon. She started off toward the back of the build- ing. "Are you ladies ready for the storm?"

"Josie and that teenage boy she tends to take care of helped me secure things around the house," Dalma com- mented as she picked up a clunky rock from the ground and placed it into the wagon.

Opal glanced at it, not bothering to ask why, and continued on. She placed a half sheet of plywood over the steps and used it as a ramp to roll the wagon up to the back porch. After pulling it inside the store, Opal paused to retie the bandanna holding her hair out of the way and then made her way to the store showroom with the three women on her heels.

"How about you and Miss Ethel?" Opal asked Bertie, trying to figure out how to get them to leave without appearing to be rude so she could finish up and head inland to her parents' house. She really wanted those cookies back.

"We're as ready as we'll be. Some of the youth from

church helped us out earlier." Bertie gazed around the store and clucked her tongue. "This place is a mess. How can you find anything in here?"

Opal held in the snarky retort wanting to slip out, that the old woman wouldn't be bothered by her mess if she'd simply stay away.

"I thought that stranger with the limp was supposed to be helping you out around here?" Ethel chimed in, finally getting around to what their unexpected visit was about in the first place.

If they wanted Opal to talk, they'd better hand over those cookies. She held her hand palm up and wiggled her fingers toward them. Ethel gave the bag back and Opal made the women wait until she'd eaten her fill, three more cookies, before saying, "You are referring to the giant, grouchy man, correct?" The sisters nodded but Dalma didn't seem to agree.

"That young man is a teddy bear pretending to be a grizzly." When Dalma's comment received three incredulous frowns, she explained, "I saw him just this morning at Growler's. He was there getting supplies like the rest of us, and when a young'un dropped her MoonPie on the floor as soon as she opened it, he was quick to buy her another one. Even took the time to carefully open it for her. And do you want to know what else that fine gentleman did?"

Opal could easily agree on the *fine* part—she wasn't blind—but she wasn't so sure about the *gentleman* part. She didn't want to appear too interested in hearing what else Dalma had to share about Lincoln, so she downplayed it with a noncommittal shrug.

"He walked my bags out to the bike for me, but when I told him I was riding it over to Josie's, he wouldn't hear of it. Loaded me and the bike up and drove me over there."

"He's still a grouch," Opal maintained, even though that was mighty gentlemanly of him.

Dalma tsked. "My Gerald lives with chronic back pain from that car accident. He can't help it when the pain gets to be so severe that he can't think past it and ends up snapping at me like a Doberman pincher."

"Pinscher," Opal corrected, deciding not to point out that Dalma's Gerald had passed away well over a decade ago. No way was she reminding the little lady of that fact.

"One pinched me right on my bottom when I tried running away from it when I was a girl, so I said it right," Dalma insisted while settling into a chair. "What was I saying . . . ? Oh yes!" She snapped her fingers. "That young man's eyes hold the same kind of pain I've seen reflected in Gerald's. Like he's barely hanging on. And can I just say Lincoln has one good-looking set of eyes even with the agony crinkling the corners. They remind me of warm maple syrup. Hmm . . . I sure could go for some of that over hot biscuits."

"Oh, my gracious, you mooning over a boy who could be your great-grandson," Bertie scolded Dalma before setting her sights back to Opal. "I do agree with her, though. Who knows what war he's battling internally behind his grimace. Sounded like that bomb tore into him real good."

"How do y'all know so much about him?" Opal pulled a rag out of her back pocket and began wiping down the antique counter she had scored from an old café that went out of business.

"Google," Bertie supplied. "There was plenty of news coverage when Lincoln made it back to his home in Beaufort after surviving a bombing. He's considered a war hero. The report said he ushered several of his team members to safety and was going back to direct more just before the bombing." The older ladies' eyes softened, even prickly Ethel Matthews.

After their little moment passed, with Opal feeling the effects of the information as well, Bertie continued, "The poor dear was making quite a name for himself in the Marines. He was already a first lieutenant and was close to making captain."

"Then why are you asking me about him? Y'all know a lot more than I do." Opal put the rag away and began shutting off the lamps around the showroom, wishing the ladies would get her subliminal message: *You don't have to go home, but you can't stay here.*

"We want to know why he ain't here helping you," Ethel demanded like she had a right.

Opal knew if she didn't give them something, the ladies wouldn't ever leave. "After talking it over in length, Lincoln decided he was more suited for a career as a stand-up comedian. I sent him away with my best wishes."

Ethel rolled her eyes, Bertie clucked her tongue, and Dalma giggled. After swiping the nearly empty cookie bag once again, Ethel led the women out the back and out of Opal's hair.

Finally left with some peace and quiet, Opal made one more pass around the storefront, double-checking that everything that could be done was done. She gave in to the notion of opening and closing the front door just to hear the bell chime one last time. After whispering a prayer, she got into the van and headed inland.

●　●　●

Later in the evening, darkness fell and took the electricity with it as the wind and rain became more aggressive. Growing tired of playing board games with her mother and snacking herself into a bellyache, Opal flopped into one of the wingback chairs in the den, where she and her parents were camped out. She watched as her mother read a book with the aid of a flashlight.

"Reading will help the time to pass if you're not going to saw logs through it," her mother said. She tapped the cover of the book in her hand just as Opal's dad released a snorting snore.

Both women snickered as they observed the sleeping man stretched out on one of the two large sofas. His motto was to sleep storms away, but the two Gilbert women had never taken to that idea. Both tended to be restless during hurricanes.

"Honey."

Opal moved her gaze from her peacefully sleeping father to her mother. She was holding out another book for Opal to consider.

"I won't be able to focus on it. Thanks, though."

"Suit yourself."

Opal sat for a while longer with one foot bouncing up and down, debating whether to munch on some licorice as a distraction or try out the book. She leaned toward the coffee table and picked up the bag, but her stomach protested, so she dropped it and sighed. "What time is it?"

"Ten minutes since the last time you asked," her mother retorted.

"Ugh." Needing to at least try to work off some of her anxiety and sugar binge, Opal grabbed a flashlight and roamed around the house like a ghost herself. With the windows boarded up and no air circulating, she was starting to feel claustrophobic. When sprinting up and down the stairs only produced the need to puke, Opal gave in and slipped out the front door for some fresh air.

She stepped onto the deep front porch, bracing her

feet wide to combat the wind, and regarded the madness once her eyes adjusted to the thick darkness. The outline of trees morphed continuously as the wind orchestrated them to bend and jerk and sway in a staccato tempo. As the wind whipped her hair around and caught the opened front of her jacket so it could push against her torso, Opal became part of the performance. She understood storms such as this hurricane were nothing to take lightly, but she couldn't help but see the force of nature as the eerie beauty it was. So powerful and mystifying.

Off in the distance, the jarring sound of something crashing snapped Opal out of the storm's spell. In the blink of an eye, another band of rain appeared out of nowhere and rushed the house, reminding her of those car wash nozzles that spray sideways. She was soaked within seconds, but before she could retreat back inside, the rain was gone and the wind grew still to the point she could feel the atmosphere's shift. Goose bumps broke out along her neck as her ears popped. Mesmerized, she eased to the edge of the porch, wrapped her arm around one of the thick columns, and peered up at the dark sky.

The barely visible clouds continued to rotate above, and their ferocious roar could be heard, reminiscent of an out-of-control freight train, but Opal could feel nothing more than a faint breeze. *The eye of the storm.*

Gaze fastened to the undulating sky, she whispered, "He rebuked the wind and raging waves, and they ceased, and there was a calm." Even though Opal had seen countless storms come and go, it never stopped amazing her how God could create a calm smack-dab in the middle of chaos.

She had no idea that come morning, she would be seeking a calm in the midst of another storm neither the Weather Channel nor the Gray Man had the decency to warn her about.

• • •

Most days, Opal was a pro at brushing off unpleasant things as easily as shooing a wayward curl out of her eyes, but the dreary morning found her resolve weaker than water. She stared at the store that felt more like home than her beach house up the street, trying to figure out which direction she should take to get things back right.

As Lincoln and her friends continued to comment on the situation, Opal kept quiet and regarded her pride and joy. She tilted her head to the left and then to the right, but not even looking at the damage sideways gave any hint as to how to get started. There were chairs and small tables that had been pried off the ceiling and now lay scattered around the tiny yard and street. Who knew what the interior held? Her dad had given strict orders not to place a foot inside until he had the place inspected for safety, so there was no telling yet what could be salvaged.

"The insurance company will probably write it off as a complete loss," Mr. Negativity spoke up, offering his two cents when Opal had no desire to give even a penny for his thoughts.

Before she could say so, Sophia shocked the entire lot of them by reaching over and pinching the fire out of Lincoln's arm. From the grimace on his face and the sudden flinch he did to get out of her reach, Opal figured her feisty friend was going for blood.

"Sophia Grace!" Josie reprimanded, eyes wide in shock.

"I warned him to keep it shut." Sophia pointed in the direction of his frowning lips as her phone started ringing in her other hand. With one last glare at Lincoln, she swiped the screen and walked off to answer the call.

Opal closed her eyes, not having the energy to figure

out how to put a halt to Sophia growing more and more sour by the day. Too many negative vibes bounced around her to think clearly. After dragging in a deep breath and slowly releasing it, she opened her eyes to find Lincoln watching her with sad puppy-dog eyes. It was a new expression for the ornery man, and one that really didn't suit him. Clearly he was there out of pity, but she asked anyway, "What are you doing here?"

Lincoln shrugged, stuffing his hands into the pockets of his hoodie as he cast his eyes to his shoes. "I just wanted to . . . check on you?" he muttered hesitantly enough to make him sound as unsure about his answer as Opal was.

The brooding man with his hair falling into his eyes, along with the cooler temperatures, had Opal right uncomfortable. She pulled the thick sweater tighter around herself with hopes of combating both. She watched him as he brushed his hair behind his ear and looked toward the building like he actually cared. Lincoln was a puzzle that had her racking her brain over the last week on how to solve, but with the damage to her business there was no room for puzzles—or the complicated feelings he stirred inside her.

Josie knelt in front of Opal's chair and took her icy hands into her much-warmer ones. "What can we do?"

Space was what Opal needed, but she was too kind to ask for it. With some effort, she pulled on a smile. "Your daddy got the ovens up and running yet?"

Josie smiled back and nodded. "Yep. He's already sent out a few rounds of biscuits to the utility workers and city crews."

"Great. I'm starving. You wanna go fetch us some breakfast?"

Josie stood. "Now that's one thing I can definitely do

for us." She walked over to Lincoln by the side of the road where he was collecting the scattered chairs. "Will you stick around? I'll bring you some breakfast too."

Lincoln hefted a chair in his bulky arms and peered at Opal over his shoulder. "I'm not going anywhere."

"Great. I'll be back as soon as I can." Josie waved as she opened the door of her little white truck and climbed in.

Sophia came around the corner as the truck drove away, worry puckering her face. "I'm sorry, Opal, but Collin is having a meltdown and Momma said he's crying for me."

"It's okay. You go take care of your son." Opal reached out and patted her friend's hand.

"But—"

"I'll be fine." Opal gave it another squeeze before dropping her hand back to her lap. "Now go."

"I just don't know what's gotten into him lately. He's never acted this way." Sophia looked close to tears as her phone went off again. Looking at the screen with a slight cringe, she answered, "I'm on my way." She hurried over to her SUV and was gone in a flash.

Lincoln was piling up the broken chairs, and after testing the legs of two others, he brought them over and lined them up beside Opal's lawn chair. "She acts like that and doesn't know why her kid does. Really?" He shook his head while settling on the chair beside her and let out a stifled grunt.

"You don't know Sophia's situation, nor what she and her son have been going through, so don't go making assumptions." Opal angled her body away from him, wondering why, on such a devastating day, she had to be stuck with the likes of Lincoln Cole.

They sat in silence as a few seagulls flew overhead. Even the birds appeared to be at a loss for words after the storm. Lincoln kept shifting beside her like he couldn't find a comfortable spot, and it took all her good upbringing to keep the suggestion that maybe he'd be more comfortable down the road clamped behind her lips.

Finally, not being able to take the tension any longer, she pivoted and asked once again, "Seriously, why are you here? After your two tirades—" she gestured toward the store where they both happened—"it was pretty clear you wouldn't be back."

He looked her square in the eyes, solemn yet stern, and asked, "Is this where I apologize for acting like an overgrown brat?"

His dry, humorous question caught Opal by surprise, but she managed to keep it off her face. "It wouldn't hurt."

"Then I apologize."

She scoffed. "That was lousy, but I accept." She had a feeling it wasn't in Lincoln's nature to make apologies for anything, no more than it was in her nature not to have a forgiving heart. Apparently, he was who he was, and one could take it or leave it. For some reason, she chose to accept him and his lackluster apology.

He nodded once and slowly rose to his feet, barely covering the wince that flashed across his face, and hobbled over to the door, which sat slightly ajar. She could tell he was in more pain than he had been during their previous encounters.

"It's not safe to be inside there," she called out. "My dad has people lined up to check things out before we're permitted to go in." She remained glued to her chair. At the small distance, she couldn't see inside the windows, so it made it easier to pretend all was right behind the door.

Lincoln stood, peeking around for a while, before reaching one of his long arms inside. He yanked something loose and came back with a chunky desk she'd fashioned out of two sewing machine table bases. The patina treatment used on the cast iron looked fine, but the barn door top was saturated. Lincoln easily tipped the heavy table above his head, carried it over, and placed it before her like an offering.

"The breeze should dry it out by the time Josie gets back with breakfast," he explained, moving over to another jumbled-up pile of chairs.

Opal remained planted in her spot and watched as he removed the cables from a few that were salvageable and tucked them into the other side of the table. Seemed he was one of those doers who always had to be moving. Or maybe it was his nerves keeping him in action. Or maybe it was his way of trying to get away from the ache in his leg. Regardless, Opal remained attached to the chair, not wanting to get any closer to facing her new reality.

Another hour slid by with her watching Lincoln limp around the yard and building as if he were on a treasure quest. A total of eleven chairs had been lined up in front of the store and a pile off to the side had grown into a mountain of broken furniture parts by the time Josie's truck pulled into the parking lot.

"Sorry!" Josie hurried over with several Styrofoam containers. Lincoln followed behind her, a drink carrier holding to-go cups in one hand and a few greasy white bags in the other. "Dad was slammed and I ended up helping him feed about half the town. You know how it is."

Opal did know how it was. She'd been behind the counter at Driftwood Diner more times than she could count during and after various storms. If people didn't have electricity, they always meandered there, knowing Jasper Slater would have his generators up and the food rolling out the kitchen.

As Josie divvied out the food, Opal picked up a cup and took in a deep inhale, letting out an appreciative moan before taking a small sip of the coffee. "Thank you."

Josie offered her a kind smile in response.

Lincoln surprised Opal by claiming the chair beside her, but perhaps that was his way of keeping her away from his line of vision. She didn't have the energy to care at the moment, so she said grace and then signaled everyone to dig in. It was a hearty breakfast of sausage biscuits, golden hash browns, and heated-up pastries Josie admitted to having left over from her hurricane snack stash. The warm meal with its heavily laden carbs was like a much-needed embrace. From all the contented sighs and moans, her table companions felt the same way.

Opal gazed around the small yard her mother had helped landscape a few years back. Even though debris was strewn all over, it still reminded her of a whimsical fairy garden, complete with thick rosebushes and garden gnomes. "This is kinda nice. It's the first alfresco meal I've ever had here." She shook her head while slicing into another piece of toast with her plastic fork. "Such a shame I've not enjoyed it until now."

The other two stopped eating and stared at her like her teeth had just fallen out and into her plate.

Chewing the bite, she garbled out, "What?"

Josie shook her head. "Only you, Opal Gilbert, would see past the flaws of a picture to find the beauty hidden among it."

Opal snickered for the first time that day. "And only you, Josie Slater, would comment on it so artistically." It felt good to laugh, so she tried it out again with the others joining in—well, one of them anyway. The reprieve was short-lived. The next inhale she took wiggled loose some

dam and before she could collect it, a sob pushed free
from deep within her belly.

Through her watery view, she noticed Josie begin to
rise while Lincoln looked downright disturbed by her
outburst. With a shaky palm raised, she beckoned her
friend to sit back down and turned her attention to the
formidable man sitting beside her. "Linc . . . May I call
you Linc?" she asked, voice coming out all squeaky.

Lincoln cleared his throat. "Suppose I can't stop you
no more than I can stop anyone else who does it."

Another sob slipped past her trembling lips and drew
another line of tears down her cheeks. "Linc, you gonna
eat the rest of your hash browns?"

He stared at her like she'd lost her mind, and maybe
she had dropped her basket, but considering the circumstances, Opal couldn't quite pick it back up just yet. First,
she needed those cheesy, greasy hash browns and . . . Her
gaze moved to Josie's coffee as Lincoln handed over the
container of hash browns.

"And, honey, may I have the rest of your coffee?"
Another hiccup, followed by another sob falling from her
trembling lips. Not only did Josie's cup slide her way but
so did Lincoln's half-empty coffee cup.

Opal sniffled and blathered, feeling like a stranger
in her own skin. She'd always prided herself on being a
free spirit. No kind of challenge was allowed to weigh
her down. As the tears fell and the blubbering sounds
continued to wobble from her lips, Opal realized just how
wrong she'd been in her thinking.

The remainder of the late breakfast went as follows:
Opal bellowed like a wounded animal and the other two
kept tossing her food to hush her up. By the time she'd
scarfed down anything she could shove into the gaping
hole the storm had torn in her stomach, her tears had

ceased and the bellowing tapered down to just a slight whimper.

"You want the rest of my apple fritter?" Josie asked with a good bit of caution as she held up the half-eaten donut.

Opal stifled an unladylike belch and shook her head. She was dizzy and bloated as it was, and no way could one more bite of food be consumed.

All eyes kept up a sweeping dance in her direction, just shy of full-on staring. She was a natural redhead, so Opal knew the cry didn't paint her face kindly. She had to be blotchy with a nose as bright as a maraschino cherry.

Later, when there was nothing left to do, Lincoln headed to his Jeep in what Opal could only describe as the fastest limping gait she'd ever witnessed. Surely he couldn't get away from her craziness fast enough. She was also fairly certain it would be the final time she'd see him run away from her. No way would he be coming back after that meltdown.

Sure don't blame him. Opal shook her head, feeling a pounding edge along her temples from the effect of the long cry. With one last look at Bless This Mess, she walked to her van and left the uncertainty for another day.

* * *

It took a few days before everyone in town had their power restored, but it didn't slow down Sunset Cove from picking up the pieces of their lives that Hurricane Lacy had scattered everywhere, and working on getting back to normal. Thankfully, most of the community had been spared, only sustaining superficial damage. While most were making progress, Opal had to sit tight until the building was thoroughly inspected. By that time, she'd been able to pick her basket back up and form a plan of action.

In a white thermal shirt, worn denim overalls rolled halfway up her shins, and high-top sneakers, Opal was ready to get to it. She surveyed the building and then the refreshment table Josie had helped her set up earlier for the volunteers, while tying a navy bandanna around her head. She didn't have time to deal with wayward curls today. No, today was all about productivity. As cars began to line the street, a giddiness overtook her. She was ready for the new beginning to begin.

Clapping her hands, she skipped over to the small group from her church. Each one was dressed in their own form of work attire. "Thanks so much for coming out to help!" She brought their attention to the two yellow-and-white-striped tents she'd rented from the events company that took up the entire side parking lot. "We need to clear all the furniture out of the building and place as much as possible underneath the tents."

The volunteers quickly formed an assembly line of sorts and began handing off piece by piece of furniture until making it to the tents, where Opal worked on arranging it all. Before they got the first tent a quarter of the way filled, a familiar Jeep pulled up, bringing with it a sight Opal had felt certain she'd never see again.

With his hair pulled up in one of those man buns that somehow worked for him, causing the frowning man to look even more intimidating, Lincoln slowly wove around the line of people snaking toward the tent until he reached her side. Opal regarded him, taking note of the high cheekbones that had been shielded by his long hair on other occasions. Even the thick scruff of beard didn't hide them. In faded jeans and a flannel shirt rolled up to his elbows, the man looked like he meant business.

"You're brave," Opal quipped as she set down a night-stand she'd fashioned from a coatrack.

Lincoln shifted his weight to his left leg and grimaced. Shifting it back to the other leg, he reached for the next piece to be handed over. It was an intricate wood bed frame she had turned into another bench. He sat it down and seemed to be pretending she didn't speak. Maybe going as far as pretending she wasn't even there.

"You're not going to say anything?" *About my crazy getting loose the other day?* Opal wanted to add the last part, but he probably already knew what she meant, so she chickened out.

Her question was met by more silence. Finally, after another ten minutes or so of remaining mute, Lincoln glanced around and mumbled, "This place looks like a circus."

Relieved he finally spoke, a smile tugged at her lips as Opal regarded the tents in a new light. "Oh, my! You're right, Linc. It does look exactly like a circus." She tightened her ponytail and allowed her imagination to carry her back to a childhood memory of a ringleader and an elephant underneath a tent her parents took her to one fall day. "I'd love to go to a circus. That's such a happy place."

Lincoln's big brown eyes cut toward her as he was handed the rocking chair she had been working on before the storm. His gaze held a curious caution, like he was gauging his chances of being able to haul tail without getting caught.

"I'm not crazy," she blurted.

"Ain't suggesting you are," he retorted, scooting the half-finished project over to the other side of the tent.

"Your eyes did." She pointed toward them before taking the rocking chair and setting it outside. *That would be a good project to take home and work on.*

After that comment, Lincoln worked hard at filling the tents and keeping his eyes to himself. When the group of volunteers gathered around the refreshments before heading out, she assumed he had taken that as his chance to make a clean getaway.

Opal watched the Jeep disappear down the side road as quickly as it had appeared earlier. The man was too squirrelly for her liking. Not standing in any one spot long enough to let her get too close. She thought that perhaps he'd shown up to help out of some remorse for being so rude to her in the beginning. Or it might have been pity. Shrugging off the uneasiness, she moved her focus to her guests and kept their tea glasses filled until all the food platters were bare and the sun was slipping behind the inlet. All in all, it had been a good day, and she whispered a quick prayer of thanks before following the caravan of vehicles home.

●   ●   ●

The following morning, Opal beat the sun to Bless This Mess. There was too much to get done before the roofers showed up for her to wait on daylight. In the grays and pinks of dawn, her poor store looked puny and battered.

A considerable amount of time, love, and money had been invested in the building in the last six years to turn back now. She'd willingly put aside any inclination of a personal life in order to keep her focus on making the business a success. Her parents were great and had always supported Opal in anything she pursued, but she longed for independence. Even when they wanted to give her the start-up money for Bless This Mess outright, she refused and had the family lawyer draw up a loan contract. Sure, she didn't pay interest, but the monthly payment was always paid on time. She had actually been on the path to paying it off early before the storm.

Sighing, she reached out to pat the charcoal-gray front door and whispered, "I wish for you to be restored. To be stronger than ever after the crew takes extra-special care of restoring you . . . Please, God, please bless my mess." Her fingers skimmed over a dent that hadn't been there before the hurricane, and she considered the flaw an added bit of character. Smiling, she gave the door one last pat and moved over to the tents to begin washing down each piece.

Armed with a bucket of soapy water and a rag, Opal took a deep breath to fortify herself, but the odor had her wrinkling her nose. The air trapped inside the tent was dank and held a mild mildew scent. Certainly not a healthy environment for furniture. She took the next little bit of time to set up large fans around the perimeter of each tent to help ward off the moisture and rolled up a few sections of the sides for better airflow.

An hour or so into cleaning, Lincoln walked through one of the tent openings. He was wearing similar work attire as the day before, and a similar frown.

"Good morning, Linc." Opal gave him her best chipper welcome, and all that accomplished was causing his frown to deepen. The overwhelming desire to figure out how to make him smile tapped her on the shoulder. Rotating the sensation away, she reminded herself she couldn't afford any distractions, Lincoln Cole included.

Without offering any form of greeting in return, Lincoln pointed at her hand. "You got another cloth?"

Opal scrutinized him, unable to figure out the man to save her life. He acted like he couldn't stand her, yet there he stood, willing to spend more time with her. She shook her head and said, "I just needed volunteers for the one day to get everything out of the store. I'm good now. Thanks, though." She dropped the large rag back into the bucket, swished it around, and then lifted it to wring the water out. Squatting beside a large dresser, she began wiping it down.

"I'm here to work." His words sounded just as uncertain as they had the day before, but Lincoln didn't wait for her response. Instead, he reached over and plucked the rag out of her hand and tore it down the middle like it was made out of nothing more than rice paper. "You take the bottom of each piece and I'll wash the top half."

"Taking charge and giving orders seem like something you're well versed in," Opal sassed but went about wiping down the bottom drawers as he'd instructed.

"I was climbing the military ranks at lightning speed for a reason."

Opal glanced up in time to catch him cringing, apparently having shared more than he'd wanted to. She decided to follow up with a snarky retort and snicker. "We both know it had nothing to do with your sunny disposition."

The only response Lincoln gave to that was a grunt of discomfort, so she let it go.

They worked in amicable silence with the ocean doing its job as the tranquil backdrop. Hours crept by, with her becoming quite impressed by how well they worked together.

"Does this cleaner have honey in it?" Lincoln asked out of the blue as they tackled an entertainment center that was now transformed into a wet bar.

A fan ruffled a red curl loose from Opal's topknot, so she stood and wound it back into place. "No . . . It's just Murphy oil soap." She picked up her rag and sniffed it, only finding the pungent scent of the cleaner.

"Oh," he mumbled, moving a few steps away from her.

Opal wiped a film of grime off the side panel and glanced at Lincoln. "I'm guessing this means you want the job?"

He didn't look at her, just kept working and answered in that tentative way he had with anything that seemed related to her. "I reckon."

"I'll probably only need you like three days a week, and the pay isn't that much." Her back and hamstrings were tiring, so she plopped on the tarp-lined ground and continued cleaning in a seated position.

"I don't need much money. Plus, I start PT with my new therapist next week, so the three days will work good for me."

Opal's eyes moved over his jean-clad leg, wondering what sort of damage it concealed. "How's your mobility?"

Lincoln leaned over and washed his rag out in the bucket, moving efficiently, not wasting a second before going back to cleaning the top of the piece. "Honestly, it's not great but slowly getting better. I'm learning how to work around it."

Opal twirled her rag in her hands and continued to watch him. The man cleaned with gusto and didn't stop until the piece was immaculate. "What do you mean by *working around it*?"

He tipped his head to the side, giving her a fleeting look before going back to work. "My leg has weak spots and the dang thing has sent me flat on my back a time or two." He chuckled, but it lacked humor. "That's on me. If I'd use my cane like I should . . ." His voice trailed off as he shook his head.

"Why not use it?"

"Because I'm stubborn."

"I already figured as much." It was the first time Opal

considered maybe Lincoln wasn't the right guy for the job. "August said you'd be able to handle this."

"And I can as long as I do what my other therapist back home has taught me. It's all about back and upper body and compensating with my right leg." He flexed his massive arms before dunking his cloth back into the bucket. "I'm strong as an ox. No worrying about that." Even though he sounded sure, the visible part of Lincoln's cheeks above his beard were elevated in color.

That little indicator was enough to make Opal realize how uncomfortable he was with discussing his injury, so she changed the subject. "I need a break and Seashore Creamery is the perfect solution." She stood and stretched out her stiff back.

Lincoln made a face, one he was making too often in her presence—brows puckered, lips pursed, stare perplexed. "It's kinda chilly for ice cream, and it's lunchtime." After wringing out the cloth, he brought it to his nose and took a sniff. Seeming to not find whatever it was he was searching for, he brought it back to the wet bar and slid it along the underside of a shelf that held slots for stemware.

She dismissed his weather and lunch observation with a flick of her wrist. "Nonsense. They wouldn't be open year-round if you could only eat ice cream on warm days, and it can be a very satisfying meal, in my opinion. Plus, I have it on good authority that they've just made a batch of seaweed swirl as their weekly special." She waggled her eyebrows, hoping to tease and tempt him, but one look at his stern face showed she had failed.

That perplexed look etched harsher on his face as he straightened to full height and stared. "Now you're talking pure nonsense. Seaweed ain't supposed to be in ice cream. That's just . . ." He wrinkled his nose and shook his head. "Nasty."

"You're making assumptions again." She dropped the rag into the bucket and dried her hands on her purple cargo pants. "I'm going for ice cream. You're welcome to join me."

He gave her a quick side-eye and went back to work. "I don't care to."

"Suit yourself." She began weaving through the tent to the side exit, knowing good and well the ornery man thought she was a certifiable nutcase, but not caring enough to correct his fallacy. Nothing was going to side-track her from the pursuit of creamy goodness.

Opal set her pace to a lazy stroll just in case Mr. Cranky Britches changed his mind. She kept listening for the stomp/limp pattern of his gait to follow, but by the time she reached the crosswalk, she gave up. Even though it wasn't surprising he chose to stay behind and sulk, disappointment still accompanied her on the way to the creamery.

"Good morning, dear," Miss Dalma greeted, startling Opal.

Opal looked over and found the tiny lady sitting on a bench. "Good morning." She tapped the side of a small laundry basket sitting beside Dalma, filled with mismatched socks. "Are you on your way to the Laundromat?" She hoped not, since the Laundromat was on the other side of town.

"Oh no. My Gerald bought me a washer/dryer set for the house." Dalma hitched a thumb over her shoulder in the direction of her house on the inlet.

Opal glanced down the avenue to where Dalma's house sat, three lots over. At least she hadn't lugged the basket too far. Miss Dalma was nearing ninety years old and had been the town's librarian for so long that even after retirement she was still referred to that way. Her mind hadn't been faring too well in the last few years, but surely that came with living close to a century.

Opal scooted the basket over and plopped down beside her while sending a text to Josie, who had taken on the caregiver role. **Just found Dalma on the bench at 53rd Avenue. Whose day is it to keep an eye on her?**

Josie texted back immediately. **Bertie Matthews. I'm on my way.**

Opal responded. **No worries. I'll take care of her. You sure?**

Yep. She sent several smiley emojis, hoping to put Josie's mind at ease. The poor girl worried herself silly over just about everybody. "Miss Dalma, where's Bertie?"

Dalma laughed dryly and rolled her eyes, looking rather youthful for such an old lady. The high ponytail capturing her long white hair and the crewneck sweatshirt she had paired with denim capri pants added to the effect. "The ole gal is snoring away on the porch swing. She naps more than a newborn."

"What's up with the laundry basket?" Opal pointed, bringing Dalma's surprised attention to it.

"Darnedest thing . . . I have no idea." She made a face and dismissed it altogether, closing her eyes and tilting her head toward the morning sun.

Opal chose to do the same, knowing it was a waste of time to try figuring out the little lady. After a few minutes, she opened her eyes and asked, "You feel like going to the creamery with me?"

Dalma's cloudy-blue eyes popped open and her face lit up. "Why, I'd love to."

Opal gathered the laundry basket in one arm, held her other hand out for Dalma, and happily led the way.

Once they'd each ordered a double scoop of seaweed swirl, Opal and Dalma decided the pier was the perfect place to enjoy their ice cream. Dalma chatted her up on basically nonsense, but Opal didn't care. After being stuck with Mr. Antisocial, who was apparently allergic to words, it was a nice change.

Opal licked a dribble of ice cream escaping down the side of the cone before asking, "Do you think I'm too far out there, Miss Dalma?"

"I say the farther out there, the better, dear. You make life interesting, but you're no wackadoodle. Don't let any sticks-in-the-mud tell you otherwise." Dalma gave her arm an encouraging squeeze. She then launched into telling Opal about a historical romance she'd just finished listening to on her iPad. It was Dalma and Josie's thing, sitting together on Dalma's back deck listening to audiobooks. Opal didn't do much reading, considering it required sitting still, but she enjoyed hearing Dalma's lively take on a story.

By the time she walked Dalma home, Opal had come to the conclusion that she'd have to start working on softening Lincoln's guarded exterior if he planned on sticking around. They'd both be miserable otherwise. She felt for sure they could become friends if he'd just give it a chance. Dalma had assured her she wasn't a wackadoodle, not entirely anyhow, and Lincoln needed to understand that too.

5

"The woman has to be completely off her rocker," Lincoln muttered as he limped over to the tents the next day and found all kinds of evidence to support his theory. The savory notes of butter and burnt sugar wafted toward him, and darned if he didn't hear the familiar sound of brass instruments tinkling out the jovial tune associated with the circus—the *dada-ta-ta-ta* that seemed to be the universal theme song.

Pulling in a deep breath of the appealing aroma that certainly smelled of childhood memories, Lincoln didn't know whether he wanted to step through the tent curtain and enter her curious world or just quietly slink away to never return. Confused and quite agitated with himself, his feet kept propelling him forward until he'd entered to find an antique-looking popcorn stand brimming full. A grinning sprite of a woman was twirling a paper cone around a cotton candy maker beside it, collecting a bright-pink ribbon of candy along the way. There she stood in blue, baggy coveralls with a name patch declaring her *Bubba*. Her red-gold curls were pulled high into pigtails. He wanted to tell her she was too old for such a hairstyle and that she should give Bubba his uniform back, but she was just too blame cute and happy for him to get the words out.

"Good morning, Linc," Opal greeted, same as yesterday in all that bubbly happiness. And same as yesterday it annoyed him.

"Mornin'," Lincoln replied in a tired voice, still trying to shake the lingering vestiges of the morbid night. It had been filled with images of the rocket attack, twisted into disjointed dreams that made waking up even more bothersome. He'd lain in bed, panting and washed in sweat, wondering if the vise grip of those nightmares would ever alleviate enough for him to find some form of peace. "I'm going to start wiping furniture down in the other tent." Lincoln scooped up the bucket she'd already prepared and started shuffling away.

"Wait!" she called out. "I've made you cotton candy."

A quick glance over his shoulder found her skipping toward him with the cloud of pink candy held high like a confectionery torch. "It's eight in the morning," Lincoln pointed out with a good bit of grit, hoping it would send her in the other direction with the absurd treat. *It's too early to deal with this.*

"Yes, but I thought it would make for a more enjoyable way to start the day . . ." She paused when he shook his head, but only briefly. "Don't look at me like I'm crazy. This circus stuff was your idea."

That had him turning completely around and giving her his full-force you-are-most-definitely-crazy look. The woman practically vibrated kookiness, but her joy was as alluring as that candy in her tiny hand. And boy, did that make him spitting mad.

"Aha!" Opal pointed the cone toward his face, barely missing the tip of his nose. "You like me in spite of my quirks."

"What makes you think that?"

"Your gorgeous brown eyes gave it away. They just

softened around the edges. That can only mean one thing . . ." Opal shoved the cotton candy torch into his free hand. "You like me, Lincoln Cole. You might as well stop lying to yourself about it." Giggling, she sashayed back to the refreshment table, the baggy legs of the coveralls swishing as she went. She could play the part of the clown in their current scenario with little effort.

He was pretty sure he had the flabbergasted sidekick role down pat.

"Your gorgeous brown eyes . . ."

Shaking off the uneasiness she pushed on him with that knowing smile of hers, Lincoln said tersely, "I do not like you! And whose clothes are you wearing?" He dropped the bucket and shoved his hat lower onto his forehead, wishing he could wear a complete face mask to help hide from the perceptive woman. Annoyed for even wanting to be there under the ridiculous tent with her, he took a harsh bite out of the side of the cotton candy and did his best not to enjoy it.

"They were my brother's until he outgrew them a few years ago. His name is Kane, but I've called him Bubba ever since they brought him home from the hospital. I tried my best to talk Momma and Daddy into renaming him, but they were set on Kane for some silly reason." Opal touched the lapel of the coveralls. "I had these made for him when he used to help deliver furniture. Now he's off to college and I'm left missing him. He wanted to come home and help me out, but it's midterm time, so I told him to stay put and focus on that. He's going to be an architect one day." She rambled off all that information with pride when Lincoln would have much rather had just a very *brief* briefing. *They were my brother's* would have been a sufficient explanation.

Three more substantial bites and Lincoln was left

with only remnants of sugar stuck in his back teeth and clutching a sticky cone in his fist. Tossing it into the garbage bin, he retrieved the bucket and attempted the trek once more to the other tent.

"You're welcome, Linc," Opal said in that singsong tone.

"Thank you." Lincoln ticked his head in the direction of the portable speaker placed on a coffee table. "Cut that racket off. I already got a bellyache as it is." Truthfully, it had nothing to do with his belly and everything to do with the all-out war raging in his thoughts and his leg. The nightmare episode and pain was pressing down on him so severely, his jaw kept locking up.

"What would you like to listen to, if not this fun musical selection?" Opal asked with a little too much sugar dripping off her lips, oblivious to the battle he was fighting against.

Lincoln knew she was being nice enough to ask his preference but sly enough to get a jab in. He couldn't fault her in that one bit. It was deserved, and it made no sense why she even put up with him. As he took in her warm smile, a longing to share with her what was tearing him apart hit him out of nowhere. His bottom lip betrayed him, right along with his thoughts, and began to tremble before he could stop it.

The flirty tease slipped away from her beautiful face as Opal grew serious and took a step toward him. Her green eyes scanned every inch of his rigid body, making him feel exposed. "Lincoln, are you okay?"

Lincoln released a harsh cough and turned his back to her, something he'd become accustomed to as of late. "I'm fine." His voice betrayed him too, presenting hoarse and weak. The happy tune abruptly stopped playing, leaving a heavy silence to hang in the air. Taking several deep breaths, he pushed the hurt and turmoil deep within and put a lock on it. Once he regained his composure, Lincoln waved toward the speaker. "Anything country I ain't opposed to." As he finally made it into the adjoining tent and placed the bucket beside a barrel table, a Sam Hunt song began filtering throughout the space.

Getting down to work, Lincoln forced his mind to drift to simpler memories. Times that were bright and promising with no dark shadows to dim the excitement. Youth ROTC, basic training, nights of kicking up dust on back roads back home, OCS, shooting the breeze with his unit during those brief downtimes, and traveling overseas to show the enemy who was boss . . .

Hours slipped by as they steadily worked. It was a relief that the woman's perceptiveness picked up on his need for just that. By lunch, the knots in his shoulders and neck had loosened and he was able to say a word or two without sounding like a frog.

After hobbling over to the Jeep, Lincoln eased the leg of his pants up and slapped on a few Icy Hot pain patches around his knee before grabbing the cooler from the back. He brought it over to the tent and even pulled on a half smile while handing Opal the sandwich he'd made her for lunch. Of course, she made too big a deal out of it, thanking him profusely for the boring turkey sandwich.

"This was so thoughtful of you." Her face lit up as she unwrapped the sandwich.

Lincoln shrugged while placing two sandwiches, a couple packs of crackers, a bag of carrots, three apples, and two bananas on the table. "Gotta eat." He placed a bottle of that weird raspberry tea she liked by her sandwich and slid an apple and banana over too. They ate in silence, him tearing into the food with gusto while Opal slowly nibbled.

Sharing the meal was pleasant enough, but once they

got back to work, somehow Opal's mute button had stopped working, and Lincoln couldn't figure out for the life of him how to press it again.

Opal jabbered on and on about nonsense while flitting near him like an annoying fly. He'd speed up to get a few pieces ahead of her, but she remained right on his heels. All the while, her heart-shaped mouth never took a break. For some odd reason, he wanted to be in the woman's atmosphere but at a safe distance. Too close and she'd suck him into her zany orbit and a catastrophic collision would surely follow. Every time she approached him with popcorn or a bottle of water or some other offering, he shuffled in the other direction.

No matter, that day ended and the next day showed up to find Lincoln going back to help Opal, all the while wondering why it was impossible to just stay away. He chalked it up to wanting to make amends for his past rudeness and he threw in some pity for her situation to round it out. Life might have sullened him, but his manners were still somewhere deep inside, and he was genuinely ashamed of how he had treated her.

It took two more days to finally get all of the pieces washed down, and in those two days, two things began to nag at Lincoln. First, the throb in his leg escalated to higher levels of pain no matter how much ibuprofen he threw at it. And second, that scent of honey nagged him until he finally understood where it was coming from.

Yesterday, Opal had to work on a dresser she had fashioned out of mismatched parts from several other dressers. It took quite a bit of sanding on a few of the drawers to get them to move with ease. There was no denying the fact the woman had a gift and knew what she was doing. Not many could come up with the strange refurbished pieces and actually create them in a functioning way. As she worked, he noticed the scent of honey mingled with the more robust scent of sawdust when he was close to her. He began hovering around just to draw in the aroma, never having imagined that the odd combination could smell so appealing.

Today the combination was slightly different, with the honey entwining with the polishing wax Opal was applying to the finished dresser. He finally figured out she carried the note of honey along with whatever project she was working on at the time. As if the piece somehow became a part of her. He didn't even realize he'd leaned in to take in another breath of her sweet air until she grew still and eyed him.

"Why do you keep sniffing me?" Opal asked, holding the pot of wax in one hand and the polishing rag in the other. Her outfit for the day was made up of Army-green corduroy pants and a flannel shirt. All of those wild curls were tucked underneath a knit cap, making her look like she should be trekking through the mountains instead of dawdling seaside.

Lincoln straightened and took a few steps back. "What? I ain't sniffing you! Just breathing." He grumbled a few sentiments under his breath while hobbling away from the distracting smell. "Sniffing you . . . Stupid . . . Can't a guy breathe? Sheesh!"

Once he had a few tables between them, Lincoln chanced looking at her and found Opal rubbing the wax into the top of the dresser while giving him a sardonic smile. The woman always looked at him like she had a secret, and that annoyed him even further. The irritation escalated and the pain in his leg joined in, and by late afternoon when Carter showed up to help load the dresser, Lincoln was ready to boil over in more than one sense of the word. Even though the air was comfortably cool, a fine sheen of sweat pressed against his skin and his gut was on fire from the vexation of . . . well . . . of everything. He was so angry that he'd lost sight of what had him so angry in the first place.

It took both guys to wiggle the furniture into the back of Opal's Volkswagen van. Of course, the weird van was the same teal color as the store with the same logo on the side. It looked silly in Lincoln's opinion and he said as much, along with several other haughty comments.

"These tents stink."

"Stop humming! You always got to make noise!"

"Why can't they be done with that roof already?"

"The wind is too loud."

His rant kept on until Carter walked over and presented him with a king-size Snickers, slapping the candy bar against Lincoln's chest.

"Eat this," Carter ordered.

"Why?"

"You're an extra-special kind of cranky today. I'm hoping that candy bar will take you from being the grumpy bear that needs to go back into hibernation and turn your tail into sweet Bambi."

"Aww. Lincoln is a cute bear. A Bambi character wouldn't fit his frame," Opal teased while narrowing her eyes at Carter. "Now stop goading Linc. He's tetchy enough without provocation today." Opal formed the statement properly, something else he'd complained about earlier—her going back and forth between country slang and proper language. She breezed by and snatched the candy bar that Lincoln had been holding out like he was ready to throw it.

"Hey! That's mine!" Lincoln watched as the lumber-jack sprite unwrapped the candy and took a big bite.

"You don't want this," she garbled around a mouthful,

her cheeks poking out. "It has nuts in it. They'll get stuck in your teeth and then you'll have something else to complain about, and I, for one, think you've reached your limit on that for the day." She took another substantial bite and chewed it thoughtfully. "Carter, would you be a peach and help me deliver this dresser?"

"Sure," Carter answered.

"That's my job," Lincoln replied at the same time.

"No worries, Linc. I think it's time you head home for a nap." Opal skipped off and hopped into the van, leaving him fuming.

Carter clamped a hand down on Lincoln's shoulder with concern set in his eyes. It was all the angry man could do not to bristle at his friend's touch. "Seriously, man. Are you okay today?"

"I'm fine. Just need a nap apparently." Lincoln shrugged off Carter's hand and hobbled to his Jeep.

●   ●   ●

The nap happened without Lincoln's permission. One minute he was sitting on the edge of his bed, trying to get a grip on his rage and the escalating pain; the next thing he knew he was waking up to a new day. The pain continued vibrating through his leg, but the rage had withered into a hazy sluggishness. Skipping the physical therapy session that morning as planned wasn't an option. Something new was wrong and he had to get it fixed, pronto.

Coastal Orthopedics and Physical Therapy was a combination clinic that Lincoln's therapist from back home had recommended. He sat in his Jeep and stared at the building. It was an unassuming tan structure with the backdrop of the ocean behind it. His eyes roamed over the deserted beach, remembering days he'd spent just south of here on a surfboard with August, Carter, and their other buddies. He shifted in the seat as he reached back to grab his cane. The slight movement sent a thunderbolt up his leg, reminding him that his surfing days were history. Gripping the cane, it was all he could do to restrain himself from bashing the dashboard with it.

Taking a calming breath, Lincoln let it out slowly as he proceeded at the same sloth-like pace to exit the vehicle before causing any damage. Using his cane like a good patient, he stepped inside and over to the reception area to sign in. A twentysomething woman sat behind the desk smacking gum, her hair dyed a unique shade of gray. It was on the tip of his tongue to tell her that shade of hair would come naturally and all too soon, but he chose to not speak at all. She'd figure that out on her own, anyway.

Lincoln tipped his head to her before limping over to the waiting area. The place was decorated in the likeness of a beach shanty. Not very original, but completely inviting, and something about the styling seemed familiar. An ancient crab trap with bleached wood planks on top serving as a coffee table caught his attention. After inspecting it, he moved over to do the same to an old rowboat split in two on the back wall. One half had been refurbished into a TV stand. The other half, split the long way, was being used as low-standing bookcases on either side of the entertainment unit.

He took a seat in one of the lifeguard stands lined in a row. The legs had been cut down to a normal chair height, and each one was dressed with a nautical-themed cushion. Before he could scope out the rest of the waiting room for other familiarly crafted pieces, a dark-skinned man in blue scrubs appeared from behind a side door and looked right at him.

"Lincoln Cole?"

"That'd be me," Lincoln answered on a grunt while slowly standing up. He offered his hand to the therapist, who returned it in a confident grip. "And you must be Marcus?"

"Correct. Are you ready to work that leg out?"

Lincoln held in the grimace, not looking forward to anyone touching the angry part of his body. "Might as well be."

The front door swung open and a waft of honey floated in. "Oh, good! I'm not late!"

Brow furrowed, Lincoln turned to find Opal standing right behind him. "What are you doing here?"

"I wanted to keep you company." Opal presented him with a hopeful smile, her bright-green eyes wide and friendly.

"I'm good." He pointed toward the door. "You're free to skip back to wherever you just came from."

Opal clapped her hands quietly. "I'm so glad to see you're in a better mood today . . ." Her gaze drifted to the cane in his grasp. "Oh, and you're finally using your cane."

Right then and there, he understood her kookiness was only a front. The woman was too sly and intuitive for his likings. Each one of her odd attributes had purpose. He just didn't know her well enough to read what was behind it yet.

Lincoln cut her a look before sliding a friendlier one to the therapist, who had his arms crossed and was looking a little suspicious. "I use my cane."

"It's the first time I've ever seen you with it," Opal interjected.

His eyes snapped back to her. "Go away."

The glare and sharp tone should have had the tiny

woman retreating. Instead, she stepped around him and gestured for the therapist to lead the way. "Marcus, I feel Linc has been joshing me over the severity of his injury. I need to know he's okay to work with me."

Marcus shook his head. "Opal, you know how HIPAA works. I'm not allowed to discuss his health with you."

She waved off his concerns. "Oh, I know. I'm just going to be a fly on the wall during his appointment. Feel free to discuss matters as though I'm not even here."

"Like that's possible," Lincoln said snidely behind her as Marcus showed them into an exam room. It was a rather large space with an exam table he chose to sit on and a section with exercise and PT equipment.

"It's your choice, Lincoln, on whether she stays or not." Marcus opened a small laptop and began typing something.

"There's no getting rid of her," Lincoln mumbled when she took the cane from his hand and propped it against a chair like a good helper. It was the first time he had someone with him during an appointment in a long time. Sure, his family wanted to support him, but he'd shut them out, wanting to prove he could do it on his own. "So y'all know each other?"

"It's a small town," Opal answered. "Everyone knows everybody."

"Opal decorated the waiting room for me. My wife and I love her eclectic furniture pieces."

"Eclectic? That's a nice way of putting it." Lincoln frowned when the other two laughed like he'd said something funny. He slid farther back on the exam table and barely stifled the whimper when he was unable to straighten his leg.

"Enough about that. I want to hear more about you not using your cane." Marcus closed the lid of the laptop and moved to Lincoln's side.

Lincoln shot a harsh scowl toward Opal, who was bouncing on a stability ball in the corner. She was wearing one of her floral grandma dresses and oversize sweaters with cowgirl boots on her feet, looking like a little girl playing dress-up.

She smiled innocently. "Did little ole me get you in trouble? Sorry."

She didn't look sorry. As a matter of fact, he was thinking she had shown up to do just that. The retort he was forming fled when Marcus pushed the leg of his track pants up and began applying pressure to the area just above his knee. Nostrils flaring, Lincoln almost came off the table.

"Opal, you didn't need to tattle. This swelling and redness is all the evidence I need to know he's not been using his cane. Why, man?" Marcus shook his head and didn't give Lincoln time to form the nonexistent excuse. "Your former therapist warned me about your stubbornness, but there's a big difference between being stubborn and being stupid. I think you're a smart enough man to know which one you're being by not taking care of this leg like you've been instructed."

"Stupid," Opal whispered, hidden somewhere behind Marcus.

Lincoln spoke out even though he couldn't see her. "I don't want you here!"

"Then tell me to leave," she fired back, the top of her golden curls coming just into view, making it clear she'd stood up from the ball.

"Let me grab some ice packs and see if Dr. Rabin is free to see you." Marcus hurried out of the room.

Opal was just sitting back down on the ball but jolted to her feet in a tizzy as she zeroed in on his disfigured leg, sending the ball rolling across the room. Gasping, she rushed over and grabbed Lincoln's hand as if it were the most natural thing to do while eyeing his mangled limb. Apart from the severe swelling, there were pocked areas and spots with purplish scarring that looked so foreign he sometimes couldn't wrap his mind around it belonging to him.

"This is all my fault." Opal sniffled while rubbing her other hand over his forearm.

Lincoln came to his senses and shrugged her hands off him. "You hardly know me. Ain't none of this your fault." He rolled the pant leg back down to conceal his ruined leg.

"You've been helping me and not tending to your leg. I knew yesterday but couldn't bring myself to send you home."

"Why not?" He tried to slide over and out of her reach, but Opal just leaned over more and was right back to holding his hand.

"Because I want you to be my friend." She sniffled again.

"Knock it off. I'm fine. Probably just overdid it and . . ." He wiped the dewy sheen off his forehead as the room grew too warm.

"You're slurring . . ." Opal's palm covered his forehead, then tested the temperature on his cheeks. "And you're burning up." The door opened, and Marcus and another guy wearing a white exam coat hurried into the room. "He has a fever," she informed them.

"I thought so," Marcus admitted while setting down a handful of ice packs and an Ace bandage. "This is Dr. Rabin. I believe you have an appointment with him next month."

"You just couldn't wait to meet me, I see," the doctor quipped while scanning the details Marcus pulled up on the laptop. He moved over to Lincoln. "May I take a look?"

Lincoln grunted out his permission and braced himself. As the doctor's hands went to pushing around his throbbing knee, Lincoln whimpered. Opal's grip automatically tightened on his hand and he squeezed it back without realizing his actions.

Dr. Rabin shook his head. "Marcus is going to wrap it with some ice packs while I grab a wheelchair. We need to move you over to the ortho side of the clinic so we can get an IV going to administer a round of antibiotics."

Before Lincoln could put up a protest, he was being wheeled down a back hall of the building with Opal by his side. She carried his cane and a worried expression, both of which had him feeling even more off-balance. Through a haze of pain and grogginess, he vaguely sensed them giving him something for the pain and fever while the IV delivered antibiotics to war against the infection set in his leg.

Hours passed with the redheaded sprite by his side, offering sips of ice water and kind smiles.

"Go away," Lincoln muttered off and on.

And off and on Opal would reply, "Play pretty now."

There was no getting rid of her, and he was too tired to put up much complaint when she agreed to drive him home once the IV bag was empty and some of the fire in his leg had calmed down.

"Your prescriptions should be ready within an hour for pickup. Stay off the leg until our follow-up next week," Dr. Rabin instructed.

"I have to work." Lincoln's protest was weak. Whatever painkiller they had given him had weighed down his mind and limbs considerably. That detached feeling he hated.

"There's no work to be done at this point. We have to pause while the crew lays new flooring, so it's perfect timing for you to neglect your health and fall ill." Opal said this in a reassuring voice, but Lincoln was learning her sweetness was only a tool she used to drive home her true meaning.

The ride home in the van wasn't his idea of comfortable, but at least he arrived at the beach cottage in one piece. Opal walked him in.

"I got it from here," he said at the door, motioning for her to go on, but he wasn't surprised when she flat-out ignored him.

Opal pulled her phone out and was rattling off a food order while moving around his kitchen.

"I ain't hungry," Lincoln complained as he propped himself up in the recliner. It was the only piece of furniture he'd handpicked for the new place. It was an oversize chair and could accommodate his long limbs pretty well. He pushed until it reclined way back and shut his eyes, promptly dozing off.

●   ●   ●

"I have your prescription and the best shrimp burger on the coast." That whimsical voice penetrated the medicated haze Lincoln was trapped in.

He peeled open one eye to find a plate piled with fries and a bun overflowing with golden shrimp and coleslaw. The other eye opened as his cottony mouth began to water. He heard smacking and looked over to find Carter sitting on his couch eating his own lunch. His friend gave him a nod but kept eating.

"Carter brought over your Jeep and took care of picking everything up," Opal offered while placing a bottle of Gatorade on the end table beside his chair.

Lincoln sat up just enough to send the footrest down a reclining notch so he could eat properly. Still with a foggy mind, he blinked and found his plate empty and half the bottle of orange drink gone. He looked around and found Carter in the same predicament but wearing a weary expression.

"What?"

Carter shook his head. "Man, you gotta take better care of yourself than this." He pointed to Lincoln's leg.

Lincoln looked down where it was elevated on the footrest and found it wrapped with fresh ice packs and resting on a pillow. He glanced around, expecting to find the pixie hovering in her grandma dress, but the only evidence she had been there in the first place was a hint of honey in the air and a seashell resting on the side table. "She gone?"

"Yep." Carter leaned forward and rested his elbows on his knees. "I can't believe she stuck around as long as she did."

"What do you mean?" Lincoln set the plate down by the seashell, ignoring it and the small note placed beside it.

"You kept telling her to leave you alone and in the next breath asking for her sandwich. Which she kindly gave you. She made sure you had your medicine while you sat there telling her to hush up." Carter shook his head. "Dude, I don't know this Lincoln Cole you've turned into. Don't really care for the punk. How about taking some time to work this mess out and find the guy I used to know?" He stood up and gathered their lunch trash. After dealing with that, he left without another word.

Ashamed, Lincoln sat there studying the full bottle of painkillers with bleary eyes. He knew he was irritable on his best days anymore, but he refused to go back down the dark rabbit hole where those pills sent him each time he took a dose. They always brought all of his anger to the surface until it spewed out in fits of rage. Apparently that's what Carter had observed. Lincoln didn't remember any of it.

Those stinging thoughts didn't just tap on his shoulder to remind him of his wrongs. They punched him square in the gut and stole his breath. Months of pain meds had helped to morph him into someone he didn't even recognize and in the end made him act in a way he'd never done sober. It was the reason he couldn't go back home.

After much effort, Lincoln made it out of the chair. With his cane helping to balance him, he grabbed the prescription bottle and limped to the bathroom, where he flushed the pills. Tossing the empty bottle into the trash, he managed to make it to his bed. He hoped he could sleep off the rest of the side effects and maybe some of his awful attitude. Once the fog was lifted and the infection healed, he had a lot of apologizing to do.

6

The seagulls decided the crisp fall morning warranted their melody. As they soared overhead, they each squawked out their salutations. With her face turned heavenward, Opal thanked the Lord for the storm being a blessing in disguise. With the roof torn off, rotting ceiling beams had been discovered. Thank goodness it hadn't collapsed before that. Also, she would finally be able to act on her idea to enclose the back porch. Now the space could be used as a proper workshop. Shelves and cabinets had been added to help store all of her supplies, which freed up more floor space in the showroom. The paint crew was due soon to finish the trim work and any touch-ups, so it was time to get the workday started. She walked around the building and spotted Josie on a ladder.

Opal looked up. "Whatcha doing?"

Josie placed a piece of tile that helped form an ocean wave in the mosaic back in its rightful spot before peering down at her. "Fixing this."

"I have a guy coming tomorrow to do that." Opal shielded her eyes with her hand and squinted up at her friend.

"I don't mind." Josie plucked another piece from a bucket and iced the back of it with mortar. "Do you remember us putting this project together?"

"Yeah." A wide grin spread across her face as she recalled the summer after graduation, when the three friends hung out fixing up the building. "We worked on it for a solid week with Sophia sitting in a lounge chair acting as supervisor." Opal had come up with the idea of the mosaic with hopes of rekindling Josie's passion for art, but Josie did as Josie had always done. She viewed it as helping a friend out and nothing more. Soon, Opal was going to set a plan into motion to change that, but for the time being, she had another pressing matter. "I'm worried that giving Lincoln a job was a mistake."

"Hmm . . . I'm not sure . . ." Josie shook her head and began descending the rungs of the ladder. She set the bucket of mortar down and dusted her hands together.

"Why's that?" Opal tucked several errant curls behind her ear.

"I think you've been good for him." Josie shrugged. "He seems suited for this place."

Opal scoffed. "He'd probably tell you differently."

"Yeah? From what I've heard from the Knitting Club, he's shown up here every day since the doctor released him last week. And every day you send him away spittin' mad."

"I knew those old ladies were keeping me supplied with baked goods for no good reason." Opal's head rolled back, looking at the blue sky.

Each day Lincoln had shown up to deliver some form of an apology. The first day was a bottle of the raspberry chai tea she loved to have as an afternoon treat. He handed it off and started hobbling toward the tents like nothing had happened. After pointing out his misassumption, she sent him on his way. The next day it was a pint of chili-infused chocolate ice cream along with a few muttered words admitting he had been a jerk. Again, she accepted the little offering and pointed him back to his Jeep.

Opal glanced at the green beaded bracelet on her wrist that was his most recent attempt at apologizing. It had been accompanied with actual words. *"I'm sorry for being so mean."* She agreed before telling him to hit the road. And boy, did he sound like a snarling beast as he stomped/limped away. "Lincoln doesn't take too kindly to being told no."

"But he keeps coming back anyway. There's a reason, and I think that reason is you. I really think he needs you. And this job." Josie paused to take a breath. "What if you make him promise to be more careful with his leg? Would you allow him to come back to work?"

Opal sighed long and loud. "I had no idea how severe his injuries were. I feel so guilty for having him standing hours on end while helping around here. Look where that landed him. I just don't think this is a good fit for him." Each time he'd shown up to argue his case of working for her, Lincoln stood there, defeated and desperate for another chance, and her arms ached to reach out and hold him. To reassure him he was going to get through this storm in his life. And it scared the mess out of her to feel so strongly for him.

Josie bent her knees to bring Opal to eye level, looked at her like some weird something was lurking in the green depths of her irises, and twisted her lips. "Who are you? And what have you done with my Opal?"

Opal focused anywhere but on her friend's scrutiny. "I . . . He . . . We . . . I don't know, okay?" She waved her hands in the air, conceding defeat in the great battle of Lincoln Cole. Admitting that she liked him and wanted to be his friend was a cinch. Easy-peasy. That was her nature, after all. But seeing him sick had flipped some switch in her and had her wanting more than friendship, and each time he barked at her to leave or to hush up was a blaring reminder she couldn't have it. Clearly the man wasn't in a place in his life to invest in a romantic relationship, any more than she was. If she was going to keep him as a part of the business aspect of her life, Opal was going to have to be extra careful not to blur the line between work and friendship.

"Just think about it." Josie hitched a thumb toward the two tents. "You're going to need extra sets of hands in another day or two to get that stuff moved back into the store."

Opal nodded but chose not to comment. Her friend seemed to read that as the conversation's closure. She picked up the bucket and moved to another section of the fairy mural.

Opal watched Josie climb a few rungs and go to work patching a section of gold-and-orange hair before moving her attention over to the large tents. If only she could think of a way to fit Lincoln Cole into her life that would be beneficial to them both while keeping them both intact—Lincoln's leg and her heart.

●　●　●

The following morning, a plan was sort of in place by the time she noticed the Jeep parking at the curb. Lincoln limped toward her, using his cane. He had his hair pulled back, giving her a direct view of his features, which were set in a scowl. His lips were already moving back to say something before she could interrupt him.

"I'm a man," he announced abruptly, that deep voice booming around the small yard. She was about to agree wholeheartedly, a mighty handsome one at that, but he plowed on, raising his left leg slightly. "This makes me feel less of one."

She stepped closer, shuffling the store's floor plans into one hand so she could reach the other out to grasp his forearm. "Linc—"

"But working here . . . doing something useful in the last few weeks . . . it made me feel closer to being whole again." He took a step back to get away from her touch, clearly not there for her pity.

She dropped her hand and fiddled with the large papers, determined not to give him any. "Good, because I need your help and don't really have time for any more of this chitchat."

Lincoln's lip curled back to protest, but he paused in confusion at her words. Obviously he had been expecting her to send him away once more. "Come again?"

Opal held up the plans. "I need your help. I have more floor space now with the addition, and to be honest, the former layout wasn't working so well. Now I have this clean slate, and I'm at a loss as to how to arrange it."

Lincoln took the floor plans and studied them. His eyes narrowed while he looked them over. "Are the floors dry yet?"

Opal clapped her hands. "Oh yes. The crew only put a clear sealant on them so all the natural beauty can show off, and they turned out so gorgeous. I knew all that old barn wood I had in storage would come in handy someday." She took the plans back and clutched his free hand. "Come see!"

They moved inside, where the sharp aroma of fresh paint and wood sealer met them. She already had a large table set in the middle of the space with two chairs tucked underneath. The plan was for Lincoln to sit down and figure out the puzzle of the furniture arrangements. She sat and spread the plans out. He took the seat beside her and swiped a pencil that was beginning to roll away.

"You need to place the bigger pieces around the perimeter. The first time I walked in, it was like walking into a wall . . ." He began drawing out the plan while discussing ideas with Opal. By the time the morning was gone and their stomachs were rumbling, they had a pretty good idea where all the furniture would be placed.

Opal hung up from ordering a pizza and asked for the third time, "You sure we can't hang the chairs back on the ceiling? I thought they looked so cute up there."

"Look, I gave in to your pizza choice. I'm not budging on the chairs." Lincoln sat back and scanned the warehouse-size room. "Tell ya what, if it's a light fixture, we can hang it. If it's just a chair, we can look at retro-fitting some racks on the walls to hang them. That will be a less haphazard way to approach it."

Opal studied the pale-teal walls, imagining his idea, and found it rather pleasing. "I love it. Our chairs can be art!" She beamed and clapped her hands.

"*Your* chairs." Lincoln began rolling the plans up. "This mess is all on you."

She giggled. He wouldn't be here if he didn't want to be a part of the mess. "Lincoln, you seem really good at this organizing and structuring."

"Common sense can go a long way." He shrugged while standing up. "Now, let's look at the office in the back to see if we can come up with a plan for that space before the pizza gets here."

"Lead the way, big boy." Opal gestured for him to go first and barely contained her grin when he gave her a stern look. She waited for him to snap something back, but he just picked up his cane and began heading to the office off to the right. "You know . . . that cane really makes you so distinguished."

"Makes me look like an old geezer." Lincoln muttered a few more sentiments under his breath.

She watched how he maneuvered the cane like it was a part of him and found it quite attractive. Of course, a big tough guy like Lincoln Cole had not just a plain ordinary cane. The one in his grasp was glossy black with the Marine Corps emblem on the handle and pewter accents. It looked as mean as him. "No, your grouchiness does that. Seriously, I like the cane."

"That makes one of us," Lincoln mumbled as he stepped into the small office.

"Should you be wearing flip-flops?" Opal noticed he had to sort of do a slide-step when he was wearing them.

"I wore boots for two tours and it was like wearing lead weights on my feet, so I really don't care if it's good or not. I'd just as soon go barefooted."

"I don't mind if you go barefooted. It's got to be better than trying to slide that left flip-flop around." Opal pointed and it seemed to be all the permission he needed to ditch them by the door.

"You still have that L-shaped desk?"

"Which one?" She could think of at least three underneath the tents.

"The one fashioned from the metal milk crates and the boardwalk top."

"Yes. I lucked out when snagging the planks after last year's beachfront remodel."

Lincoln combed his fingertips through his beard, deep in thought. Opal thought the beard made him even more distinguished, the way he kept it neatly trimmed to show off those sharp cheekbones and the long column of his neck, but she decided not to comment on that.

"What?" she asked when he remained quiet.

"The bookcase you've made out of the wood wine crates should go along that wall with the desk next to it." He pointed to the left wall that had no window.

She could envision the rustic wood-and-metal pieces against the pale-teal walls. "Those two pieces will look good together. What else?"

"A small love seat or two chairs in the corner, but that's it for in here. You had it too cluttered before."

Before she could argue, the bell she'd replaced on the front door chimed. "Pizza!" She dashed off.

"Here. Let me pay," Lincoln called from behind her, but she kept on skipping to the door.

"It's a work lunch. It's on me." She met the young delivery guy at the door and handed over some cash. "Hello, Jamie."

"Hey, Miss Opal." He handed her the pizza.

"Seriously? I'm only twenty-six. I've not earned the old lady title yet." She waved him off when he tried giving her some change. "Let that tip be a reminder that I'm not old."

The young man chuckled and stuffed the money in his pocket. "Yes, ma'am."

"Jamie!" she said in a warning.

He laughed again and darted out the door before she could smack him.

"You know us Southerners say *ma'am* to any female, infant or geriatric, doesn't matter the age," Lincoln said as he settled back at the table in the middle of the room.

"I know, but I sure don't like those manners aimed at me." She set the pizza down and popped open the lid, releasing a garlic-infused steam. Licking her lips, she asked, "Will you say grace?"

Lincoln shifted in his seat.

"It's simply thanking God for this meal. You can handle it." She waved a hand in his direction. "The pizza is gonna get cold."

Huffing, Lincoln bowed his head. "Thank you for this food. Amen." When his head rose again and he aimed his brown eyes at her, she returned it with a glare equal to his.

"I'm giving you another shell before you go home today." She pulled a piece of pizza from the box and took a substantial bite, loving the crunch of the super-thin crust.

Lincoln followed suit, folding his piece in half before chowing down. "Why?" he asked around a mouthful.

"Slowly but surely, Lincoln Cole, God is going to answer a lot more prayers on your behalf." She tipped her head sideways and held his gaze. "I can't wait to witness what you do with them."

He stopped chewing and stared. "That shell you left at my house was for my healing." He chewed a few times and swallowed. "You realize my leg won't ever be whole again, don't ya?"

"Oh, so you found my shell?" she asked, sidestepping his comment. Truth be told, the prayer was for the healing of his soul. Not his leg.

"Yes." Lincoln tossed his crust into the box and crossed his arms, frowning. "I'm really sorry for how I treated you that day. . . . It was beyond kind of you to take care of me in spite of that. Thank you."

Opal swiped his discarded crust, ready to eat it, but then froze. "You apologized and thanked me in the same breath?" Her eyes rounded, causing his to narrow.

"It was two breaths; now let's just drop it." He reached for another slice of pizza, effectively closing their feelings-sharing segment of the day. "Now, about that back workroom . . ."

The afternoon flew by with Lincoln sketching out a

plan for the workroom, suggesting they use several pieces she'd crafted. Opal thought back to the wishes she made for the selected furniture and was surprised at how fitting they were for her at that moment in time.

The milk crate desk—*please bless this person with some structure.*

The wine crate bookcases—*please bless the owner with a rich understanding of what their next adventure should be.*

The storage cabinets made from old kitchen cabinets— *please let the next owner fill these shelves with what they love and understand the importance of cherishing it all.*

Lincoln picked out each piece and Opal was in pure wonder over how God was using him to bless her mess. She wanted to point all this out but knew it wasn't time yet. He wouldn't appreciate it and she just knew there was going to be a time it would really impact him, so she kept it to herself and only offered him knowing smiles throughout the day.

That smile remained on her face until Opal got into her van to head home. It vanished as soon as she turned her key and nothing happened. "Oh no!" Frantically she looked at the time on her phone before trying to crank the engine again.

"What's wrong?" Lincoln appeared at the driver's-side window she had rolled down. Her windows remained open most of the time so she could enjoy the briny air that fortified her life.

"My van is dead." She wrinkled her nose and turned the key again to show him.

"Sounds like the starter." He leaned into the window a bit.

Opal looked at the time again. "Can you get the starter started? I'm close to being late for supper with my parents."

"This is a vintage VW van, so that part will probably

need to be ordered and replaced." He stepped back and looked behind her van to where his Jeep was parked. Sighing, he said, "I can give you a ride."

She perked up. "Really?"

He nodded.

"But they live a good twenty minutes inland. Surely that's out of your way."

"I ain't got any plans except for eating a few sand-wiches and watching a football game."

"Oh, who's playing tonight?" Opal did a mental check of the Monday night lineup. It was the Packers versus . . . she couldn't remember.

Lincoln opened her door and beckoned her to get out. "You don't strike me as the ball game–watching type."

"Well, there you go assuming again. And let's be clear, you really stink with your assumptions." Opal walked over, climbed into the Jeep, and waited until Lincoln fas-tened his seat belt and easily cranked his vehicle. "Head west on 17. Just so you know, my dad and I scored tickets to the Super Bowl last year. Great game, even though our team lost."

Lincoln cut her a dubious look before turning onto the main highway. "You seriously like football?"

"Love it."

"Favorite team?"

"Hello! Panthers, of course. But my favorite quarter-back is hands down Aaron Rodgers. Green Bay is holding that man's talent back by not having a strong enough offensive line, if you ask me."

Shaking his head, Lincoln muttered, "Opal, you are one surprisingly unique woman."

She thought he was talking to himself more than to her, but she answered brightly anyway. "Why, thank you. Turn onto Gilbert Highway another mile or so up on the left." She turned slightly in her seat and studied his profile. "Now, tell me your favorite team. And if you say Patriots, you can stop the Jeep right here and let me out."

Lincoln barked in laughter. "Good thing it's the Saints then."

They volleyed football stats back and forth until they made it to her parents' street.

"Linc, I have a request."

"What?" He remained focused on the road but his frown deepened.

"How do you feel about fried chicken and collard greens?"

"I'm a country boy, so what do you think?" He glanced at her briefly.

"How about pecan pie? You like plain ole pecan pie?"

"Sure." Lincoln tapped the top of the steering wheel, keeping time with the Lee Brice song on the radio.

"Oh, thank goodness."

"Why do you say that?"

"Because I want you to join my family tonight for Thanksgiving. Well, everyone but Bubba. He's still away at college." She smiled warmly, hoping to sell him on staying for dinner.

"Thanksgiving is over a week away."

"Yes, but my folks will be out of town visiting my brother and some girl he wants them to meet, and so we're celebrating tonight. To make it up to me, Momma is making all my favorites." Opal directed him to pull in at a gated driveway. She fished a small remote out of her purse and sent the wrought-iron gate sliding open, revealing a three-story plantation-style home just behind it.

Lincoln put the Jeep in park and squinted at Opal. "Who are you?"

"What do you mean?"

"Who are your parents, Opal *Gilbert*?" Lincoln asked her, even though it was obvious he'd already pieced that answer together.

"Daniel and Mira Gilbert," Opal answered nonchalantly.

"*Senator* Daniel Gilbert is your father, the man for whom that last road we took is named." Lincoln hitched a thumb over his shoulder.

"Yes."

He snorted and shook his head in disbelief. "All this time I've been picturing a set of hippie parents living in a tent by the river, thriving on the land and each other's love."

Opal snickered. "You and your assumptions . . . Will you please stay?"

He looked down at himself as he scratched the side of his neck. "I don't think I'm dressed appropriately for Thanksgiving."

"Jeans and a Henley shirt. It's basically what I'm wearing." She pointed to her flare-legged jeans with several patches dressing them and her tie-dyed long-sleeved T-shirt. "No worries."

With apparent reluctance, Lincoln put the Jeep in drive and began moving down the long driveway. "Are you adopted or something?"

"Nope." She could say more about him assuming things again but chose not to rile him up before they even made it to the door.

Opal let herself and Lincoln in even though he whispered his protest. "This is my family home. It would be insulting to my parents if I knocked." She glanced at his empty hand. "You forgot your cane in the Jeep."

"I'm good."

"Linc—"

He came to a halt, his face lighting with an idea. "I can go get it."

And give him the chance to run? Nope. "It's fine. We'll be mostly sitting." They walked through the massive foyer and around the table set in the middle that was brimming over with fall foliage and several plump arrangements of orange and yellow mums. "Hello! Your favorite daughter is home!" Opal called out as she grabbed Lincoln's hand, even though his fingers refused to hold hers in return, and guided him to the kitchen near the back of the first floor.

"You're our only daughter!" Her mother's voice drifted down the hall.

They pushed through the heavy double doors and were engulfed in aromas of the holidays. Savory meats and sugary-sweet desserts perfumed the air in warmth. Opal's mom turned from the stove, wiping her hands on the apron tied around her narrow waist, and froze. Her eyes skated between the giant man beside Opal and their entwined hands. Lincoln must have noticed because he wiggled free from her grip and put a little space between them.

"Momma, I'd like you to meet my friend Lincoln. Lincoln, this is my mom, Mira."

Lincoln stepped forward and took her shocked mom's hand. "Nice to meet you, Mrs. Gilbert. . . . We just work together."

"My, you're so tall . . ." Her mom shook off the surprised look and replaced it with a friendly smile. "Welcome to our home, Lincoln. So glad you could join us. . . . Let me go get Daniel. He had a few e-mails to tend to . . ." She kept smiling and tucked a much-tamer red curl back into her neat chignon as she hurried off.

"I think I'm gonna head out," Lincoln whispered and began to turn.

"Oh no, you don't." Opal grasped his upper arm. "Help me set the table." She pulled him over to the buffet in the adjoining dining room, where the china and silverware were waiting. It was the smaller of the dining rooms and was where she and her parents always took their meals. The other fancier space down the hall was for dinner parties with officials and other public guests.

Lincoln gathered the silverware and followed behind her around the table. "You owe me after tonight."

She released an unladylike snort. "I've put up with your moody behind for the last month or so. After tonight we can call us even." She looked at him, his lips poked out far enough to trip over. "Stop pouting. We'll watch the game later while we eat our pie. You'll survive."

"I'm not so sure . . . ," Lincoln muttered under his breath just as her parents walked in.

Another round of introductions. Opal summarized Lincoln's injury overseas and how he'd been working with her ever since the hurricane. She grew a little more comfortable when her dad commented on his military service, thanking him and then moving on quickly to talk about tonight's game.

As soon as her parents vanished into the kitchen to grab the food, Lincoln whispered harshly, "Your folks are dressed in their Sunday best." He flicked his shirt. "I thought you said we were dressed okay?"

Her mom wore a pale-green sheath dress that reminded Opal of mint ice cream and her dad was in an oxford shirt and chinos—basically what they wore on a daily basis. "That's as casual as those two get. They're misdressed, not us, so chill." She patted the chair beside the one she was settling into. "Take a load off."

Lincoln plopped his big form into the chair. "I don't like you very much."

"If you say so." She smiled sweetly at him and winked as her parents reentered the room.

After her dad said grace, all appeared to be well until they were eating juicy fried chicken and her parents began making small talk.

Mira passed Lincoln another fluffy yeast roll and asked, "Are you permanently disabled, Lincoln?"

Lincoln studied the roll in his hand. "No, ma'am. Just not up to par enough to defend my country anymore."

The table fell silent until Mira chose to plow on with her interrogation. "Surely you had a backup career plan. I hope you took advantage of the free education the government provided for you." She smiled sweetly, but it didn't have Opal fooled. Her mom was in full-on snooping mode.

Lincoln shifted in his chair beside Opal. Without looking any further than his plate, he answered, "Nothing's free . . . but I did earn a master's degree while serving this country."

No one acknowledged Lincoln's sharp retort, but Opal's dad perked up when he mentioned the degree. "That's great, young man. What master's degree did you earn?"

Lincoln gave Opal a measured look, one that said she was going to pay for this, before focusing on her dad. "Astrology," he answered with pride.

Opal's mouth fell open but she quickly snapped it shut and muttered under her breath just so he could hear, "And you call me the hippie?"

Both her mom and dad looked stunned stupid for a few beats, which was exactly how she felt.

"Astrology," Daniel repeated, trying out the word,

and by the looks of his scrunched-up nose and twisted mouth, he didn't find it too appealing.

Mira cleared her throat on a dainty cough. "What does one do with such a degree?"

Lincoln shrugged his shoulders. "I haven't figured that out just yet. All's I know is that I sure do enjoy gazing up at the stars and pondering their meaning." He took an obnoxiously large bite of his roll and garbled out, "But I'll let you know when I do." He nodded and smiled with his cheeks poked out from the mouthful of food.

Opal didn't consider her parents snooty or judgmental, but they were most definitely picky when it came to their only daughter and the company she kept. Taking a moment to see Lincoln through their eyes—a scruffy war veteran with no future ambition—she understood the lack of potential they saw on the surface. Fact of the matter, their eyes were missing a major portion of Lincoln Cole, and one night wouldn't be enough time for them to see him as clearly as she did. Although he'd certainly thrown her for a loop on the whole astrology thing.

His admission shut down the twenty questions game her parents were playing, much to Opal's relief. After Lincoln helped her mom with the dishes, refusing her pleas to just go sit and enjoy the game, they took their pie into the den and cheered on the Packers as they took the game in overtime.

The ride home was quiet until they neared the beach. Opal couldn't tamp down her curiosity any longer and quipped, "You majored in astrology? I didn't realize that was a thing."

Lincoln chuckled and shook his head. "No."

Confused, she looked over and saw the smirk etched along his handsome face. The dashboard lights glanced off the mischievous twinkling in his eyes. "Why would you lie like that?"

"Your mother was being a little too nosy. That's what she gets."

Opal tsked. "That wasn't nice." She tried to give him a stern look when he glanced over, but it floundered when he grinned wide, looking right proud of himself. And too handsome for his own good.

The grin dropped from his face as suddenly as it had appeared. Clearing his throat, Lincoln asked, "Opal, may I ask you a question?"

Her own smile fell away when she caught the sincerity in his voice. "Sure," she answered with caution.

Lincoln cut his eyes in her direction before returning his attention to the road. "What does one do with a degree in astrology?" he deadpanned, cracking her up.

She reached over and playfully popped him in the arm. "My house is two more up on the right, smart-aleck." She giggled. "Seriously, what did you earn a degree in? Moodiness? Old geezer antics? Stubbornness?"

"If you must know, I have a master's in architectural engineering."

"For real?"

He turned in and parked beside her beach house. "For real."

"Well, that makes sense. You were very precise on the floor plans today. Man . . . I think I should probably give you a substantial raise."

He chuckled. "No need. I'm good there. Plenty of savings and good investments." He opened his door, stepped out, and rounded to her door, opening it like a true Southern gentleman. "Thank you for supper tonight."

Opal hopped down. "I feel like I owe you an apology for that."

"No, you don't. Your parents were just being good parents. And that meal was worth the interrogation. You probably need to let them know we are only working together. I think your mom is probably scared to death I'm gonna pull you into the *hippie* side of life and teach you how to read the stars." He quietly chuckled.

"You're not my friend?" Opal's cheeks heated, not understanding why he fought to keep her at a distance.

Lincoln shrugged one of his big shoulders. "I suppose we could try."

Opal rummaged around in her bag until her fingers landed on the smooth surface of a seashell. She pulled it out and pressed it into the palm of his hand.

He studied the shell underneath the streetlamp before glancing down at her. "What's the wish this time?"

"That we succeed in our friendship." She left him with the shell and started toward the house. "Good night, friend."

Lincoln murmured something behind her, but she didn't quite catch it. The Jeep didn't pull away until she'd made it inside and had flicked on a light. Sighing, she peeped out the window and watched the taillights flash once before turning onto the road. The man was undoubtedly the most complicated friend she'd ever had.

7

The woman was nothing but complicated, and Lincoln wasn't so sure how much more he could put up with. They spent the better part of the following week in the workroom while movers set up the store according to his specific directions. Each day he would come in, and each day she had a job set up for them to tackle.

Today they sat across the worktable from each other, sanding wood spindles.

"Don't think for a minute I don't know what you're up to." His words came out just shy of a growl, sending her head to pop up.

"What are you grumbling about now?" Opal rolled her eyes at him and went back to brushing the sheet of sandpaper against the old milk paint.

"Each day we're either back here in this room working on a project or doing the same in the front yard. Sitting. All we do is sit." He sanded a stubborn spot before dropping the finished spindle in the bin beside the table. It was like those danged things were multiplying right before his eyes.

"Stand on your head and do the work for all I care." Opal delivered the jab sweetly as always, and it made his skin itch.

He scratched his cheek before picking up another spindle. "I don't like you."

"So you keep saying." She eyed the spindle in her grasp, tilting her head one way and then the other. "For someone who doesn't like me, you sure do like to watch me."

His eyes skittered back down to the sandpaper clutched in his fist, hating that she never bit her tongue when an opportunity to call him out on something presented itself. "Train wrecks are always hard to look away from," Lincoln lied right through his gritted teeth.

Truth be told, he couldn't help himself. When Opal was in the same space as he was, his eyes instantly gravitated to her. Sure, she was a unique beauty, but it was also the sweet spirit radiating from her in so many ways. Her knowing smile that tended to hitch more on the left. The teasing twinkle in her green eyes. The fluttering of her long eyelashes when she was deep in thought . . .

"You're staring again." Opal hummed, her eyes twinkling. Just as that heart-shaped mouth of hers popped open to deliver more tease, the bell over the door chimed. "Saved by the bell." She hopped up and skipped out of the room, leaving him still itchy and irritated.

Moments later, the back door opened and Josie carried a gigantic canvas inside. When she realized she wasn't alone, her feet nearly cleared the floor.

"Oh!" Josie slid the canvas behind her back, not hiding it in the least. "I, uh . . . I didn't think anyone was back here."

"Clearly." Stifling a grunt, Lincoln stood and motioned for the canvas. "I already saw it, so you might as well let me see it."

Josie's bright-blue eyes widened. "Oh . . . I . . . uh . . .

It's actually for Opal. I'll just come back later . . ." She took a step backward, but he reached a long arm out and swiped the painting. "Hey!"

Lincoln turned his back to her protests and checked out the painting, finding it quite fitting. A barefooted redhead sat on a tall stack of furniture that looked like it was teetering on the edge of calamity. She wore a royal-blue ball gown gathered around her knees and she was laughing, her head tipped back.

An eyebrow shot up as he glanced over his shoulder at Josie. Her face was high in color. "You painted this?"

"Y-yes . . . ," she stuttered, studying her flip-flops.

"Wow." Lincoln turned around and narrowed his eyes. "Why on earth are you working at a diner when clearly you should be creating art like this full-time?" He held the painting a little higher.

"Umm . . ." Josie cleared her throat and toyed with a thin leather band wrapped around her wrist. While she fiddled with it, Lincoln took a moment to give her a thorough once-over, thinking she looked like she should be on a surfboard out in California, with her white-blonde hair and eyebrows, or rubbing elbows with other artists at an art gallery with his buddy August Bradford. Even in the understated outfit of baggy jean shorts and a tank top, she was obviously meant for more than the small diner she was hiding out in. Whoever this Josie Slater was, she didn't have him fooled.

"It's not a choice at the moment," Josie finally whispered.

Lincoln didn't need to know the details behind her statement. He could easily recognize a fellow victim of circumstance, so he chose to drop it and redirected his focus to the beautiful painting. A smile pulled at his lips

before he could stop it. "You captured our pixie in paint."
He looked up and found her eyeing him instead of the
canvas. "What?"

Just as Opal entered the room, Josie stepped behind her
and peeked over the top of Opal's curly red hair, pretending
to tremble in fright. "You're smiling. It's scaring me."

Lincoln scowled. "You're not funny." Even though he
thought it was pretty funny the timid blonde actually
knew how to joke around. "I know how to smile. Just
need a decent reason."

"Aww! And Josie's painting of me did that for you.
What an honor." Opal grinned and he wasn't sure if she
was being sincere or teasing. That little condescending
quirk of hers made his eye twitch.

"Where should we hang it?" Opal asked Lincoln,
always acting like his opinion meant more than anything
in the world.

He glanced around the workroom. "If you're going
to hide us back here most of the time, you might as well
give us something to look at." He pointed to the bare wall
beside the back door.

"That's a great idea." Opal propped the canvas that
was almost as tall as her against the wall and took a few
steps back to admire it. "Will you hang it for me?"

"Sure." Lincoln strode over to the exact drawer that
housed the needed supplies and tools. He'd helped orga-
nize the entire place, so he knew it like the back of his
hand by now.

"Are you ready to reopen the doors Friday?" Josie
asked.

"Yep. Everything is set," Opal commented.

Lincoln worked on hammering a nail above his head
while the women chatted.

"That's great news, Opal." Josie sounded genuinely

thrilled for her friend, and that made Lincoln soften to her a little more.

"I'd love for you to create a few pieces to put on display in the storefront," Opal said in that sugar-sweet coercing tone.

"I'm not sure I'll have time . . . ," Josie mumbled.

Lincoln hung the canvas and adjusted it a few times before letting go and deciding to get on the meddling bandwagon. "If this is the quality of your work, you should be in galleries all around the world. That alcove wall up front needs something spectacular like this." Lincoln looked over at the blushing blonde and nodded his head toward her painting. "Seriously, Josie."

The tall woman fidgeted, seemingly uncomfortable with being the center of attention. "Thank you," Josie mumbled. "We'll see."

Lincoln had heard that phrase enough growing up to know it meant a *church no* and wouldn't be happening. Again, he figured it was best to drop it. He put the supplies away and went ahead and put some of Opal's away as well. He'd been bound and determined to get her into an organizing routine, but so far she was looking like a lost cause.

"Okay. So you two have been angels in the last few weeks, helping me get my mess back together, so as a thank-you, I'm cooking y'all supper tomorrow night at my place." Opal did her little happy clap and bounced in place. Lincoln found her quirks silly a few weeks ago, but they had somehow grown on him, even if she still annoyed the daylights out of him.

"Sounds good to me," Lincoln was quick to say. If she cooked anywhere close as good as her mom, he was in for a treat. His mouth watered just thinking about it.

"You've been working so hard, Opal. Why don't we

just go out to eat and celebrate," Josie offered, nodding her head exuberantly beside him.

"No, no, no. You know how much I love to cook." Opal flicked a wrist in the air, and Lincoln was glad she was dismissing the idea of going out to eat. He was burned out on sandwiches and was hankering for some home cooking.

"And I love to eat. A lot." Lincoln caught the grimace on Josie's face before she smoothed it away. "What?"

"Nothing," Josie stuttered out. "I just don't want to put Opal out, and you shouldn't either. Why don't we have Daddy put together a low-country boil at his place." She directed this to Lincoln with her eyes rounded and began nodding her head like a maniac.

"I'm game for the low-country boil. No need in giving yourself whiplash to convince me." Lincoln shook his head and stifled an eye roll.

"Enough now. I'm cooking for y'all. Be at my house around six. I'm going to lock up." Opal walked off.

Josie groaned once she was out of earshot.

"What was that all about?" Lincoln asked, feeling like he was missing something.

"Nothing. Just hope you bring your appetite," Josie muttered while trailing Opal.

Lincoln arrived at Opal's place right at six the next day with his stomach growling. He'd forgone snacking that afternoon in preparation. The tinkling melody of wind chimes dancing in the breeze greeted him as he stepped out of his vehicle. He shook his head, thinking only Opal would want to add to the natural song of the ocean. He'd been to her house a few times but the sight never ceased to catch him off guard. The faded-orange hue of the clapboard siding and the robin's egg blue on the shutters reminded him of Easter.

"Only Opal," he muttered while taking in the beach house. He wouldn't admit it out loud to her, but it was cozy and welcoming. Much in the same manner as its owner. He read the plaque on the front porch railing, *Beach Haven*, and thought the name fit it to a T. The owners of his cottage had named it *Seashore Wishes* and he was starting to believe it was a sign.

He heard laughter on the back deck, so he headed that way and found Opal and Josie setting dishes on a patio table underneath a bright floral umbrella. Temperatures were in the upper sixties with just a subtle breeze, so dining outside sounded appealing. His back stiffened when his eyes landed on the she-devil they called Sophia Grace as she placed napkins under each plate. He'd been able to dodge most of her visits, but seemed his luck had run out.

Opal tucked one of those errant curls with the faded ends behind her ear and looked over as she picked up a glass pitcher filled with what appeared to be lemonade. Her green eyes lit up when they landed on him. "Linc! You made it!" she said, sounding like there was some doubt that he would.

"Of course I made it. I'm hungry." He took his time maneuvering the steps with his cane, trying to come to terms with depending on the annoying stick.

"Look who came into town to surprise me for the reopening!"

Lincoln regarded the brunette, who was wearing that sour look she wore the last time he saw her, and didn't see where she warranted Opal's enthusiasm. Against his better judgment, he took the only vacant seat next to Sophia and noticed she smelled like his favorite Italian restaurant back home. Garlic and herbs wafted around on a briny breeze, setting his mouth to watering. "We eating lasagna or spaghetti?" His question made Sophia's face bloom in shades of red.

"No, what makes you think that?" Opal asked while filling glasses with lemonade.

Lincoln leaned over to Sophia and sniffed, but before he commented, a foot made sharp contact with his good shin under the table. He glared at Sophia and she glared back. "No reason," he mumbled while leaning down to rub the sting away.

"I'll be right back." Opal flitted through the open sliding-glass doors, humming all the way.

"What's up with you? And where's the pizza?" Lincoln asked Sophia.

Sophia clucked her tongue, having the audacity to act perturbed with her nose in the air. "Don't know what you're talking about." She quickly grabbed up her glass of lemonade and downed half of it. Josie sat on the other side of her and looked just as guilty for some reason.

Opal was back in a flash with a platter of golden-brown biscuits. "It's a new recipe I found. I tweaked it a bit though." She placed them in the middle of the table and took a seat.

"Where's the rest of the meal?" Lincoln asked, wondering where the meat and sides were.

"Oh, that's the neat part. The biscuits are stuffed, so they are an entire meal in themselves."

Lincoln surveyed the platter, knowing his appetite was bigger than what it held. "I hope you have more than that."

Sophia coughed and Josie choked on the lemonade she was guzzling. "No worries, Lincoln. Eat all you want." Sophia flicked a manicured hand in the direction of the platter and grinned way too wide.

Opal began loading everyone's plate with two biscuits.

"I think Lincoln should try it first, being as he's kinda the guest of honor," Sophia commented, ignoring her plate.

"I'm hardly a guest of honor, but I'd be glad to test this biscuit out first." He picked up the flaky bread and took a big bite and began chewing with things crunching between his teeth.

Lincoln was raised on scratch-made biscuits formed from lard and buttermilk. The golden bundle of deception he held was nothing like those delicious dreams. No. Whatever that thing pinched between his thumb and forefinger was, heavenly it was not. With each chew the fishy travesty seemed to grow in his mouth. Even though his eyes began to water, he was able to see everyone at the table watching him. Josie and Sophia looked as miserable as he was, their faces puckered. Blinking the tears away, he noticed Opal was looking on expectantly. Lincoln had no idea what she was hoping for, but he knew for certain that he was about to let the woman down.

He took his napkin and tucked it around his mouth and spit the awful-tasting biscuit into it, using a clean section to wipe his tongue. "I think they went bad somehow." He gagged. "What'd you put in them?"

Opal took a tentative bite. "I took the idea of salmon cakes and stuffed it inside a biscuit." She inspected the inside of the pastry while chewing. "They taste fine to me."

Lincoln downed a long swig of his lemonade. "Why'd it crunch?"

"Oh, I like to use the cans of salmon with the fish bones. It's added calcium and texture."

Lincoln rubbed his gut and studied the other two women suspiciously. "Ain't you two gonna at least try it?"

"Opal, I'm sorry, honey. But Ty has this event coming up and I have to squeeze into a cocktail dress, so I'm off carbs." Sophia appeared completely disheartened, but Lincoln wasn't fooled by her act. He'd had breakfast at Driftwood Diner that morning, where he watched Sophia and her baby boy share a fat stack of French toast, which was nothing but carbohydrates.

"And I'm trying to be supportive and not eating carbs in front of her." Josie scrunched her face and shrugged her shoulders.

Lincoln cut a glare at Josie, recalling how supportive she'd been that very same morning when she swiped a bite of French toast while taking a moment to chat with her friend.

"Okay." Opal took another bite.

"What's that red blob on your chin, Josie?" Lincoln pointed at it.

Josie's eyes bugged out of her head as her hand darted up and wiped away the evidence that was obviously marinara sauce. "This lemonade is outrageous, Opal. May I have another glass?"

Opal narrowed her green eyes, watching the group for a few beats before standing. "Sure."

As soon as she was inside, Lincoln tossed the rest of his biscuit and the remaining biscuits on the platter to the seagulls waiting patiently by the railing. "No carbs, but you can eat pizza and had no problem at breakfast this morning."

"There's a few slices left in Josie's truck," Sophia whispered, extending a peace offering.

"You couldn't warn a guy?" Lincoln chugged the rest of his lemonade, unable to get the foul taste from his mouth.

"You didn't notice me protesting a bit strongly at the store yesterday?" Josie spoke up.

Lincoln looked over at her and found her making that silly face she had sported then.

Sophia pointed to her face. "That is a warning look. You ever see us wearing that look, you better take notice."

He scratched the side of his beard. "But her mom is an amazing cook."

"Opal is exceptional at a lot of things. Cooking is not one of them," Josie supplied.

"Yeah, just a few months back she made us cookies with pickle relish in them. And, honey, just let me tell you one thing, dill has no business in a chocolate chip cookie. Makes my stomach hurt just thinking about it." Sophia's prim face puckered again.

"Why not tell her the truth?" Lincoln reached over, swiped Sophia's glass, and finished it off in one long gulp.

"She's one of the dearest people you'll ever meet. We don't want to hurt her feelings," Josie whispered just as Opal's humming grew closer.

Opal came back out with another pitcher of lemonade and refilled everyone's glasses. "I sure hate that y'all can't try out this new recipe," she said to Josie.

Lincoln snorted.

"What's that about?" Opal asked him.

Lincoln ticked his head in the guilty women's direction. "Opal, I'm about to prove I'm your *true* friend. One that's honest, unlike those two." He shot Sophia and Josie a glare before redirecting his attention to her. "Straight up, you can't cook. Those things on that plate are an abomination against biscuits. As of right now, you're off KP duty indefinitely."

"KP?"

"Kitchen Patrol," he clarified. "No more cooking for you. Stick to creating your unique furniture and making your wishes. That's what the world needs from you. Not fishy biscuits."

Opal sat back, stunned by his admission. She searched

the other two for more answers, but they were too busy studying their laps. "Umm . . . thank you?"

Lincoln tipped his head in one quick nod. "You're welcome." He stood and helped her out of her chair. "I'm starving. Let me take you out to supper."

"What about those two fibbing friends over there?" Opal asked as Lincoln settled his hand on the small of her back and began directing her down the deck steps.

"Those two fibbers are stingy, too. They already ate pizza. If they're still hungry, they can finish their stash in Josie's truck." After helping Opal into the Jeep, he limped around to the driver's side and climbed in. "You seriously had no idea about your cooking skills?"

Opal snickered. "I know it's unusual and you know by now I like unusual. But it sure has been fun watching those two soldier through my experiments without ever saying a thing about it." She giggled again, and again he was reminded that her silliness was only a cover for the sharp-witted woman behind the curls and eccentric outfits.

Lincoln took her to a barbecue joint he'd stumbled upon a while back. They ate their fill of pulled pork, ribs, and all the fixings while Opal chattered nonstop, but for some reason he didn't mind so much.

His cheeks actually hurt from laughing with Opal during their meal, but Lincoln couldn't wipe the smile off his face as he parked beside his beach house. Even the constant throb in his leg didn't dampen the best evening he'd had in quite a while. And even though he tried not to see it, Opal Gilbert was one intriguing woman. She didn't just wing it with her refurbished pieces. The pixie knew how to properly do things, like how to use the right hardware and the proper technique to stain a piece so it didn't look like an uneven gaum. A lesson she patiently taught him when he'd flubbed his first attempt.

With the smile still in place, Lincoln climbed out of the Jeep and slowly maneuvered to the back porch. He wedged his cane beside the porch steps and eased down to sit on the top one while watching the sky paint itself in vibrant hues of orange and purple over the ocean. Breathing in the salty air, he leaned back on his elbows and scanned the beach as his phone chimed. He dug it out of his pocket and winced at the number. Taking in another less even breath, he sat up and hit Play on the voice mail and listened.

"Hey, sweetheart. It's Momma. . . . I just . . . I just wanted to let you know that your dad is mostly better . . ." She sniffed and breathed heavily into the phone. "I . . . we . . . miss you. And I think you need to make this right, sooner rather than later. Your dad will forgive you, Son. All you need to do is ask." She sniffed a few more times. "I hear you're faring pretty well there. That's good. That's what I had hoped for, but I never thought you would shut us out like this. Please call me soon. We love you."

The heavy meal churned in Lincoln's stomach as he shoved the phone back into his pocket. With a watery gaze, he stared at the ocean without seeing it. The only thing he could see before him was that last day in Beaufort and the look on his father's face right before Lincoln turned his back on him and the rest of his family. He'd felt less of a Cole man in that moment than he did lying in the hospital after that first surgery.

If only it were possible to take it all back. To hit the Rewind button . . .

Slowly standing, Lincoln wiped at his damp eyes and limped inside to hide from that mistake for a little while longer.

8

"Are you sure this is how you want to spend one of your last nights of freedom?" Sophia questioned Carter's fiancée, Dominica, as the women set up their foldout chairs on the quiet beach. The sun had long set and granted the night a clear sky twinkling with millions of stars.

"It's an honor to be included in a Sand Queens meeting for the very first time," Dominica replied, her subtle accent sharping the ends of each word.

"I'm tickled you wanted to spend it with us, Dominica, but we could have thrown you a true bachelorette party." Opal regarded the beautiful Cuban woman, considering her a breath of fresh air for Sunset Cove. Dominica's family and friends weren't due to arrive in town for another few days, so there was no way Opal would have let her spend the evening alone while the guys celebrated.

Dominica giggled nervously. "No thank you. This is more my style."

The women settled down and studied the ocean before them. Opal loved how the foamy crests of the whitecaps appeared to glow at night as the moonlight danced along the top of the water. With each languid roll of the waves touching the shore and the subtle roar off in the distance on a melodious repeat, she could have easily closed her eyes and dozed off.

"Has Carter told you where y'all are going yet for the honeymoon?" Sophia spoke, breaking the trance as she began handing out thermoses filled with her homemade hot chocolate.

Dominica took one and held it in both hands. "We've done our fair share of traveling the world. I wanted something more private and cozy, so he's taking me to the mountains."

"That is so sweet," Josie commented as she passed out thick slices of pumpkin bread.

"How *romantic*." Opal swooned a bit before focusing on the treat. She took a deep inhale of the spicy aroma before taking a bite.

"Isn't a log cabin in the mountains a little *cliché*?" Sophia added with a dramatic eye roll.

Opal scoffed. "Don't be so cynical. Just because you've had a rough patch with Ty doesn't mean you have the right to rain on Dominica's romance parade."

"Seriously, Sophia. That wasn't nice," Josie spoke quietly.

Sophia dropped her uppity air for a look of remorse. "I'm sorry, Dominica. I didn't mean anything by that. The only cliché here is me. High-profile couple on the rocks." She groaned at her own angst and slumped further down in her chair. Sophia worked for a successful PR firm that represented some of the biggest names in the professional sports world, namely her NFL star husband. Those two couldn't do one thing without the media reporting on it and padding it with false accusations.

"Is Ty coming into town anytime soon? It's been ages since we've seen him." Josie spoke in her soft voice again.

She towered over the others by almost a foot but had a knack for making herself seem small. Opal had been praying that the woman would grow in her confidence, because she was one spectacular woman in Opal's eyes.

"Probably not. They're gearing up for the playoffs. Besides, the only way I could probably get him in this town would be to knock him out and have him shipped here." Sophia flipped her hoodie over her head, which was already shielded by a hat.

Opal studied her friend. Even though the ball cap and hoodie hid most of the brunette's features, her mouth was set in a hard line and her slouching shoulders were indicators that something was weighing her down. "What happened?"

Sophia shrugged. "I suggested we move back here and try for a fresh start, but Ty's dead set against it. Said I was being selfish for even suggesting it." After a brief pause, she admitted, "Things just aren't like they were in the beginning . . ."

"Aww, sweetie, maybe after Ty gets past the playoffs, things will smooth out for y'all." Opal reached over and held Sophia's hand, hoping to offer some comfort. She knew her friend well enough to know there was more going on than what she had mentioned.

"I hope so, for Collin's sake. The poor baby isn't handling all this uncertainty very well. He's been acting out."

"Collin's a toddler. He's supposed to act out." Opal winked at her and the women laughed.

"This is true," Josie agreed before taking a sip of hot chocolate.

The laughter broke the sad mood and the friends moved the focus back to Dominica and her approaching big day. She happily chatted about the wedding details while everyone enjoyed the pumpkin bread.

After about an hour, the snacks were long gone and Josie was nodding off to sleep.

"Ugh! We are too young to be this boring!" Sophia flicked a hand at their semicircle of chairs.

Opal was ready for when she spoke the words. Giving her friends a rascally look, she asked, "How about something cliché then?"

Within the hour, the three Sand Queens and their honorary queen were pulling off said cliché while sneaking around the parking lot at the Palmetto Fine Arts Camp, which was currently under construction. Tonight, it was serving as the playground for Carter's bachelor party. Music boomed from the woods, where Opal knew the guys were goofing off. Their boisterous yelling and raucous laughter blended into the songs blaring out from the camp speakers. Luckily, they were in the middle of the country with no residents for miles, so they could successfully act like hooligans without disturbing the peace.

Opal handed each woman a handful of washable paint pens and orders to give each guy's vehicle a feminine touch. She looked down the row and easily spotted Lincoln's Jeep. Eyes set on the goal, she hurried over and began with the tire cover, turning the black circle into a neon-green peace sign with hot-pink accents. After that, she worked on the passenger's side, thinking Lincoln was the true hippie and needed reminding of that fact. Fluffy flowers and hearts decorated the side before she moved to the driver's side. A large rainbow took up the back part. Once she finished it, she scooted up to the door and decided on adding another peace sign with the word *groovy* underneath it.

Proud of herself, Opal stood up and came face-to-face with a scary sight—glaring eyes and severely pinched brows watching her from the other side of the driver's window.

Yelping, her feet cleared the ground by at least a foot. "What are you doing in there?" Opal whisper-screamed while clutching her chest.

One of those thick eyebrows arched up while the rest of his face remained frozen in the scowl. "It's my Jeep. You mind telling me what you're doing to it?"

She hid the paint behind her back and forced an unsteady smile to her lips. "Making it pretty?"

"Get in," Lincoln demanded. A combination of guilt and shock had her scurrying around to the other side and hopping inside. Before she closed her door, he barked another order. "Leave the contraband outside."

Opal dropped the paint pens, wiped her guilt on her jeans, and shut the door. She steeled herself, waiting for him to lay into her, but after a few minutes passed in silence, she chanced a glance at him. With his head resting on the steering wheel, the thick locks of his hair served as a curtain around his face, blocking out whatever was bothering him.

"Linc . . . what . . . ?" She began to ask him what was wrong, but the past two months had taught her a thing or two on how to maneuver the rocky terrain of Lincoln Cole, and asking that question would only plow her right into a roadblock. Clearing her throat, she began again. "What's so wrong with painting up this ugly beast?"

He tilted his head just enough for a dark eye to peep from the mass of brown hair. "Please tell me it's washable paint."

"I'm assuming." She kept her reply short, hoping to draw the other eye out. She had to bite her lip to hold back the giggle when it actually worked.

Lifting his head, Lincoln said, "It better be some fine art skills then." His dry retort was her undoing and sent the giggle slipping out.

"I can't believe you were hiding out here and caught me red-handed. I officially fail at pranking."

"Who says I'm hiding?" His voice was sharp and his glare sharper.

"Aren't you?" She continued to navigate the conversation with caution.

Lincoln let out a rugged sigh and leaned his head back. Eyes fastened to the roof, he muttered, "They're having a paintball gun battle in the woods."

Opal's first thought was that surely there was a tactic he could use to perch hidden somewhere so he could participate, but then reality popped her in the back of the head from her foolish thought. And that made her want to pop Carter in the back of his head for not considering their evening's entertainment choice wouldn't be very entertaining for a soldier still healing from wounds he endured during an actual battle. Surely Lincoln found nothing amusing about playing war games in the dark.

"Where do the guys think you're at?" she asked after a punctuated silence swept through the vehicle.

"I told Carter my leg hurt and I was calling it a night."

"Is it hurting?"

"It's always hurting," he mumbled, pushing both hands through his hair. After giving the ends a swift tug, seemingly to demand they stay out of his eyes, Lincoln reached over and cranked the Jeep. He glanced in the rearview mirror and began backing out.

"Whoa!" Opal's hand lashed out and gripped his forearm. "I'm here with Josie, Sophia, and Dominica."

He ignored her protests as he circled the parking lot until finding the other pranksters working on painting an ocean along the back of Carter's tailgate. He rolled his window down and said, "I have Opal."

Josie's eyes bugged out, taking in the side of the Jeep

where Opal knew her crime was on vivid display. "What are you going to do with her?" Her question came out all squeaky as she fidgeted.

"Don't know yet. Depends on how mouthy she gets." Lincoln rolled the window up, leaving Josie standing there looking like a frightened kitten while Sophia and Dominica hid behind the side of Carter's truck.

Opal gave her friends the meanest look she could conjure and mouthed, "Cowards." She turned her sights on her surly driver. "Look, Linc, I'm sorry for decorating your Jeep. I'll wash it all nice and clean tomorrow. Promise." Her hand moved to the door handle, ready to make a break for it once he reached the first stop sign.

"Nah. I'd rather you make this wrong right another way."

Her belly flipped, thinking the worst. "I'm not that kinda girl, Lincoln Cole. You let me out right now!"

He snorted with no humor at her demand and kept driving. Didn't even come to a complete stop at the sign, so there was no way she could escape unless she was willing to test out her tuck-and-roll skills. Knowing that would end in an epic fail, she reached over and pulled on her seat belt and then commenced to huffing and puffing in protest.

Lincoln kept his eyes on the road and finally gave some explanation. "Back home, when I'd have a lousy night, I'd take the top off the Jeep and cruise back roads with the radio cranked up. You know of any good back roads around here, Opal?"

Opal uncrossed her arms and sat a little straighter. "If dirt roads will make my wrongs right, then I'll lead you all over this here fine county."

"Deal," he agreed. "I'm gonna swing by the firehouse to lose the top, and then you can lead the way."

She perked up some more. "Can I drive?"

"No. You can copilot."

Her shoulders drooped a bit. "Fine." She only managed probably the shortest pout in history by the time they pulled up in front of the firehouse. A night cruising around with Lincoln was more appealing to her than it probably should be. The fluttering of her heartbeat and the smile stretching her lips couldn't be stanched if her life depended on it.

As soon as he parked off to the side of the two-story brick building, they both hopped out and made quick work of removing the top.

"Seems you've done this a time or two." Lincoln looked over at her as they carried the top to the shed.

"Bubba has a Jeep."

"Kane?" He nodded his head toward the cement floor and began lowering the bulky top.

"Yep. You two have a lot in common, actually." She brushed her hands off on the sides of her jeans and followed him back to the vehicle. "Anyway, we've done this very same thing many a restless night."

"Good. At least you can make up for this gaudy hippie graffiti." He glanced at his door before opening it and climbing in.

The fact that he had caught on to the theme of her artwork so easily had a giggle slipping out of Opal before she could contain it. She had other pressing matters to tend to at the moment, so she reined in the laughter and tried straightening her face into a serious expression. "I'll agree to be your copilot on two conditions."

Lincoln gripped the steering wheel and frowned. "What?"

She pulled one of the hair ties from her wrist and held

it out to him. "First, you need to pull your hair back so I can see your face."

He accepted it but asked, "What's my hair have to do with riding back roads?"

"I want to be able to see your handsome face, if you must know."

Lincoln turned in his seat to face her head-on, hair still hiding most of his face. "You see too much when you look at me. I don't like it."

His honesty sent an odd mixture of emotion rolling over her. "It's not my fault you tell me so much with your expressions, but I promise not to share your secrets. They'll stay just between us."

A wariness set along his features as he hid the hair tie in his closed fist. "What's your second condition?"

"Around these parts, it's not considered proper dirt road cruising unless we have ice-cold bottles of cola and peanuts."

Opal's second condition somehow got the man to working on pulling his hair back in the hair tie at record speed. "I like the way you think sometimes, Gilbert. Where's the closest store?"

The heaviness floated away into the night sky above, and the lighter nuance of his comment had her grinning ear to ear as she pointed over her shoulder. "Down the road, about a mile on the right. The first dirt road is only another mile past it."

Without further discussion, Lincoln finished fixing his hair in a messy ponytail and began driving up the road to the store.

They each grabbed two bottles of cola apiece and a pack of dry roasted peanuts. As they waited to check out, someone let out a long whistle from behind them.

"Well, well, well, if it isn't Opie-dopey."

Opal cringed before turning around to face a night-mare from her past. "Opie-dopey? Really, Ray? No one has called me that since high school." She rolled her eyes at the preppy guy who took it upon himself to taunt her any chance he got and had several other doofuses follow-ing his example.

It wasn't easy being the politician's daughter, and add-ing her free-spirited personality to that made for an easy target. Nobody called it bullying, but that's exactly what she endured. All because she didn't look or act in the way most decided was the norm. Never did she want to fit that definition, so she ended up paying a price for it with being constantly teased and called inappropriate names. *At least he chose one of the less offensive names to recall,* she mused to herself.

"Aw, come on, Opie. You know you earned your weirdo status, but I'm game to get down with the freaks. How's about I take you out for a drink. Just no weirdo outfits." Ray laughed like it was the funniest thing until the formidable man behind her leered over her shoulder. Lincoln's rigid stance pressed close to her, and Ray's taunt-ing eyes froze as the shadow encased them both.

"Who are you?" Lincoln asked with enough grit in his voice to scare even Opal.

She was about to back away from the confrontation when a strong arm secured itself around her waist, a wall of muscle pressing firmly against her back in a united front.

"Ray Owens. I'm a friend of Opal's from back in high school." He reached a shaky hand out and Lincoln ignored it. After getting the hint, Ray retracted his hand and swiped it over his forehead, looking right nervous.

"Opal's never mentioned a friend named Ray.

Certainly never mentioned an idiot dumb enough to call her a ridiculous name. What are you, two?"

Ray stammered out a shaky laugh. "Come on, man. I was just joking around. I mean . . . look who we're talking about." His head tilted toward her with his eyes growing round.

"No way are you talking about this woman standing in front of you. She's one of the most creative and kindest people I know. You'd be wise to take note of that and to also take note I won't be putting up with anyone treating her with anything less than absolute respect." Without another word, Lincoln used his hold on Opal to spin her around and place her away from the hurtfulness the guy had just pushed on her.

Opal was used to having Lincoln's strong personality aimed against her, but it was remarkably comforting to have it used as a shield of defense for her.

Opal remained quiet while Lincoln paid for their snacks, watching him add several packs of candies to the pile but not focusing on the types. No, her focus was on how good it felt to finally have someone on her side. Sure, she had the Sand Queens and her family, but having Lincoln on her side was a completely new idea. She'd always been mindful of the fact that she was the sidekick or third wheel. This time she had a partner in crime. Someone to lean on, and not just partially.

With his arm still fixed around her waist, Lincoln walked them outside and helped her load up, going as far as reaching in and latching the seat belt for her. He fished a glass bottle of cola out of the bag, used the side of the Jeep door as an opener to pop the lid off, and handed it over.

"For what it's worth, I truly hope my words have never cut you down like that idiot's did just now." He took an uneven inhale and pushed it back out before meeting her eyes. "I'm angry at myself. Not you. But I think I might have taken that out on you some since we've met . . ." Lincoln leaned into the open door and whispered a confession. "I moved here to find myself, but all I've managed to do so far is to become even more lost."

Opal reached over and smoothed her palm down his cheek and considered his confession, knowing exactly what he needed when he leaned into her touch. It was the same thing she needed right then, too. "I think maybe we need to head down south about a mile and grow a little more lost for a while. Whaddya say?"

The remorse and anxiety ebbed away from his face and a sad smile lifted his lips. "I'd like that."

Her eyes widened in mockery. "Finally! I found something Lincoln Cole likes!" She let out a hoot and stomped her feet.

Lincoln shook his head but kept the small smile in place. "I also like the smell of honey," he admitted.

Opal had a feeling he meant a good deal more with the simple admission. "It's okay if you like me, Linc. I like you too."

Those rich-brown eyes watched her for a few moments, looking like an entire war was going on within them, until he blinked a few times before managing to share a small smile with her. He playfully flicked her hoodie onto her head and walked around to load up.

It didn't take long before they were cruising with the country tunes cranked up. A steady twang of Florida Georgia Line, Lee Brice, Sam Hunt, and many others made up the back-road playlist of their languid night. Never did he get the Jeep over twenty miles an hour, as if he didn't ever want the night to end. Certainly they were working on leaving the night on, as one of Hunt's songs reminded her at one point before dawn.

As the Jeep crept down a bumpy back road, Opal sang along to a Lady Antebellum song while she funneled peanuts into her second bottle of cola. She cut off midchorus and commented, "Soda should only ever come in glass bottles. Cans and plastic are such a crime to the taste of cola, wouldn't you agree?"

"Affirmative." Lincoln's head was keeping time to the beats of the song as he held his bottle out to her. "You mind?"

"Not at all." Opal settled her bottle between her legs and steadied his on top of her thigh to fill it with peanuts.

Once she handed it back, Lincoln surprised her by saying, "Thank you."

"Great day, Linc," she teased. "It's only a few peanuts. And you'll be grumbling come next week when you're fishing them out from underneath this seat. I kinda lost a few a *few* times."

"You'll be the one grumbling. You're having a GI party with this Jeep next week."

"GI party?"

"You made the mess, inside and out, you get to clean it. Fair's fair."

Opal guessed that was another one of his military terms that meant cleanup duty. Shrugging it off, she asked, "Then what on earth are you thanking me for?"

Lincoln took a generous gulp and chewed a while. "I'm thanking you for this." He pointed the bottle toward the road, where the headlights illuminated nothing but trees and dirt.

She'd normally let tease flow in such instances, but he was finally being up-front with her, and by golly she owed him the same. "I know I'm different than most folks, and most folks like to take it upon themselves to make me feel bad about that. I appreciate you sticking up for me and my kookiness tonight."

He gave her a sidelong glance and shook his head. "You're not kooky, so stop trying to act like you're so special like that." He took another swallow, chewed for a while, and then chuckled. "You reckon pretty boy back there 'bout wet his pants?" Lincoln tipped his head back and laughed at himself, and the sound of it warmed her from head to toe.

Now he was the one teasing and Opal really liked it. Before she could tease back, he grew serious and stopped the Jeep in the middle of the dirt road. His dark eyes drilling home an unyielding point even before he spoke it. "Anyone ever talk to you like that again and I won't be as kind as I was to that guy tonight. He got off easy compared."

Opal nodded her head and chose to sit back and enjoy the moment, because right then she realized Lincoln was more than just a friend. More than just a partner in crime. The man was becoming a part of her soul.

As Danielle Bradbery began singing "Sway" on the radio, Lincoln let off the brake and continued rolling down the rutted road. The vehicle swaying as slowly as the song's melody had Opal's nerves settling down. She hummed along and watched a shooting star paint a streak across the dark-purple sky.

"You just made a wish, didn't you?" Lincoln teased, ending the punctuated pause in their conversation.

Opal smiled, keeping her eyes directed to the night sky. "You know it."

Lincoln didn't ask her to share her wish, and for that she was thankful. He certainly wouldn't care for the idea of her wishing him to fill more of her nights just as he filled it then—rolling down back roads, sharing snacks and thoughts felt so right to her. She just wasn't sure the man in the driver's seat would agree.

They rode around until the first hints of the sunrise warmed up the sky. Lincoln pulled up to her house and appeared reluctant to leave, so they simply sat in silence and watched the sun completely rise over the ocean. Once it appeared settled into place, Opal reached into her pocket and pulled out a sand dollar she'd found while exploring the beach with the Sand Queens. She handed it over to Lincoln and said in a gentle voice. "Finding one of these intact is almost impossible anymore, but look what I found last night." She traced her fingertip along the natural etching on top of the snowy-white shell where it rested in his palm. "I wish that wherever you end up finding yourself, you'll remain intact. You're one rare find, Lincoln Cole, just the way you are."

He said nothing, so she left it at that and made her way inside. She peeked between the blinds of her bedroom and watched him sit there for the longest time, looking down at the shell in his hand. Apparently that tiny token gave him a lot to think about. Her eyes grew heavier, so without even changing, she snuggled in her bed and dozed off with sounds of country music and the newness of Lincoln's laughter floating through her mind.

9

Ever since he returned from overseas, churches made Lincoln's chest tight, as if it were being squeezed in a vise clamp. And weddings had always made his skin crawl, feeling like an army of ants was doing the jitterbug on each of his nerves. Both of those prickly feelings, paired with the dress shirt and tie he wore for the occasion, had his mood teetering toward all-out crankiness. Luckily, Carter let him off the hook and didn't push him into being part of the wedding party, so he was able to perch on a pew in the back. Another good thing about the bride and groom was they weren't into frills and such, so the ceremony was short, sweet, and to the point.

The reception, on the other hand, was an entirely different story. It was held at Carter's brother's restaurant and was over-the-top with a DJ, a bountiful buffet of all things seafood, and a dance floor. The high energy of the celebration was so intense the walls were practically vibrating from it.

Lincoln sat at his table in the corner of the room and took it all in while working through his third plate of food, trying to ignore the pulsating ache in his leg and the other nagging one in his chest.

"You just gonna stay in this corner all night and be antisocial?" Carter asked as he walked over with a generous slice of red velvet wedding cake. He set it beside Lincoln's plate.

"August did it by breezing in to be your best man and then ditching you at the altar as soon as you kissed your bride."

"Yeah, the punk forgot about another commitment in San Francisco. He needs to slow down, but you don't have the excuse of being too busy."

"You see I'm busy eating my weight in all these good groceries." Lincoln sliced off a wedge of the deep-red cake and shoved it into his mouth. "Great day, that's good stuff." After he swallowed the bite, he added, "You haven't figured out how to chain August down somewhere around here?"

"Oh, I have a plan." Carter rubbed his palms together. "He made a promise to me years ago, and I'm about to collect on it."

"That all you gonna tell me?"

"For now. I have more pressing matters that require my attention at the moment. Like, say, hurrying this shindig along so I can take off with my bride for our honeymoon." Carter waggled his eyebrows, eliciting a chuckle from Lincoln.

"Congratulations, man. You did good." He tipped his head in the direction of Dominica, dancing with her father.

Carter looked over at his bride, beaming with pride. "I know, right?" He shook his head and kept staring with a hand resting over his heart. "That woman is all I see."

"I can *see* that." Lincoln snorted and took another bite of cake, knowing he would be going for seconds on that as well. "For the two of you to be so creative, I'm right disappointed in this color scheme you got going on." He waved his fork around at the similar decor that the church was dressed in earlier. "Black and white with some red here and there. Seriously?"

"It's charcoal and frost with accents of crimson, I'll have you know." Carter quirked a dark eyebrow at Lincoln, as if the names of the colors were truly significant and unique.

"Same difference. At least August's blue hair added some flair at the ceremony." Lincoln smirked at his friend before popping a few shrimp into his mouth, choosing to go back and forth between the savory and sweet fare situated before him. "How long are you gonna hole up in the mountains?"

"Just a week so we can be back in time to settle in our home before Christmas."

Lincoln gave Dominica a cursory glance. Her warm skin tone stood out against the white lace gown. She reminded him of summer. "I figured you'd take that tropical beauty to an island somewhere."

Carter smoothed his lapels and straightened the crimson rose pinned to the left side of his jacket. "Dominica has to stay out of the sun, plus she needs rest, and traveling too far tends to drain her."

Lincoln set his fork down, irritated at himself for forgetting so easily about Dominica's recent diagnosis of lupus. Carter had filled him in about it one night over burgers, explaining all the complications. The list was extensive and dismal. He figured he could either apologize for being insensitive or try playing it off. He went with what he thought Carter would appreciate more. "You ain't got me fooled. You taking your woman somewhere covered in snow so she'll have no choice but to stay wrapped in your arms for an entire week."

"You caught me." Carter raised his palms briefly before growing serious again. "You better still be here helping Opal out when I get back, you hear me?" He swiped a few hush puppies from the bowl Lincoln was hoarding and began munching on them.

"I reckon I'll stick around, so long as the creek don't rise." Lincoln grabbed his glass of red punch and took a long sip.

"Good. Now, I'm gonna mosey on over yonder and cut a rug with my ole lady." Carter tipped an invisible hat in Lincoln's direction with Lincoln doing the same, before sauntering away.

Lincoln chuckled to himself and went back to chowing down on cake and seafood. If ever someone could pull him out of his shell and lighten the heaviness, it was definitely Carter Bradford. Well, a certain sprite of a woman was starting to get pretty good at it too. He began to scan the crowd for that shock of golden-red hair, but before he could find her, a sour-faced brunette wearing a black dress came over and flopped in the chair beside him.

"Ugh. These shoes are killing me." Sophia bent down and began working the clasp free on one of her strappy red heels.

Lincoln shoved another bite of cake into his mouth and chewed while watching Sophia chunk the shoes underneath the table before sinking deeper into the chair. She looked more exhausted than the wedding shindig warranted, but he made no comment on that.

"You don't hang around Shy Spice and Silly Spice all that much," he spoke, surprising them both.

"Spice?" Sophia scoffed. "That's so unoriginal and beyond cheesy." She pulled a compact out of the glittery bag hanging from her wrist and checked her face.

Even though she acted tired, the woman's hair and

makeup were immaculate, so he didn't see any reason for her to be dabbing powder along her nose. Instead of pointing that out, he chose to question instead. "And 'Sand Queens' isn't cheesy in the least?" He gave her a bored look and finished off the cake in one giant bite, hoping his impolite manners would have her scampering away.

"Touché," Sophia conceded, kicking her feet up in the vacant seat beside her.

Seemed she was going to stay awhile, so Lincoln began gathering his plates to try for a getaway. Before he could, she started up a conversation.

"So . . . what spice am I?"

Sighing, Lincoln set the plates down and leaned back in his seat with his eyes focused on where most of the guests were having the time of their lives on the dance floor. He thought of a few words that fit the bill but weren't all that nice, so he said "Sour Spice" instead, and it earned him that sour look the woman liked to wear.

"Why sour?" She glowered, looking right intimidating for such a petite debutante, as she slicked some lip gunk on her pouting lips.

"You walk around looking like you're sucking on lemons. Seriously, aren't you happy for the newlyweds?"

The flinch was so subtle it should have gone undetected, but Opal wasn't the only one good at reading body language. Lincoln saw it and almost felt bad for being the one to produce it.

"I don't mean to be like this," she whispered, slumping down even more while putting the compact and lip gloss away. "Life has worn me slap out lately."

Lincoln studied her out of the corner of his eye. She was too spunky to be so defeated. He nudged her arm with his. "I was just messin' with ya. The first time we met, you pinched the fire out of me. Seems only fair

I get to tease you a bit, but there's nothing sour about you. Please don't take what I said to heart." When she remained quiet with her eyes cast down, he was compelled to add, "You're actually Sassy Spice, and I think sass is a respectable quality to have."

Sophia gave him a dubious look but followed it with a small smile. "I've been called that a time or two."

"Back to my original point, you don't hang out with the girls much. Why's that?" Lincoln saw Josie about as much as he saw Opal, but not the woman sitting beside him.

"I don't live around here anymore, but Collin and I visit at least once or twice a month, so you've been warned more sass will be here near Christmas."

"Collin was the other ring bearer who helped Carter's little nephew carry that sign down the aisle today?" He recalled the sign saying something about it being too late to take a ride because here comes your bride, and Zachary practically dragging the toddler down the aisle.

"Yes. He's only sixteen months old, but he thinks he can keep up with the big kids already."

Lincoln checked out the fat diamond ring that looked like it was weighing her tiny hand down. "Is your husband here?"

Sophia squirmed a bit and shook her head. "Ty is a pro ball player. With . . . with playoffs coming up, it . . . it was impossible for him to make it."

The stuttering coming from beside him had Lincoln fully turning to look at her. Gone was the confident, feisty woman he was just bickering with and in her place was a flustered mess. He thought over what she'd just shared, causing a lightbulb to start flickering. "Ty Prescott is your husband?"

Her posture grew rigid. "You know him?"

"I watch football, so yeah."

"Oh . . . that's . . . umm . . . nice."

Lincoln felt like a fish out of water with this woman, and instead of coming up for air with this conversation, he was getting deeper and closer to suffocating. Then the lightbulb came on completely and had him cringing. He recalled a few headlines that had recently been circulating around the sports world about Ty Prescott, and they weren't high accolades on his rushing yards. No, they were gossipy stories pertaining to the famous running back's personal life. Partying and womanizing—two things that shouldn't be attached to a married man with a child.

The subject needed to be changed and in a hurry. Tugging on his suddenly too-tight collar, Lincoln asked, "Why was Josie a no-show tonight?"

Sophia huffed a little laugh. "When August is in town, she ghosts on us."

"Why?"

"Because Josie is hopelessly in love with him. Has been since high school."

Lincoln almost swallowed a mouthful of punch wrong, wondering why this was the first he'd heard of it. "Then why is she avoiding him?"

Sophia shifted in her seat. "Shoot. I probably shouldn't have told you . . ." She sighed. "Josie believes it's best to avoid him if she can't have him."

Looking back, Lincoln should have caught on to how squeamish Josie acted each time he or Opal brought August up. He almost asked Sophia why Josie didn't think she could have him but figured it was because the guy couldn't get still somewhere. Josie seemed pretty rooted to Sunset Cove and certainly wouldn't be one to chase after a man. He'd noticed her scampering around the little town doing for others all the time like it was her mission.

Lincoln caught sight of Zachary zooming by with several balloons tied around his torso, but no tiny suit followed behind him. "Where's your little guy?"

"My parents took Collin home. Poor baby was wiped out."

"Can't believe he and Zachary near about knocked the wedding cake over." Thinking about it had a smile blooming across his face.

"Oh, wow! Put that thing away," Sophia protested as a hand shot up to shield her eyes.

He wanted to laugh at her silliness and sigh in relief that her sass had returned to lighten the mood, but with effort, he schooled his features into a scowl. "Better?"

Sophia peeked from the side of her hand. "Much. Thank you." She snickered, making Lincoln's lip twitch.

"Looked like Collin had himself a large time tonight. That was nice of your parents."

"Yes, but what's even nicer than that is you taking up for Opal the other night. That Ray Owens needs a fist to his face. He better not cross my path anytime soon." Sophia crossed her arms, looking ready to go to battle for her friend.

"Opal told you about that?" It still steamed him that anyone would be so cruel to such an amazing woman. She'd mentioned that was the norm of her youth. Between being a little eccentric and being the wealthy senator's daughter, kids had plenty of material to work with. Lincoln told her it was just jealousy, but the small smile she gave him made it clear she didn't buy it. He then told her, if he could rewind time, he would have been her bodyguard and beat them all up for her. That earned him a genuine smile and a kiss on his quickly heated cheek.

Lincoln rubbed his palm over his bearded cheek, remembering how good it had felt, as Sophia's words faded to the background. Shaking off the enchantment of Opal Gilbert, he mumbled, "Huh?"

"I *said*, of course Opal told me. She told more than just about Ray, too. Just so you know, the Sand Queens don't really keep secrets from one another."

Lincoln muttered an oath under his breath and set his sights on a search for the little yapper. He found her by the punch bowl, talking animatedly with an elderly couple. Each time he looked at her—more often than he should—a mixed feeling of peace and yearning washed over him. It felt good but uncomfortable and he had a suspicion that she liked keeping him tied in knots.

"Here's one of our secrets I'll share with you." Sophia tapped him on the shoulder to get his attention. Once he pulled his eyes away from Opal and focused on her, she continued, "Opal may be dressed in a ditzy flamboyant package, but that's a mere disguise. Underneath is one wise soul who sees everything and loves it all. Good or bad."

Lincoln's eyes flickered back over and found Opal staring at him. She didn't react like most women would when being caught staring at a man—blushing and looking away. No, his little sprite threw her hand up and waved with a big smile on her pretty face that made his lips turn up in spite of him trying to tamp them down. Opal glowed with a natural beauty he'd not seen much in his lifetime. He tipped his head slightly toward his table companion without taking his eyes off of Opal when he realized Sophia was yammering on about something. "What was that?"

Sophia sighed and started again. "Here's your *warning*. Opal doesn't love with just a piece of her heart. She loves with her entire being."

Lincoln expected her to add more, but Sophia fished her shoes from under the table and gathered her purse. "Wait. Where's the warning in that?"

"You think about what I said long enough and you'll figure it out." Sophia turned her attention to the dance floor and just stood there staring for a few beats. Sighing, she mumbled, "To love and be loved like that . . ."

Lincoln followed her line of vision and found Carter and Dominica dancing. The couple appeared to be in their own universe, holding each other and stealing small kisses. They certainly wore their happiness with pride. "Like what?"

"Carter and Dominica's love clearly includes respect, affection, and friendship," Sophia said as she twirled the diamond ring around and around her finger, making it clear her marriage held none of those particular qualities.

They watched as Carter smoothed the back of his hand down Dominica's rosy cheek. The man looked drunk with the love he had for his bride. Lincoln would file that away to tease his friend about at a later date.

"They're right sickening, if you ask me," Lincoln lied, hoping to pull Mrs. Sass back out. Instead, her eyes became glassy. She was evidently too far gone for him to rile up.

"That's a sickening I wouldn't mind putting up with." She sniffled and shook her head. Moments of more sniffing passed before she whispered, "Lincoln, are you a praying man?"

Her question zinged from out of left field and knocked the wind out of him. Clearing his tightening throat, Lincoln muttered, "Not like I should be."

Sophia picked up a folded napkin and dabbed the corners of her eyes with it. "That's too bad."

"You in need of prayers?" Lincoln asked before he could stop himself.

"My *family* is in desperate need of prayer." Standing, Sophia offered him the saddest smile he'd ever witnessed before walking away.

Time slipped by as Lincoln sat there pondering the deep yet vague conversation he'd just had with a practical stranger, who suddenly felt more like a little sister he needed to protect than not. Foolishness showed up and sat heavily on his shoulders. For that was what he'd been lately with his faith. And here was someone requesting his prayers on their behalf and he didn't feel like he was in a strong enough position to help them out.

Please, God, forgive me for my foolishness. He began the prayer as the vise grip around his chest tightened, but he knew he needed to put the lid firmly back on all the hurt and confusion that had gnawed at him over the last few years. If not, he'd probably be carried out of the wedding reception in a straitjacket.

After a few deep breaths and more punch to quench his dry throat, Lincoln was able to bottle it all back up for the time being. He also resolved to have a talk with Opal about what was going on with Sophia and her family.

He watched on as Carter dipped Dominica mid-dance. She giggled as he righted her and placed a kiss on her smiling lips. Lincoln wished he were brave enough to love someone that confidently, that openly.

Just as that thought flickered through his head, so did a pixie flicker up to his table.

"What are you thinking about?" Opal asked, her face high in color and feet bare.

He blinked out of his daze and let out a nervous cough. No way would he be sharing that particular wish with this particular woman.

Her eyes softened when he didn't speak. "Aww . . . You're happy for them, aren't you?"

"Why wouldn't I be?"

Opal stood beside him and swayed back and forth. "You wanna dance?"

Lincoln raised an eyebrow at the same time he picked up his cane to drive his answer home. His leg wouldn't be able to handle any type of dance moves. Not even the languid sway of a slow dance was possible, especially after the intense session he had with the therapist the day before.

"Oh, my friend." Opal shook her head. "You're too busy focusing on the obstacles and keep missing out on all the potential solutions."

Before he could protest or grouch some type of response, Opal shoved a chair against the side of his and sat close. She leaned over like she was going to hug him, which was pretty much what she did. With her arms around his neck, Opal began to gently sway to the rhythm of the slow song playing through the speakers.

"Dance with me, Linc," she whispered close to his ear, her breath tickling the side of his neck and sending an army of goose bumps down his spine.

Surrounded by Opal's warmth and the scent of honey assailing him, it didn't take much for Lincoln to agree. He stretched one arm over the back of her chair and encircled her waist with the other. It was silly for all of two seconds before he was lost in the sensation of dancing with the vibrant woman who'd pranced into his life and was turning it upside down.

Opal let out a contented sigh that had him pulling her a tad bit closer. Testing the newness of having her in his arms, Lincoln didn't find it as bothersome as he'd expected. Even though she was a pint-size to his giant-size, the embrace was a perfect fit with him finding an abundance of comfort in her petite arms. He knew he looked like a strong tower beside her, yet inside he felt certain he was the more delicate, weaker one of the two.

With her soft cheek resting against his bearded one, Opal hummed along with Brett Young as the singer belted out his song "In Case You Didn't Know." Lincoln made note of it, knowing each time he heard it in the future, he'd remember this nondance with Opal in his arms and he'd recall it being the best dance of his life.

"You look beautiful tonight," he whispered, unable to stop himself.

Lincoln sensed her laugh more so than heard it as Opal began sliding her fingers through the ends of his hair. Her affectionate gesture feeling familiar yet so new. "Glad I could pull that off for one night at least."

"You pull it off every day, Opal." He pulled her closer when she tried to lean away. No way did he want her searching his eyes at the moment. His words already gave away enough.

They swayed through a few more slow songs, and he secretly enjoyed every minute of having an excuse to hold her close and loathed when she finally pulled away to fetch them another glass of punch. Her warmth and ever-present fragrance of honey lingered as he watched her walk away, needing her to hurry back. And when she did just that, he couldn't contain the smile it produced.

Later in the night, the silly woman talked Lincoln into a chair version of the Macarena. He figured he couldn't look any dumber than the people doing the same moves on the dance floor. Opal wiggled further into his heart when she swiped them both another piece of wedding cake with a side of crab cakes.

Before he knew it, the time was close to midnight and the crowd was standing by the doors as they cheered for the departing couple. Whistles and catcalls rang out as they disappeared into the night.

What that couple had found together was a rarity, and Lincoln didn't blame Carter one bit for wanting to celebrate it. His stomach tightened just as his chest had been doing throughout the night as he finally admitted to himself the appeal of being in love. Rubbing his chest, he left those girlie thoughts at the wedding reception. Or that's the lie he told himself all the way home.

10

A coastal Christmas around the southern parts of Sunset Cove always looked a good bit different from, say, a Christmas up north, but late December had ushered in a heat wave and was making the traditional celebrations look even more different than usual. With humid temperatures lingering close to uncomfortable, not even the ugly Christmas sweaters were taken out of the attic to wear. Or if they were, it was only for a short stint at a holiday party that was holding one of those ugly sweater contests.

Always the optimist, Opal didn't let the tropical atmosphere put a damper on her festivities. The cheery redhead smoothed the skirt of her green-and-gold sundress, loving how the jingle bells she'd sewn along the hem jingled their sweet tune every time she moved. The red sash around her waist had a few as well.

"You look like Malibu Barbie, Christmas edition," Kane teased, snickering at his own joke as he climbed into the passenger seat of Opal's van.

"Why, thank you, Bubba. And you look like a college kid in serious need of doing some laundry in those holey shorts and ragged T-shirt." She smiled with narrowed eyes before climbing in the driver's seat. His shirt was red and the shorts an Army green. Both paired in a Christmas theme with his Santa hat, so he was one to talk. "You'll be over teasing me once you see my gift for you." She put the van into gear and headed away from her parents' estate.

"You didn't have to get me anything." Kane twisted slightly in his seat and set down several canvas bags filled with Christmas dinner leftovers behind them. "We got enough food to last weeks."

"That's what I love most about Mom's inability to cook in small portions." Opal took a left at the end of the driveway and turned up a station playing nothing but Christmas carols. Then she bumped up the air-conditioning to combat the eighty-degree temps heating the interior of the van to stifling.

"How's the store doing now that you're back up and running?" Kane asked as he adjusted the vents to get more cool air flowing in his direction.

Opal glanced at him, amused with how the air vent had his coppery curls dancing along the edge of the Santa hat. "It's been so busy, and I'm not sure I'll ever get caught up on the custom pieces, but no complaints on that."

"I'm home for another week. I can help out some."

The van tires began vibrating the familiar sound they made when crossing the old drawbridge. Opal looked out and found a few boats twinkling in the early night. Some were even decorated with Christmas lights. Smiling, she turned her attention back to the road. "Tucker Bradford is going to start helping me deliver furniture after school, starting in about two weeks, so I'd appreciate you giving me a hand while you're home."

"You talking about August's brother?"

"Yeah. He's a year behind you in school." Opal turned onto Front Street, slowing the van so they could take in the Christmas lights sparkling from the palmetto trees and beach houses.

"But I thought Momma said you had a hippie astrologist helping you." Kane cranked his window down and let the ocean breeze move through the van as they approached the old pavilion that was closed for winter.

Opal shut the radio off so they could get the full effect of the holiday scene before them. "Linc is neither a hippie nor an astrologist . . . Well, he may be part hippie, but that stubborn man won't ever admit to it." She pulled the van to a stop in front of the Ferris wheel, where colorful lights raced around the circle with the music chasing it. "I just love this place."

"Yeah. I'm glad the owners figured out a way to let us enjoy it in the off-season."

And did they ever. The entire park was lit up and the lights were synced to several vibrant songs, making them dance between the hours of seven and midnight throughout the months of November and December.

"So what does that guy do to help you out if he's not delivering furniture?" Kane questioned. His eyes were pinned on the lights flickering to the jovial beat of "Rockin' Around the Christmas Tree" that made the carousel look like it was moving while standing still.

"Linc helped me get the store put back together after the storm. And now he's been helping me catch up on the custom orders. He's quite handy."

"He's not an astrologist?" Kane turned to face his sister.

Opal leaned forward in her seat to peer around him. "No. Linc was just messin' when he told Momma and Daddy that, and I kinda think it's fun to not correct their misconception. He actually has a master's in architectural engineering."

"No way. Why's he working for you then?" Kane's brows pinched.

Opal reached over and playfully popped his arm. "You're a Nosy Nelly tonight. And what's so wrong with him working for me?"

"Just trying to make sense of why the guy is hanging around . . ." Kane's eyes widened. "He your boyfriend?"

Opal snickered. "Not hardly. He's a Marine, but an injury caused him to have to retire. Now he's trying to figure out a new path." Opal shrugged. "I don't mind him dawdling around the store until he forms a plan."

"What if you're his plan?" Kane made a kissy-face and waggled his eyebrows in true little brother fashion, earning him a shove.

"You'll be set straight after y'all meet. Trust me, the man doesn't really care for me."

Kane looked like he wanted to ask more but let it go and turned his attention back to the dancing lights for a spell.

After a couple more songs, Opal put the van into gear and went a few more avenues over to where her store sat on the corner.

The light coming from the back of the building instantly caught her attention. "Humph."

"You leave a light on by accident?"

Opal leaned up and peered out of the windshield but found no vehicle in sight. "No. We've been closed the entire week for Christmas, and I drove by a few times. Surely I would have noticed before now."

They both quietly climbed out of the van and began casing the building like they were the robbers instead of whoever it was inside making a bunch of racket.

"Oh, wow. The back porch is gone," Kane whispered as they crept around the side of the building.

"We closed it in and made it into a workroom," Opal whispered back while trying to peep in the window, which was impossible since the antique plantation shutters they'd installed on the interior were closed as usual. A shadow moved from behind them.

"Let's go in like gangbusters," Kane whisper-yelled as if psyching himself up to do just that.

"Let's not and say we did," Opal retorted, stepping up to the back door and knocking.

"Knocking? Are you serious right now? It's your store!" Kane grabbed a rake that was propped by the door and held it up like a baseball bat. "Eek!" he screeched like a little girl when the door flung open to reveal a giant, causing the rake to scrape against the metal awning over their heads. As the rake flayed around, it snagged a string of Christmas lights in the tongs and shorted them out.

Opal rolled her lips in to contain the laugh before pulling on a warm smile. "Merry Christmas," she offered in her singsong voice as her brother wrestled with the lights from beside her. She hoped he wouldn't electrocute himself in the process.

The giant's eyes did a quick sweep of her outfit, sending one eyebrow arching up, before looking over at her sidekick wielding the garden tool. "Put that down before you hurt yourself," Lincoln ordered before stepping back inside.

The first thing Opal noticed was the cane was absent and the limp more prominent. "How'd you get here, Linc?" she asked while following close behind him. She already knew how he got in, being as that she'd given him a key a few weeks back. He was only supposed to help her three days a week but showed up most every day to at least putter around some. Sundays were really the only day they spent apart, and she tried remedying that to no avail, but she was hopeful he'd come around to attending church with her eventually.

His broad shoulders shrugged. "I rode my bike."

"You have a bike?"

"As of this week I do. My therapist said it's good exercise at that last appointment, remember?"

"I'm pretty sure he said *stationary*," Opal countered.

"You go with the dude to his appointments?" Kane chimed in, reminding Opal of his presence.

She looked back just before he closed the door and noticed the rake swaying in the breeze where it remained snagged in the lights. "Linc is my friend, so yes."

"She goes because she's nosy," Lincoln supplied.

"Only because you're a fibber." She glared at Lincoln as he turned around.

"You must be Bubba." Linc jerked a chin in Kane's direction.

Kane grinned while straightening his red Santa hat that jingled from his effort. "Yeah, did my good looks give me away?"

"The way you wrestled with those poor unsuspecting lights looked like something your sister may have taught you." Lincoln's lip twitched as he shook his head. "How does a straitlaced senator end up with two silly elves as offspring?"

Opal pranced in a circle, causing her own bells to jingle. "You like our outfits. Don't deny it."

"This coming from a hippie astrologist?" Kane taunted back as he glanced at Lincoln's bare feet peeping out from the fraying hem of his jeans.

"Something like that," Lincoln agreed.

Opal couldn't contain the giggle any longer at the silliness of the conversation. "Linc, what are you doing here?" She looked around and noticed a drop cloth covering a mountain of something in the corner of the room. "What's underneath that?"

Lincoln rubbed the side of his bearded face with his palm. "Just something I've wanted to work on . . ." He stood in front of the concealed project as if to hide it.

"Okay," Opal simply said, letting him have his secret for the time being. From the narrowed look, Lincoln was skeptical nonetheless. "I wanted to give Bubba his Christmas present," she told him, then moved her focus over to Kane. "Lincoln helped me design it."

Without prompting, Lincoln led them into the main showroom, flipping on lights as he went. Near the back of the store sat the draft table with a huge red bow dressing it.

"Aww, man, this thing is sweet." Kane rushed over and ran his hand over the smooth surface. "I've never seen so many different rulers in all my life."

"Took us an entire weekend to gather them from all over the state," Lincoln mumbled and crossed his arms, but Opal could tell he was proud of the finished project. She was pretty sure he had enjoyed their adventurous weekend of junking too, but she kept that to herself.

"Lincoln helped me fit them all together to form the top, and then he suggested we cover them with acrylic glass so you'll have a smooth surface to work on."

Lincoln demonstrated how to angle the top while Opal set a pencil on the ledge they had fashioned from a yardstick.

Kane studied the table with a wide grin. "I love it. Thanks, y'all." He bent to check out the legs, which were made from metal tubing and dressed with large L-shaped metal rulers.

"This was all your sister," Lincoln said, quickly giving Opal all the credit as he always did with each of their projects.

"Nonsense. You redesigned the entire thing after I shared my plans for it." Opal rolled her eyes.

"Just tweaked it a little." He shrugged.

Opal caught a subtle hint of his citrusy cologne and realized she'd stepped closer at the same time Lincoln did, like some kind of gravitational pull, and from the amused clearing of Kane's throat, her brother had noticed too. Not giving him a chance to call her out on it, Opal stepped back over to the table. "Let's load it up."

Lincoln limped over to grab his shoes, but Opal halted him. "No worries. Bubba and I can manage it. Just get the front door for us, please."

Once they had it loaded and Kane was piled back into the passenger seat, Opal feigned the excuse of needing to grab an invoice. She hurried inside just as Lincoln was about to pull the cloth off the mountain. As soon as he spotted her, he stopped.

"You want a ride home?" she asked, looking for a reason to spend some more time with him.

"Nah. I have some more work to do."

"You sure?"

He nodded with a closed-off demeanor. One that was a clear indicator for Opal to leave it be. Reluctantly she did.

After the draft table was unloaded at Kane's condo, Opal divvied out the plastic containers of food.

"Man, there's enough to feed an army," Kane mumbled before popping open the lid of a container filled with cookies.

"True," Opal agreed while snagging a gingerbread man and biting his head off. She knew for a fact there was enough to feed at least one soldier. "Okay, Bubba, I'm heading out."

"Thanks again for my drafting table. That thing is

killer." Kane wrapped her in a bear hug before going back to the cookies.

She was out the door and heading back to the store in record time. Sure enough, the light was still on when she arrived. After grabbing up a few of the canvas bags of food, she let herself in this time without knocking.

Lincoln sat on the floor in front of the furniture piece and was applying an antiquing glaze. He glanced up and actually blushed.

"That's the neatest thing," Opal whispered as she set the bags down and walked over to the chair/table combo.

"You think so?" Lincoln wiped a rag over the table leg, removing most of the brown glaze to reveal an aged-teal hue underneath. "I, umm . . . I used the broken tables and chairs from the storm."

"So there's more than just this one?"

Lincoln tipped his head over to the cloth covering other pieces, so she stepped over to it and pulled the cloth off. Underneath two more chair/table combos sat complete. One with a weathered-cream finish. The other with an aged-peach hue.

She heard him grunt and then shuffle about but kept her sights set on the furniture. It was only when his breath touched her exposed neck that she realized he'd moved to stand behind her.

"It seemed wasteful to not salvage them somehow. And I thought you could put these in the front yard for customers or whoever to use. I've already sealed these two and will do the other once the glaze is cured. That should protect them from the weather."

Opal tried to disguise the shiver his warm breath elicited by reaching out to run her fingers along the textured top. "They sort of remind me of school desks." She glanced up and over her shoulder and smiled. "I love them. They'll be perfect in the garden."

"It's not much but . . . merry Christmas," Lincoln murmured, surprising her by brushing a hand down her shoulder and continuing until his long, warm fingers were entwined with hers.

His thumb swept over the back of her hand, and it was so gentle and tender that tears pooled in her eyes. Hundreds of words rushed through her thoughts to share with him, but sometimes no words are needed and this was one of those times, so she held them all in and just experienced the unexpected moment with this withdrawn man showing her an intimate side for the very first time. It was merely holding hands, yet it was such an extravagant gift coming from Lincoln Cole.

It was over well before she was ready when he slowly released her hand. Opal turned and met his brown eyes. They reflected a warmth and, dare she say, love that she knew was shining from her green ones. Again, she kept those words to herself and said, "Thank you, Linc. It means a lot."

He cleared his throat and looked over her shoulder. "Glad you like them."

"I love them!" She grinned and placed a palm to her chest, her heart pounding against it. "Man after my own heart, taking broken things and refurbishing them into something new."

"I just don't like things being broken." It was a weighty statement delivered with a strained voice and sounded like he was talking about more than just furniture. He met her eyes briefly before dropping them to his bare feet.

Opal looked there as well, loving this little quirk about him. He wore flip-flops or worn Converse sneakers mostly, but any time they were alone, he'd shed them and walk around barefoot like the country boy he was. He shifted his weight off the bad leg, catching her attention. Knowing he needed to get off his feet, she pointed over to the bags of food. "I brought us some food. Momma cooked it all, so it's safe to eat. You think we can try these two out?"

Lincoln's answer came in the form of him pulling the chair/tables out and placing them side by side. Opal didn't know if that was so he could sit beside her or to keep her from looking at him head-on. Either way, she happily set out the leftovers and was over the moon when he led them in grace without her prompting him first.

By the time they got to the dessert container, Opal couldn't stand it any longer. Between bites of a chocolate layer cake, she blurted, "Why didn't you go home for Christmas?"

Lincoln paused in his chewing and fixed his eyes down on the fork in his hand. "I don't rightly know if I'd have been welcome."

Opal scoffed. "They're your family. Of course you'd be welcome." She smiled with tease, but when he didn't return it, her lips sloped into a confused frown. "Why wouldn't you be welcomed home?"

Lincoln pushed a piece of pie crust around the container, studying it with a pinched expression. When he remained silent, Opal reached over and tucked the thick locks of hair behind his ear so she could see him. At her touch, his gaze connected with hers. The first glance was sharp with the edges of his eyes crinkling, but as she moved her palm to the side of his face, they softened.

It lasted for only a handful of seconds before Lincoln's shoulders stiffened. As a flush crept over his face, he said resolutely, "It's none of your concern."

She watched him mush the crust into nothing but crumbs as she spoke. "When my friend spends Christmas alone because his family wouldn't want him around, I find that concerning. If I'd known—"

"You'd what?" His eyes darted back to hers as he tossed the fork into the container. They were glassy now.

"I would have invited you to spend it with my family at least. And at most, I'd have driven down to Beaufort and had a heart-to-heart with your family on how they're treating you."

"I deserve to spend it alone. Trust me."

The hoarseness of his voice made Opal's chest hurt. Oh, how she wished he would just open up to her. "If you'd explain—"

"No. Now drop it." The giant seemed to deflate into a defeated, feeble man as he scrubbed his hands down his face. He rose to his feet and went over to the coatrack, grabbing the plaid button-down and shrugging it on over his T-shirt while sliding his feet into his flip-flops.

"I don't like leaving things broken any more than you do." Her words had him glancing up. "I don't know what you broke with your family, but hiding out in Sunset Cove isn't the way to fix it." Opal stood and walked the few steps over to the old hutch they used for storage. She reached into one of the drawers, plucked out a broken clamshell, and handed it to him. "I wish for your relationship with your family to be mended."

Lincoln studied the shell in his palm for a moment before slipping it into his shirt pocket but said nothing in response.

Opal knew her small window to speak candidly with him had closed, so she moved back over to the chair/tables and began collecting the mostly empty containers. She didn't expect anything but a door closing to signal his departure, yet she was disappointed all the same when he did exactly as she had predicted.

"Stubborn man," she muttered to the empty room.

As she gathered her belongings and locked up, Opal knew that something was simmering just below the surface with that man. How long would it be before he erupted? And would it be safe to be around when he did?

11

The New Year finally ushered in some cooler temperatures, making life a bit more tolerable. Too bad it did
nothing to improve Lincoln's outlook on things. Opal was
right, hiding out in Sunset Cove wasn't fixing anything.
But he didn't know where to start. More than just his leg
had been affected by the injury, and the damage had bled
into his family. Especially his father. Colonel Jefferson
Cole didn't put up with weakness in any form, never had
in Lincoln's entire life.

When Lincoln came down with chicken pox in ele-
mentary school and wanted to do nothing but whine and
scratch, his father had him scrubbing bathroom floors
with a toothbrush. Said it would keep his son's hands
busy and his mind off the itch. At age sixteen, Lincoln
wrecked his mom's car and ended up with a broken
wrist as a result. He thought the injury was punishment
enough for running off the road and wrapping the car
around a tree. His dad didn't. As punishment, Lincoln
wasn't allowed pain meds to help alleviate the throb of the
broken bone. Jefferson didn't want his son to forget that
being neglectful came with painful consequences. Lincoln
hadn't either.

Never one to baby or offer sympathy, Jefferson had offered his son the customary icy reception when Lincoln came out of the first surgery that took place in a military hospital in Germany. Lincoln would rather have woken up to find no familiar faces than that of his father. Still woozy from anesthesia, he lay in recovery as his old man gave him a thorough dressing-down. He had a jagged memory of being told in so many words that if he'd been paying better attention and used the common sense God gave him, he could have avoided being in the line of fire. Lincoln didn't argue, simply mumbled several *yes, sir*s while lying there in pain and embarrassment. The injury seemed to cause his dad more pain than it caused him, and that made for one long, agonizing recovery.

Before his thoughts could settle on what had happened to drive him to Sunset Cove like a coward, the whimsical humming that had become a part of his daily life grew louder as the pixie wandered into the workroom.

"We've been slammed today." Opal smiled warmly and placed an order slip on the table in front of him, sending her armful of bracelets clattering together.

Lincoln wasn't in the know on fashion, but he suspected those gaudy bracelets really didn't go with a pair of faded jean overalls and the trucker hat she was wearing.

"Ain't that a good thing?" Lincoln wiped his hands on a rag before picking up the paper. Skimming it, he found it to be an order for a set of church-pew chairs.

"It's a great thing," Opal replied as she bent close to inspect the barstool top he was painting, the scent of honey wrapping around him.

Lincoln inhaled greedily before setting the paper down and going back to work. "Do you already have a church pew we can cut down?" he asked as he dipped his brush into the bronze paint. He worked it over the black base coat and wiped off the excess, leaving a metallic sheen on the antique tractor seat.

"Actually, my church had some flood damage during the storm and a few of the pews didn't take kindly to the moisture."

"So is that a yes?" Lincoln flicked an impatient look toward her before redirecting his focus to the seat. He couldn't understand why the woman always rambled on and on about something instead of giving him a clear answer.

"We've gotta go see an elder of the church after work, but I'm pretty sure he'll be willing to let me buy the damaged ones." She picked up the other seat that was ready to be bolted to the wrought-iron bottom. "These things are heavy. Did the girls understand that when y'all discussed the stools?"

Lincoln added a little more bronze to the edge. "Yes, but they said the tractor seats were sentimental to their dad. There's really no way to make them into stools without using a heavy bottom too."

Opal used the seat to mimic a few bicep curls before she sat it down. "Okay. Oh, I meant to tell you a few more customers were going on and on about the store's new layout. Kudos to you, sir." She reached over and gave him a one-armed hug, sending even more of that sweet scent to engulf him.

"Glad I could help," Lincoln muttered, aching to return the embrace. Her comfort felt too nice, and he knew if he didn't keep some distance from her touch, he'd likely end up clinging to her like a favorite stuffed animal. With that not being an option, he leaned away until her arm dropped from his shoulder.

Opal tapped the seat top in front of him. "Even though they're going to weigh a ton, the stools will be really neat.

I'm sure Mr. Stevens will love them. It's sweet of his daughters to want to surprise him with them. Just let me know when you're done and I'll have Tucker deliver them."

And there she went poking at his other sore spot again, shining a glaring light on his weakened state. "I think I can handle delivering a few stools," he snapped. "I ain't a total invalid."

Opal raised her palms. "Okay." As she narrowed her green eyes at him, the bell chimed over the front door, saving him from whatever sweet snark she was formulating. "Do let me get that before you whack me with your cane." Nope, she got it out anyway. Breezing out the door and toward the front, he heard her say under her breath, "Cranky ole man."

Lincoln grunted in response and tightened his grip on the paintbrush. Inhaling the lingering scent she left behind, he focused on the project. He'd been floundering since leaving the military, but the last two months had shown him some direction. Remodeling furniture and fashioning new unique pieces from old ones was quite appealing and he liked it. Problem was he didn't think it was fair to Opal to have to put up with him.

He was past his limit on managing his pain today. When he reached that point of agony, he couldn't stand the sight of someone else. Luckily, it seemed all he had to do was bark a little in her direction and she would scurry out of the workroom and leave him alone. The quaint room with its shiplap walls and that large painting of the fairy herself was becoming his place of solace.

Closing time came and went, but Lincoln was determined to finish what he'd started. By the time he completed applying the bronze finish to the seat and had the supplies put back in their designated spots, as well as straightening up the mess Opal had left scattered about, all the front lights were turned off and Opal walked back in. She held her hand out to give him what he was guessing to be another shell. The way that little routine of hers was going, come springtime he'd have a bigger collection of shells than the beach across the street. He automatically held his palm out to accept it and was confused when he peered down at the small packet of sugar she placed there instead.

"What's this for?" he asked, glancing between the packet and Opal.

She shrugged her shoulder, looking timid for some reason. "You've been snapping at me all day in that sour tone of yours. Figured I did something to irritate you, so I thought I'd try to sweeten you up a little." His mouth opened to respond but she continued. "Seriously, if I've bothered you or made you mad, I apologize."

Lincoln let out a pensive sigh, feeling right ashamed of himself for taking his aggravation out on Opal. She was always the target of his frustrations as of late, even when she didn't instigate it. "I ain't sore at you, Opal. My dang leg is killing me today . . ." He groaned and ran his hands through his hair. Releasing the long strands sent them swinging back into his face as he plopped down in his chair. "I'm the one who should be apologizing."

Opal walked over and wedged herself between him and the table. "Your leg hurts because that bike ride to work is putting too much tension on your knee."

"Oh, so now you're a doctor?" He heard the snarl in his tone, so he took a deep breath to push it away as he went to stand, but Opal wasn't having it.

She placed both hands on his shoulders and made it clear for him to stay in the chair when she moved closer to stand between his knees. "No, but I've talked to Dr. Rabin."

With his jaw nearly locked to hold back from yelling, Lincoln gritted out, "He ain't supposed to be telling you anything about my leg."

Opal somehow moved even closer, her tiny nose almost pressed against his. "We didn't talk about *your* leg. I asked him about this hypothetical ole grouch's leg, and he answered hypothetically that the grouch needed to stay off the mountain bike." She reached out and smoothed his hair away from his forehead, tucking strands behind his ears. "Linc, please don't be stubborn when it comes to your leg."

He inhaled a shaky breath, feeling like the invalid he swore he wasn't. "I just want my leg to get better, stronger. It needs exercise, not all this sitting around. I'm growing weaker by the day."

"How about we figure out another, safer exercise for your leg?" Opal asked in a lower tone as her fingers kept working through his hair, the soothing motion calming him down.

Lincoln was close to drooling. Licking his lips, he mumbled, "It's not your problem to solve."

"What if I want it to be?" Opal's question had his eyes opening to meet the vivid green of hers.

"Why would you?"

"You're my friend."

"So you keep saying."

"You already agreed to as much."

"Yeah, and a friend wouldn't treat you the way I have. You don't deserve me taking my misery out on you. It's just . . . sometimes the pain gets to be too much, like it's tearing me apart and I can't get past it." Lincoln scanned the room before settling on her. "Opal . . ." He began to choke up, feeling like a complete loser. "Maybe it's best I find work elsewhere. I really don't want to take it out on you. I do try not to, but I end up doing it anyway."

Her hand stilled in his hair and then dropped to her side. "You think a little snark from big ole you is enough to scare me?" She scoffed. "You're giving yourself too much credit."

"It ain't fair to you," he gritted out.

"You want to know what's not fair to me? You not going to church with me. Now that really hurts my feelings. And you refusing to try my squid ice cream the other day. Almost had me in tears." Opal rattled off more silly nonsense, trying to brush off all the heavy he just laid out there.

Hurting too severely and too weak to deny Opal anything, Lincoln let her brush it off. He leveraged his hands against Opal's tiny shoulders and gently moved her aside so he could stand and step away from the uncomfortable conversation. "Let's go to church."

She clutched her chest and went all doe-eyed. "Be still, my little heart."

"Knock it off," he said in a played-up grumpy voice, picking up his cane and waving it around for emphasis. "Or I'll whack you."

• • •

Sure, he'd been kidding the day before about whacking the exasperating woman with his cane, but as Lincoln held it in a death grip while staring down at his dismantled bike, the teasing had disappeared right along with his front tire.

Nostrils flaring, he limped back inside the store and was ready to breathe fire. "What'd you do to my bike? Where's the tire?" he yelled and stomp-limped into her office.

Opal didn't even spare him a glance as she kept focusing on the computer screen. "I put the tire away for safekeeping, but no worries. My dad sent over one of his golf carts from the estate. You're welcome to use it indefinitely."

Lincoln grabbed the back of her chair and twirled it around. Leaning forward, he gripped the armrests and leaned forward to deliver to her his best glower. From the nonchalant gaze she returned, his intimidation tactic failed as usual. His lips snarled back in preparation of him laying into her overmeddling, but she had the audacity to place her index finger against his lips to hush him.

"Use the golf cart and stop being so stubborn." She rolled back around and began shutting the computer down. "Go home and get your swimsuit. I'll be there in about ten minutes to pick you up."

"Pick me up for what?"

"Swimming is the safest exercise for your type of injury."

He bit back a sarcastic retort of her not being a doctor and said instead, "It's too cold."

"The pool at the camp is heated. Carter gave me permission for you to go out there in the evenings."

Lincoln rubbed his jaw and squinted down at her. "I don't think that's a very good idea."

"Why not?" One of her auburn eyebrows arched up. Seemed she already knew the answer by the slight smirk on her face.

Lincoln was already struggling to come to terms with his feelings for the woman, and the idea of spending evenings alone with her at a pool in hardly any clothes would be a reckless move. By the challenging stare she was giving him, he was going to have to suck it up and endure it or face the embarrassment of admitting the truth that he found her attractive and didn't trust himself enough to keep his hands to himself. *Yep, not saying that out loud.*

Knowing there would be no winning the argument, Lincoln tossed his hands up in surrender. "Never mind." Shaking his head, he turned and left through the back door, where he noticed for the first time the shiny blue golf cart. Sliding onto the seat, he headed in the direction of his rental. He wouldn't ever admit it to Opal, but never riding that bike again was perfectly all right by him. He knew that was the cause of the escalating pain he was experiencing but was too stubborn to throw in the towel. Thankfully, Opal saved him from having to.

● ● ●

A few hours later, Lincoln found himself fighting an entirely new type of battle. One he was sure he could win, but not really caring one way or the other. "Do it again, and I promise you'll regret it," he warned while keeping a firm grip on his gun.

Eyes narrowed, his enemy slowly raised his high-powered weapon and took aim. "It's a risk I'm willing to break."

Before Lincoln could blink, he'd been struck again. "Willing to *take*!" he yelled as he popped off several quick rounds of his water gun, hitting Zachary in the neck and the shoulder.

The little boy cackled like a hyperventilating hyena as he tossed his empty water gun to the side and did a cannonball back into the pool, sending a mini wave to splash Lincoln. As soon as Zachary's head popped out of the water, Lincoln made a lunge for him.

"Come here, you little rascal!" Lincoln grabbed the

kid up and slung him over his shoulder. After tickling Zachary until they were both out of breath, Lincoln handed him over to August. "I'm spent," he declared, wading over to the steps and climbing out of the pool.

"You ort to be. The two of you have been horsing around for at least an hour straight." Carter tossed him a towel and retrieved another for Zachary. "Sure did hate that Opal couldn't stick around and enjoy the pool too."

Lincoln kept drying off, ignoring his friend poking fun at him. As soon as he'd made it home, he'd called Carter and begged him to have Dominica need Opal for something or other and for the boys to go swimming with him. Lincoln knew he had played the coward card but knew it was also for the best.

"You ain't much of a friend if you have this outrageous pool and don't allow her to use it already," Lincoln fired back, hitching a thumb toward the lagoon with the waterfall. *Pool* wasn't even close to describing what he'd just swum in.

"It was just completed and hasn't even gone through inspections yet." Carter wrapped a dry towel around his nephew and sent him off to the cabana to change clothes. After the little guy was out of earshot, he moved a little closer to Lincoln and whispered, "You wanna tell me why you're afraid to go swimming with Opal?"

"I'm not afraid," Lincoln lied, and by the lip twitch from his friend, Carter knew it too. "We already spend too much time together. I just needed some space."

"If you say so, man." Carter walked off while letting out a chorus of clucks.

Lincoln made quick work of changing into some dry clothes and headed to the front of the camp, where he thought the guys would be waiting to take him home. Of course they weren't, but the redheaded sprite was. She sat in the idling van, ready to escort him home. He yanked the passenger door open and climbed in.

"Next time I'll drive myself," he mumbled, fastening his seat belt.

"Oh, Linc, you're more than welcome. I was happy to set up the swim for you. And it's my pleasure to drive you home this evening after you pretty much banned me from the pool." Opal offered her sweet smile and batted her long eyelashes at him before putting the van into gear and rolling down the long driveway.

There was no getting anything past the woman, and she sure didn't mind calling him out on it either. Crossing his arms, Lincoln muttered, "Thank you for setting this up. The swim actually didn't hurt."

"But my company would have," she said in a flat tone, eyes focused on the road.

Lincoln didn't know what to say, and Opal seemed to be in the same predicament for the very first time, so the ride home carried an awkward silence. Once she parked in his driveway, Lincoln rushed to gather his belongings so he could get out of the van and away from the awkwardness, but Opal stopped him.

"Wait a sec. You owe me a favor."

He took his hand off the door handle and gave her a sidelong glance. "I do?" He owed her more than just a favor but was a little too prideful to admit it out loud.

"Yes. Now roll your window down."

Lincoln opened his mouth to question her, but Opal held a palm up to hush him as she rolled her own window down. Pressing his lips together, he did as he was told.

"Now, reach beside the seat and recline it as far back as it'll go." Opal had her seat laid back in a blink. She propped her short legs up on the dashboard and settled her arms over her head, appearing rather relaxed. "I'm waiting, Linc."

Sighing, he gave in to her request and did the same, minus propping his long legs up simply because there was not enough space for that. Tense, he held himself still and waited for her next instructions. When nothing came for several minutes, the echoes of the ocean waves just on the other side of his cottage caught his attention. Focusing on those sounds, the tension slowly began to fade until he gave in and closed his eyes.

"Hold my hand, Linc," Opal whispered, making his shoulders retighten.

He rolled his head in her direction and found her tiny hand stretched toward him. "Why?"

"It's part of the favor. Just go with it, please." She wiggled her fingers and when he did nothing but stare, she quipped, "You held my hand at Christmas, remember?"

Yeah, he remembered. He couldn't quit remembering. It felt too good. Too right. And it scared him, knowing she was becoming a lifeline for him and that she deserved better than a crippled grump with no ambition past surviving the day. Yet he was too weak to deny her, so he reached out and gathered her hand in his. And just like that, the goodness and rightness of Opal Gilbert overtook him. He didn't ever want to let go.

It took longer this time for the tension to wane, but eventually it did, leaving Lincoln free to savor Opal's touch and the tranquil melody of the ocean.

"Isn't the sound of the ocean the sweetest lullaby ever composed?" Opal released a delicate sigh, one filled with peaceful contentment.

"Yeah," Lincoln managed just over a whisper, only agreeing because her sweet voice added the perfect layer of harmony to it. His body was spent from swimming and was too tired to keep his guard up, so he began synchronizing his breaths to the ocean's tune. In . . . Out . . . So soothing, it lulled him into a light doze.

Snuggling against the seat, he lifted their entwined hands and held them to his cheek, relishing the comfort of her soft skin. Releasing a contented sigh, he pressed his lips against the back of Opal's hand. Realizing what he'd done, his eyes flew open and locked with hers. There was no shock of horror on her face, only a faint smile, so he gave in and placed several more kisses on her hand before slowly letting it go.

"See, Linc, my company didn't hurt," Opal whispered.

The squeeze of his heart begged to differ, but he conceded with a subtle nod. Rubbing the sleep from his eyes, Lincoln reached for the lever and sent his seat upright.

Opal did the same and then plundered in her bag for a few beats before handing him a shell.

"What's the wish with this one?" he asked, eyeing the tiny hermit crab shell.

"That you would let me in." She waited until he met her eyes to speak again. "I promise you it won't be as painful as you think."

And that was where Opal Gilbert was wrong. Lincoln had barely survived that bombing attack and was still bleeding out from the wounds he'd helped to inflict on his family before escaping to Sunset Cove. If he accepted Opal's love only to turn around and lose it when she realized he was no good for her, it would finish destroying him.

"You deserve better." Shaking his head to whatever she was about to follow that comment with, Lincoln closed the van door and made his way up the porch and on inside the house. He paused there long enough to drop the shell inside the bench by the door where all the other wishes were being held for safekeeping. Looking at the plunder, he really did wish her prayers would be answered on his behalf.

12

There was nothing more magical than late nights on the beach. With the ocean crooning its secrets to the moon and the sandy shore, Opal always felt like she was in a private world where nothing was impossible. Never a cynic, she loved to get carried away in the breezy romance the night ambience promised to deliver, but she was beginning to worry that Sophia had started to rub off on her. The star-studded night sky, the indigo ocean with its whitecaps, the moon bleaching out the sand . . . it all had somehow grown dull and less mysterious as of late.

"We're all wrapped up, looking like gifts waiting for Christmas morning," Josie said on a snicker before taking a sip from her thermos.

It was the Sand Queens' monthly meeting with the beach, but the chilly night was making it a tad uncomfortable.

"Yeah. And most would call us silly for being bundled up so tight. It's only in the fifties," Sophia scoffed as she wrapped the scarf another loop around her neck.

"Our Southern bones don't come insulated enough for temperatures under sixty," Josie chimed back in.

Opal simply nodded, not caring to add any commentary. In the last week, she'd grown more silent than she'd ever been. It was Lincoln's fault. The man's hot-to-cold, tender-to-prickly attitude left her totally perplexed and at a loss on how to respond.

"Where'd you get that hat, Opal?" Sophia asked, drawing her attention momentarily away from thoughts of Lincoln and his twitchy cold shoulder.

"I found it in some of Bubba's hunting gear he left at the house." Opal tugged the camouflage hat by the ear flaps down further on her head. It was frumpy but was doing a great job keeping her head nice and warm.

"Oh, I didn't know if you maybe snatched it from Lincoln." Sophia shrugged.

Opal might have been preoccupied with her confusing thoughts on the man but wasn't too far gone to not realize the teasing lilt in her friend's voice.

"Linc's not a sharing kind of guy, and we aren't on friendly enough terms for me to be snatching anything from him." Opal gave Sophia a pointed look, conveying that she wanted to drop it.

"He's mighty cute," Josie offered, unaware of the look.

Sophia snorted. "*Cute* is not the right word to describe that beast of a man."

"More like devilishly good looks with enough razor-sharp edges to flash a warning," Opal added before she could stop herself.

"What's going on with the two of you?" Josie asked while wrapping the wool blanket over her head and shoulders, clutching it under her chin.

"I haven't a clue. He seemed to soften up a little at the wedding but has gone back to being prickly ever since."

"Have you confronted him about it?" Sophia asked, always the one to go for being up-front on matters.

"Sort of . . ."

"That's not good enough. You need to be clear.

Men don't get subtle hints and offhand comments from women. We might as well be talking like the teacher from Charlie Brown, because that's all they hear." Sophia crossed her arms and huffed out a cloudy breath before mimicking the *wanh, wanh, wanh, wanh.*

"Yeah? And how's being clear and up-front working out for you with Ty?" As soon as Opal said it, she wished she could suck the retort back in.

The party she'd attended last weekend with Josie up in Charlotte flashed through her thoughts and had Opal cringing even more. Sophia had begged them to go to show their support to Ty and his team, but they had really only made the trek to support Sophia. And by the looks of things, Opal was glad they did.

The night of the party had been tense with Ty spending the evening with one woman or another trying to wrap themselves around him like an overzealous monkey. It was all Opal could do not to march up to the women and give them a lecture on having some decency and respect for themselves. Her palm itched to smack Ty upside the head for allowing it.

Opal sighed. "Sophia, I was just popping off at the mouth. I'm sorry, girl."

"No. You're absolutely right. Ty is a perfect example. I've tried to be subtle with him, and look where it's gotten me." Sophia's gloved hands flailed around in the air, her cheeks growing even more rosy.

Josie squeezed Opal's shoulder. "I'm with Sophia on this one. Let Lincoln know how you feel."

"What if *I* don't even know how I feel?" Opal gave her friend a wobbly smile before brushing her situation off and focusing on Sophia. "So things haven't improved?"

"We're seeing a marriage counselor, but it seems like we're going nowhere with it."

Sophia and Ty had been trying to reconcile for the better part of the last year. Opal hated to admit it out loud, but it seemed her friend's assessment might be correct.

The three friends sat out on the cold beach for a while longer, allowing Sophia to vent, until their thermoses of hot chocolate were drained dry and their bodies were chilled to the bone.

After a hot shower to warm up, Opal climbed into bed with her thoughts on the brooding soldier. Each time she thought about him suggesting he should find another job, her heart squeezed and she could hardly swallow. She'd allowed Lincoln Cole to become a part of her business plan for Bless This Mess without much thought. The idea just fit. And even though she fought long and hard against it, he ended up being a part of her life plan as well. The thought of him not being there was unfathomable, so she tamped it down the best she could by trying to focus on her next furniture project until she finally drifted off to sleep.

The break on Sunday from Lincoln did very little in making Opal feel any more enthusiastic about their situation. Trepidation was more like it, and that dreadful feeling followed her all the way to work Monday morning.

With the doors closed to the public, Mondays were dedicated to working on custom orders. The day was cold and rainy and had the mostly mute pair stuck inside together with the awkward tension making it even more uncomfortable. Lincoln spent the better part of the day playing dodge Opal. Each time she'd get near, he seemed to find a reason to limp off in the other direction.

"Do you even know how to grow a sit?" Opal asked in a snippy tone, tired of their game of chase that she'd found herself playing unwillingly.

Lincoln glanced over his shoulder briefly before going back to rummaging around in a drawer. "What are you whining about?"

"You're always moving here, there, and yonder today. Seriously, it wouldn't hurt you to get still somewhere." She glared at his broad back before focusing on taking the hardware off the old doors she planned to turn into tabletops.

"If I stop moving, my leg starts throbbing like a tooth-ache," Lincoln explained with a good bit of annoyance.

"And whose fault is that?" She gave him no time to answer before plowing on. "*Yours.* If you'd stop skipping doctor's appointments and actually do as you're told, that leg wouldn't be in the shape it's in."

Her scolding words had him swinging around, red-faced. "My leg wouldn't be in this shape if that enemy fire didn't rip into it." Lincoln nearly growled the words.

"Do you have PTSD?"

"No. I have PO'D." He stood there, clenching his fists, a severe-looking scowl on his face.

Opal blinked slowly until his meaning registered. He definitely had a lot of pent-up anger.

Working as closely as they did, she'd learned in the last few months how to pay attention to his mannerisms and what they revealed. Her favorite was when she'd catch him staring at her with his handsome face tilted just a little to the side as if to admire her better. How he twisted his lips one way and then the other while working on a furniture piece. But there were days such as today when his mannerisms sent out a warning to proceed with cau-tion. His rich-brown eyes narrowed until forming creases at the corners. The firm press of his full lips. The continu-ous flexing of his jaw.

Aware that the fuming man needed some space, Opal

left him with the unfinished doors and chose to tackle some paperwork in her office. All the while she heard him muttering to himself and slamming things around in the back.

Closing her eyes and leaning back in the chair, Opal took a moment to try to calm down. It was beyond frustrating that Lincoln chose to wear misery and pain as if it were his cross to bear, deliberately brushing off the doctor's advice on how to take care of his leg and ways to manage the pain. The question was why? She had no clue because the stubborn man refused to open up. And she was frustrated with herself because she had no idea how to get him to confide in her. Keeping whatever it was bottled inside was just as unhealthy as his injury. Along with that misery, it seemed his broad shoulders were carrying around a considerable weight of guilt. Yet another mystery to Corporal Lincoln Cole.

Opal decided to take the girls' advice and be up-front with him. She procrastinated a little longer until the noise in the workroom died down. Rising from the desk and taking a fortifying breath, she swiped a small trinket box and carried it with her.

"I've taken all the hardware off the doors and stripped the first coat of paint off them," Lincoln said as soon as she entered the room. He was using a wire brush to clean the rust on the hinges he'd spread out along his worktable. A task she was supposed to do, but he was finishing it for her as maybe an apology, something he often did after one of his tantrums.

Opal walked over and placed the box in the middle of the table. His eyes automatically drew to it. "This used to be a plain old desk clock. The kind you wind up. I found it on one of my junking trips, but the clock hands no longer worked. I took it apart trying to figure out how to fix it, but days later—after I accidentally broke the long hand in two—I knew it was time for the clock to become something new." She flicked the tiny clasp up and opened the clock face, which had been fashioned into the lid for the trinket box. "Telling time was an important job, but eventually it needed to be restored for a different purpose." She held out the box and allowed Lincoln to peep inside, where she'd tucked sentimental items— several photos of her family and the Sand Queens, her grandmother's locket, a pendant her father received after winning his first election, and the first penny the store's register ever held.

He cut her a sidelong glance and scoffed, apparently unimpressed. "Do you really think God took me out of the military to tinker with weird furniture?"

"You and I both know it's more than that." Opal closed the lid of the box and walked it back to her office with Lincoln heavy on her heels. She made note of the heavier limp his gait held. It was another mannerism she closely observed most days to help gauge his pain.

"What else is it about then?" He raked his hands through his hair, gathering the locks in a ball before releasing the curtain back to hide his cheekbones. They were one of Opal's favorite features of his face, probably because he was so stingy with sharing them.

Opal crossed her arms and planted a hip on the side of her desk. "You have no guess? No idea why there's so much tension between us?" She watched him closely and saw it in the depths of his rich-brown eyes and wondered if he'd ever fully understand she'd find his truths there every time. Sure, he was in constant pain, but there was more to the strained atmosphere than that. He'd even expressed it twice—holding her hand at Christmas and then kissing the back of her hand the other night in the van. He wasn't oblivious about it, but boy, was he stubborn.

Lincoln took a step forward, towering over her. His mouth opened a few times but hinged back shut when it seemed he couldn't articulate whatever it was trapped on the tip of his tongue.

"I'm going to be completely honest with you. I was perfectly fine before you stormed into my life. I had a business plan that needed to be accomplished, one that would rightfully earn me my independence. I certainly didn't have time for distractions." Opal circled a hand between them. "But maybe God knew I needed you. And maybe you needed me."

"Seriously?" He barely managed gritting out the one word between working the muscle in his jaw. "Blowing most of my leg off to bring me to you?"

"No! You're not listening . . ." She pointed to the box. "Sometimes things happen. They change us, and life leads us to other paths."

"I didn't want this path and I certainly didn't want to like you!" His words had enough bite to have Opal flinching a step away from him. "I can't take this anymore!"

"Fair enough." She turned toward the computer to shut it down, knowing she'd laid it out there for him to shoot down. It shouldn't have been surprising, but the rejection left enough sting to make a burning sensation sweep over her eyes. She expected to hear him stomp away but wasn't prepared to be twirled around and swept into his warm embrace.

Opal only managed a small gasp before Lincoln's tense lips crashed into hers. Confused, all she could do was stand folded in his massive arms while he kissed her good and proper. Lincoln kissed like he was starved, reminding her of his large appetite for food. Never stopping with a small portion, the man set in to get his fill. He had most certainly set out to get his fill at the moment, and all she could do was generously serve it to him.

It lasted until they both needed air. Lincoln slowly ended the kiss and placed his forehead against hers. "I like you too much, Opal Gilbert." His voice broke as if finally admitting to his feelings caused him pain.

"I don't mind, Lincoln Cole." She trailed her finger-tips down both sides of his neck. "I don't mind it one bit."

Lincoln opened his eyes and angled to meet hers. "Opal, may I please just hold you for a while?"

She didn't like the way his request sounded like it had an expiration date, yet she nodded in agreement anyway. The words wouldn't be shared out loud, but there was no denying she was in love with Lincoln and would gladly give him this small comfort.

He stepped over to the small love seat in the corner of her office and sat, pulling her onto his lap. His strong arms gathered around her with a fierce gentleness, hold-ing on as if she were his most prized possession.

"I've just wanted to hold you for so long . . . ," Lincoln whispered, tucking her head closer to him.

A few more truths were revealed as they held each other while listening to the rain tap a rhythmic beat on the tin roof above them. Lincoln Cole knew a thing or two about kissing. And Opal Gilbert might have been ill-prepared for what revealing her truths would set into motion.

●   ●   ●

Most folks thought Opal was a flighty woman who hadn't enough sense to grasp fear as much as she should. Opal never saw fit to correct them on their misassumptions, but she had fears just like anyone else.

A good kitschy horror flick with a staggering Frankenstein or masked murderer might not have done much to spook her, but put one of those demon-possessed tropes on and she'd vanish from the room quicker than an apparition doused with holy water. Growing up on the sprawling estate just inland of Sunset Cove, lizards and snakes were common and fascinated her to the point of setting out on amphibian expeditions, but let a spider or palmetto bug scurry by and she'd be fleeing the scene like a guilty vandal. And sure, Opal was known as a social butterfly, but that was how she combated her fear of rejection. Rejection had been a torturous part of her adolescent years, due to her not fitting into the normal box at school.

She'd learned to brush off most rejections, making her look brave perhaps, but right now she was paralyzed with fear of it as the beast of a man stared her down. She wanted to keep him more than her next breath, but even though he'd given in and admitted how he felt about her, Lincoln still kept a wall erected between them. It was a little flimsier than before but still there, nonetheless.

They'd spent most every evening after work for the past week exploring the newness of their relationship. He seemed to favor snuggling with her on the couch, even dozing off a few times. Last night's nap ended with him screaming out. He apologized profusely, but she told him to knock it off.

What was unnerving about it was the haunted look in his eyes afterward. Of course she asked again if he suffered from PTSD, but he said no, the nightmares only showed up when he was stressed, and his therapist had gone over coping mechanisms with him before discharging him. Opal was relieved that he'd gone through therapy, but she didn't feel any better because that meant he was stressed, and that made her wonder if she was the cause of it.

"You listening to me?" His gravelly voice growled the question, snapping Opal out of her thoughts.

She narrowed her eyes and gave him her best mean face. "What?"

"We can handle this one of two ways," Lincoln said, returning her mean face. Or that's what he was going for, but his lips refused and kept tilting into a playful grin.

Opal fought off her own grin and bucked against him. "I'm a grown woman. I'll handle things however I see fit. You don't boss me around." She tried again to wiggle from underneath him but his hands clamped against her sides once more, sending her into another fit of screeching giggles. "Stop tickling me!"

"Tell me yes and I will." Lincoln dug into her sides again until Opal squealed for mercy.

"Fine! We'll waste what I cooked and order something, you big ogre!" She bucked against him again, and this time he stopped tickling her and rolled over. Both lay sprawled out on the worn wood floors of her living room, staring at the whitewashed-plank ceiling while panting. She reached over and slapped him, but before her hand could retreat, he grabbed it.

"What was that for?" Lincoln asked, pulling her hand close and delivering a kiss to the back of it.

"For tickling me," Opal said breathlessly, still trying to catch her breath. "You're mean."

"Not mean." Lincoln flipped her hand and placed a kiss on the palm. "And you know it."

Sure, she knew it, loving this playful side of Lincoln Cole. He'd let the grumpy facade slip since that monumental kiss last week, revealing a big ole teddy bear underneath. Funny how little Miss Dalma had been right about him all along.

Opal and Lincoln kept their distance during working

hours, but as soon as the store closed for the day, they morphed into forms resembling lovesick teenagers. Who knew holding hands, snuggling on the couch, or wrestling around her living room floor would have been so appealing? It was beyond appealing and all-out overwhelming, but Opal couldn't quite let go of the fear of him changing his mind on the idea of them as a couple. Time would tell, she supposed, but in the meantime the only thing to do was enjoy the gift of his affections.

"Next time you're gonna let me choose supper. Fair is fair."

Lincoln rolled his head in Opal's direction, giving her a perfect view of his handsome face. He'd trimmed his beard, so those full lips were on better display as he pouted them out. "As long as it's nothing nasty."

"Our definitions of this word differ." That was something else she feared. What if Lincoln grew tired of her weird approach to odd food or fashion or life in general? She shook off the anxiety those thoughts conjured and scooted over until she was close enough to lay a kiss on those pouty lips. "You like me, right, Lincoln?"

He closed the gap between them when she leaned away. After he finished laying a perfectly convincing kiss on her, he murmured, "I think I've made that clear at this point." With one more kiss, this time quite chaste in comparison, Lincoln rolled to a sitting position and then slowly rose to his feet to help her do the same. "Now, as I was saying before you got all mouthy, we are tossing that concoction in the pot and ordering Chinese or a pizza."

Opal followed him to her kitchen and watched what she had thought was a stellar attempt at making sukiyaki go into the trash. At least Lincoln was direct about things he didn't see eye to eye with her on, like her cooking skills. That gave her a little bit of hope to combat the fear of rejection. Perhaps when he grew tired of her quirks and was ready to move on, he'd be up-front with that as well.

As Lincoln stood at the sink, scrubbing the rubbish stuck to the bottom of the pot, Opal sidled up behind him and wrapped her arms around his lean yet solid waist and held tightly. "Thank you."

Lincoln kept washing the pot as he looked over his shoulder. "For what?"

"For being honest about not liking my food. And for kissing me. I really appreciate the kissing."

His chuckle was so deep that Opal felt it reach her where she clung to him. "You can show your appreciation by ordering delivery. I'm starving." He finished rinsing the pot and placed it on the dish rack before drying his hands and turning around to face her. "And after that, I wouldn't mind kissing you some more."

Grinning up at him, Opal ran her fingertips through his dark beard and giggled. "Sounds like a plan."

Opal couldn't help but wish for the plan to become a more permanent part of her life. But until Lincoln dealt with whatever problems he had with his family and made peace with them, there was no use in trying to move their relationship any further. A few times, words almost slipped out demanding that he open up to her about what he was hiding from, but she held them back. She knew they would probably make her ornery soldier turn tail and flee as fast as his gimpy leg would carry him.

13

Weakness was never an acceptable role for a Cole man to portray. If any ailment was to pop up, the knee-jerk response was always to buck up and take it like a man. Lincoln wanted to live up to the expectations of his father even if they were estranged. That weakness in his leg, though . . . he'd tried bucking up and taking it like a man. He'd even hoped getting lost in the newness of his relationship with Opal would ease the pain. No matter how many sweet stolen kisses he'd collected from her in the last few weeks, the nagging weakness wasn't getting any better. Lincoln had given it his all but—

"Did you hear me, Mr. Cole?" The doctor's voice pulled Lincoln out of his thoughts about that certain red-head and pushed him back to the blaring reality of being in the doctor's office getting news he didn't want to hear.

Lincoln glanced up from his clasped hands and squinted his eyes at Dr. Rabin. "Sorry, what?"

"I've spoken with your orthopedic surgeon, and we both feel it's in your best interest."

"So you want to cut my leg open just to poke around?"

The doctor tossed the rubber gloves and pulled up Lincoln's file on the laptop. "Your mobility isn't progressing as predicted. After discussing this with Dr. Sykes, we suspect there may be some shrapnel causing the recurring infection, and there may be some other possible improvements to be made since the last surgery."

Lincoln exhaled sharply. Another surgery would have him back to square one. "I just ain't all that inclined to having my leg sliced open again."

Dr. Rabin typed something in Lincoln's file before looking up, his bifocals perched on the end of his nose. "Our goal is to get your leg to a healthier state. If not, amputation may be the only option."

"Oh," Lincoln mumbled, the wind knocked out of his sails at that one word. He looked around the room, wishing his meddling pixie were there to hold his hand, but she had prior obligations at her church. She had offered to tell them she couldn't make it, but Lincoln had insisted that she go since he knew how important her church was to her. He'd grown dependent on her presence in such a short time, yet another reason he felt so weak that day. All two hundred and fifteen pounds of him were on the verge of falling apart, and he knew that if Opal were there, he could handle it much better. "But I thought swimming . . ." He swallowed past the lump in his throat. "I've been swimming the last month . . ."

"And that's great, but we still aren't where we need to be. Your pain level shouldn't be a constant seven or eight. Our goal was to have it down to around a three by now."

"I've been managing."

The doctor slowly shook his head. "I'm putting you on another round of antibiotics for the third time in the last two months for an infection in your leg, and your limp is more prominent than it was a month ago. Son, that's not *managing*." He placed his hand on Lincoln's shoulder, but the gesture offered no comfort. "I've had several conference calls with Dr. Sykes. He's the best of the best and knows your leg better than I do. He and I both agree you need to go back to Beaufort so he can perform the surgery, but I'll be honored to assist him in helping to give a war hero a better quality of life."

Lincoln felt the heat rise up his neck and cheeks. "I'm not sure I deserve such a title."

"I've heard there are about a dozen living, breathing soldiers who would say you deserve that title and then some. Seriously, schedule the operation and I'll be there."

To say yes would mean Lincoln had to go back to Beaufort and face the mess he'd made before running away. The fevered hurt in his knee seemed to travel up to his chest just thinking about it.

"Give it some thought, and when we do your follow-up next week, let me know your decision." Dr. Rabin typed something into the laptop but paused to glance at Lincoln. "I'm sending a prescription for the antibiotic to the pharmacy. You need something for pain?" When Lincoln shook his head, the doctor let out a snuff of laughter. "You are one stubborn man."

Lincoln couldn't disagree with that statement. He promised to give the doctor his answer on surgery at the next appointment. "Thanks for coming in to see me on a Saturday."

"No problem. You served our country and now have to live with what that sacrifice has cost you, so it's my honor. Glad you didn't put it off."

Lincoln snorted. "A certain someone wouldn't let me."

The doctor joined him in a chuckle. "Tell Opal I said hey."

"Will do." He hurried out of the office as quickly as his fevered leg would allow and, against the doctor's orders, headed to the church festival instead of going home and propping his leg up.

The church normally held an annual festival in October, but the hurricane had canceled those plans without permission. So they decided to hold a sweetheart festival instead. Seemed the entire coastal town was much like Opal when it came to bothersome circumstances. They didn't let anything keep them down for long before choosing a way around the obstacle life pushed in their way.

He pulled up to the church and took in all the glittery hearts and streamers dancing in the air. Everyone appeared to be dressed in the Valentine's theme colors of white, pink, and red. He glanced down at his hunter-green thermal shirt, knowing Opal would have something to say about it, but it didn't deter him from stepping out of the Jeep and going on a search to find her.

Among the dessert booths stood his pixie wearing a pink shirt with the words *All You Need Is Love* splashed across the front in silver glitter. Red tights with a pink tutu completed the outfit. A smile tugged at his lips as he moved closer and leaned to the side to find pink high-top Converses on her tiny feet.

"Please tell me you didn't make any of these treats." Lincoln quirked an eyebrow while moving his gaze from her cute getup to the bounty of chocolate goodies.

Opal giggled. "I dipped strawberries into plain ole boring dark chocolate, just as Josie demanded."

Lincoln inspected the three-tiered platter of berries and was right impressed. "They're beautiful."

"That was all Jo. She painted them with the white chocolate after I dipped them."

Opal plucked one with swirling white hearts from the platter and held it to his lips and grinned wide when he only took a tentative bite. After a few thoughtful chews, he leaned toward her hand and snatched the rest of the berry in one bite.

Before she could make another comment, Lincoln grabbed her hand and pulled her around the side of the building. After he glanced both ways and found the coast clear, he bent down and caressed her lips with his and found the sweet taste of cocoa and berries. "Hmm . . . I think chocolate-dipped strawberries are my new favorite food."

He went in for another kiss, but Opal dodged his lips and giggled. "For someone who doesn't too much like me, you sure do like kissing me."

"We both know me not liking you is just hogwash." Lincoln took hold of one of her soft curls and rubbed it between his thumb and forefinger. "You're all glittery. My own little fairy."

Her green eyes narrowed. "Stop sweet-talking me and tell me what the doctor said. You have another infection in that leg, don't you?"

He groaned, resting his forehead against hers. "Can't we just kiss?"

Opal pushed against his chest, so he reluctantly took a step back. "Linc—"

"Yes. It's infected. Got an antibiotic, though." Lincoln rattled off the information in a robotic tone while running a hand through his hair. He omitted the spiel about the surgery, knowing that was a can of conversation he had no desire opening while hiding behind the church.

"And you should stay off it, correct?"

"Yes," he answered on an exasperated sigh. "But I wanted to see you." Lincoln *needed* to see her but chose not to sound as desperate as he actually was. He knew as soon as he allowed Opal to get close enough, he'd grow attached. It was too late to dwell on that now, so he tried wrapping his arms around his newly acquired haven of comfort, but she took a step out of reach.

"You've seen me. Now go home." Opal pointed a pink-tipped finger toward his Jeep.

"What if I wanted to help out here for a while?" He moved in and used his thumb to wipe a tiny speck of chocolate off the corner of her heart-shaped mouth.

"That's sweet, but you need to go home and prop that leg up." She gently shoved him. "I'll bring supper over in a few hours."

The promise of food and a visit made her brush-off feel less irksome, so Lincoln nodded instead of protesting further. "As long as you bring some of your strawberries."

Her entire face beamed and it made a nice warmth flood his chest. "You got it. Now . . ." Opal pointed again. "Home and rest."

Lincoln leaned down and brushed a soft kiss on her cheek. "Yes, ma'am."

By the time he picked up the medicine and had propped up in his favorite chair, Lincoln's body was spent and more fevered than earlier. His phone alerted him to a new message. Hoping it was Opal saying she was on the way, he quickly fished it out of his pocket but cringed when he looked at the screen. Hesitantly he hit Play and listened to the voice mail.

"Hey, sweetheart . . ." His mom's voice trailed off, sounding unsure. "I . . . we miss you and wanted to check in. I haven't heard from you since . . . and, well . . . You should have come home for Christmas or at least called. The holiday just wasn't the same without you . . ." His mom hesitated and cleared her throat before whispering, "Son, it's time we fix this. I . . . *we* love you." Her heavy breathing filled the line for a few moments before the voice message ended.

Lincoln placed the phone on the end table and dropped his head into his hands. If his mom's words weren't enough of a reminder that he needed to face what was waiting for him in Beaufort, the angry heat and nagging twinge in his leg definitely drove the point home. He popped a few ibuprofens, hoping they would ease the ache in his leg and the pressure of a nasty headache that was building at a rapid pace.

While listening to the ocean waves rushing the shore just outside, Lincoln concentrated on taking even breaths. As the tears built behind his closed eyes, he began to pray. *I'm broken. My family is broken. Please, God, help me mend this mess* . . . He continued to pray until the tears subsided and he dozed off.

The sweet scent of honey mingled with the savory smell of fried seafood, and it was such a delicious combination it had Lincoln's eyes slowly opening and his mouth watering. He blinked a few times to find his fairy perched on the side of his chair, her smile soft and concerned.

"You okay, sleepyhead?" Opal whispered as though she feared startling him.

"I am now." He reached over and pulled her onto his lap, mindful of avoiding his bum knee. The pain still shot down his leg, so he shifted her until all of her weight was placed on his right side. She squirmed, seeming to want to be let up, but Lincoln only wrapped his arms more firmly around her and held on for dear life.

Opal sighed and rested her head on his shoulder. "You miss me or something?"

"I did."

"That's just too hard to believe. Was it only a few weeks ago you were doing everything in your might to run away from me?"

"'Cause I'm an idiot." He tucked her closer, needing some reassurance that he truly wasn't alone.

"I won't argue with you about that." Opal began

threading her fingers through his hair, instantly soothing some of his aches. "I've brought you a flounder sandwich and some onion rings."

Lincoln swallowed just as his stomach rumbled. "Feed me, woman."

Opal wiggled out of his lap and grabbed the to-go containers. They spent a while eating with her filling him in on the festival. "They raised a good bit of money for the homeless shelter."

"That's good. I like how y'all pick different groups to support each year." He took another bite of his savory sandwich and chewed thoughtfully. "What will they do with the money?"

"They plan on buying some hygiene supplies." Opal munched on an onion ring, looking a little lost in thought.

"What is it?" Lincoln asked before taking a sip of his tea.

She shrugged. "I have a pile of old bunk bed frames in storage I scored from an Air Force base that was shutting down. Been thinking about doing a fund-raiser where you and I restore the beds and have the community donate mattresses for them. And then we donate them to the shelter."

There she went again, taking something that was deemed worthless and wanting to restore it to a grander purpose. Lincoln admired her and deep down wanted to be more like that himself. "How many sets are there?"

Opal twisted her lips and squinted as if she were calculating in her head. "I'm not quite sure. A whole bunch of them."

"Figure out a total and I'll handle ordering the mattresses."

"Yeah?"

He nodded and reached over to swipe a handful of her

onion rings. "Yeah. I'm in the know on where to get stuff like that." He winked before popping one of the crispy circles into his mouth.

"Anything else happen at the doctor's office today?"

Lincoln looked up but quickly averted his eyes, knowing she'd see the truth in just one good glance. "Yeah. The doc said to tell you hey."

"That's it?"

"Close enough." He chugged the rest of his tea and gathered the trash. "You up for driving me around some back roads?"

Opal narrowed those beautiful green eyes, and he waited for her to call him out. Instead, she let out a long sigh and stood. "If you're gonna dodge the conversation, I'd be crazy not to take you up on letting me drive your Jeep." She dusted a few crumbs off her pink shirt, sending a sprinkling of glitter to the floor as well, and headed for the door. "Come on, big boy. Let's go get lost down a dirt road for a spell. Maybe it'll help loosen the truth from your lips."

Lincoln wouldn't be surprised if she'd already wiggled the truth out of Dr. Rabin. Nonetheless, he slowly stood from the chair with the aid of his cane and hobbled out behind her.

As the night moved slowly along with the lazy drawl of country music filling the quiet, Opal eased off the road and parked on the edge of a field that seemed to hold the entire moon and stars in its grasp. She turned the radio off and reached for Lincoln's hand, but that wasn't enough for him, so he pulled on their joined hands until she was wrapped in his arms. With the crickets chirping and the wind bristling through the trees, he tried kissing away his regret. It had become a permanent part of his daily life, but when Opal was near, it was more tolerable.

"Tell me, Mr. Astrologer, what are these stars trying to tell us?" Opal whispered against his lips, making them turn up into a crooked grin.

He sat back on his side of the Jeep and focused solely on her as he spoke. "When I gaze at those sparkly jewels, all they seem to tell me is wishing ain't as out of reach as I had thought. They've given me permission to want more than I should."

His answer seemed to make her eyes light up even more. She tilted her head toward the sky and asked coyly, "The stars tell you all that?"

Lincoln's eyes never left her as he reached over and traced the corner of her right eye, wanting to make himself perfectly clear. "My stars tell me so much more."

"You know you've really surprised me."

"How so?"

Opal smiled and shook her head. "I figured after that first kiss you would make a run for it and I'd never see you again."

"Then you don't know me all that well." Lincoln was well aware that he failed in many aspects of character, but one he held firm to was that when he made a decision, he stuck to it wholeheartedly. Perhaps Opal didn't understand what she was getting herself into by pursuing him, but that was neither here nor there as far as he was concerned.

"I feel like we've gotten to know each other rather well in the last few months." Opal paused and moved her attention back to the glowing moon. "I'd like to know you better . . . Maybe we can take a trip to Beaufort together so I can meet your family."

Lincoln's body was already heating from the fever creeping back on him, but the mention of his family had his skin prickling. He tried coming up with an answer, but nothing came to him. After several minutes of silence, he asked gruffly, "Can you take me home?"

"I didn't mean to upset you. Don't you want us to grow closer?"

Of course he did, but shame and uncertainty blocked the path at the moment. "I ain't sore about that . . . I just need another round of medicine."

Opal reached over and tested the temperature of his forehead. "Oh, you're burning up again." She hurried to crank the Jeep and start the short trek home. "You should have told me earlier. Going out tonight probably wasn't a good idea."

As the beachfront came into view under the street-lights and a bright full moon, Lincoln tried turning in his seat to face her. He had to stifle a groan when his knee made contact with the console, but he had something to say and needed to swallow past the pain to get it out. "Will you give me some time to get my health squared away before we go meeting parents and stuff?"

Opal glanced at him briefly before returning her attention to the road. "You've already met my family. In fact, you're invited to Bubba's birthday party next month. Momma's doing all the cooking and—"

"You know what I mean."

"Maybe you need to square away some things with your family too."

There she went calling him out on the very issue he was avoiding. It was the thing that had been nagging him the most since trying to mend his relationship with God. He also recognized the pattern that followed his prayers. The more he prayed, the more his family was pushed in his face. He gazed out the window, up to the clear indigo sky. *Okay, God. I hear ya. But I don't know how . . .*

Opal parked and hopped out of the Jeep and was

inside waiting for him with a glass of water and his medicine before he could limp up the steps.

"Thank you." He took both, downing the pills with
over half the glass of water. By the time he tipped the glass
away from his lips, Opal was holding out a conch shell.
"What's the wish?"

"My wish is that you listen to the doctor and do as
he suggested." She fished another small clamshell out of
her purse and dropped it onto his palm beside the other
one. "I also wish that you'll listen to God and to your
heart. They'll tell you how to square things away with
your family." She reached up on her tiptoes and gave him
a sweet kiss before leaving him with a lot to think about.

It was time to start listening for a change, instead of
ignoring his problems. Certainly the latter was only making things worse.

14

Meddling is how everyone always liked to refer to Opal's helping. A meddler is what they had called her for as long as she could remember. Still, being used to it didn't mean she cared for it all that much. They were all mistaken, in her opinion. What she did was help. Sure, it took folks time to see it that way, but almost always they did in the end.

Of course, Lincoln loved attaching the term to her name every chance he got, but he was the one forcing her hand. He'd brushed off the doctor's advice on surgery and wasn't making any moves to reconcile with his family, so he'd just have to deal.

As she regarded her newest meddling, Opal knew she was right to plan on begging for forgiveness later instead of asking for permission. And there sure was going to be a whole heaping lot of begging.

"So he needs more surgery?" The graying brunette with delicate crow's-feet lining her dark eyes glanced at Opal over the rim of her coffee cup.

"Yes, ma'am. Of course you know how stubborn your son can be." Opal picked at her breakfast absently as she watched Anita Cole do basically the same with her own meal. It was Opal's favorite, fried eggs and cheesy hash browns, at her favorite restaurant, Driftwood Diner, but uneasiness had squelched her appetite.

"That he is." Anita glanced around at the rustic dining area that was filled with chattering patrons and sighed heavily. "Lincoln doesn't know I'm here, does he?"

Opal fidgeted in her seat. "No, ma'am, but after we eat, I'd love to show you some of his projects at the store. He'll be out most of the day . . . You'd be proud to know that word is getting around about his architectural engineering background, and he's already signed on to help with a few reconstruction jobs."

"You don't have to sell me on how remarkable my son is, Miss Gilbert. I already know." Anita's dark eyes narrowed, looking so much like her son that Opal couldn't hold back the small smile.

"Of course you do. I just wasn't sure how much he's shared with you since moving here. And please call me Opal."

Now it was Anita's turn to fidget, and that was all the answer Opal really needed, but the woman replied just above a whisper, "We've not talked since he left Beaufort. I've called and left messages, but he won't return them." She paused to take a sip of coffee. After she set the cup down, her focus stayed on the chipped mug. "Things happened before he left, and that's between us, but for what it's worth, I really appreciate you reaching out."

"You're right—I don't know what happened between y'all, but I do know Linc really regrets it. He wants to make amends, but he doesn't know how."

Hope lit Anita's eyes. "He said all that?"

Opal nodded as she pushed an egg around her plate, leaving a yellow yolk trail. "In so many words. To be honest with you, I think he's so ashamed over whatever it was he did that he doesn't feel worthy of a second chance."

"Again with his stubbornness." Anita's eyes crinkled as she smiled and patted Opal's hand. "This is a start, though, and I'd love to see his work. He always loved tinkering around my father's shed growing up. I'm just glad he's finally doing something to make himself happy."

"Did being in the military make him happy?" Opal couldn't help but ask.

Anita let out another pensive sigh. "Most of the Cole men for many generations have served our country. I think my son felt obligated to do the same and he did an outstanding job, always went above and beyond his call of duty, but I honestly never thought it suited him."

That answered a few of Opal's questions but also formed new ones. Ones that didn't need to be answered in a public place with a practical stranger. She was appreciative nonetheless for some insight on Lincoln Cole.

After settling their bill, Opal and Anita headed over to the store. Opal began in the small yard and showed off the chair/tables, which Lincoln's mother oohed and aahed over. She led Anita around the showroom, pointing out each piece Lincoln had a hand in designing. They were in the midst of talking over a hutch that he had refurbished into a baby's changing table when the giant man limped inside and froze.

In fraying jeans, flip-flops, and a faded Hank Williams Jr. T-shirt that declared *A country boy can survive*, he should have looked cute and compliant. But Lincoln Cole was anything but. Intimidating and irritated was more like it.

Now that Lincoln was standing face-to-face with his mother, Opal could see so many shared traits. Anita was rather tall with dark hair and eyes, leaving no doubt he took mostly after her. But the stern rigidness of his stance and the deep scowl must have come from his father, because it looked nothing close to anything Anita would ever be caught carrying.

"Mom?" Lincoln's voice barely rasped the word over a whisper. His narrowed eyes slid to Opal, causing her face to heat in record speed. "You." And that word came out sharp enough to leave a mark.

Even though the blush scalded her cheeks, Opal stood straighter and squared her shoulders to ready herself for battle. "Yes?" she asked nonchalantly.

"You did this." Lincoln pointed to his mother.

"Son," Anita scolded, "no sense in being so rude." Anita stepped closer and Opal was prepared to watch the woman whack him in the arm like her petulant son deserved. Instead, she wrapped her arms around him and began to softly weep.

Lincoln kept his eyes fixed on Opal as he hugged his mother. An entire conversation was conveyed in that blazing stare in those few short minutes. Anger, confusion, a little hurt, but there was also a hint of gratitude that he would probably deny if she pointed it out.

Once Anita regained her composure, both Coles put on an affable facade and went to pretending nothing was amiss between them. It wasn't at all what Opal had expected nor desired for the outcome of the reunion. She wanted the air cleared, not for the issue to be shoved away like an insignificant piece of junk mail.

Lincoln kept his mouth on a mostly mute setting, but his eyes gave away the battle raging within him and Opal knew it was going to boil over at some point. Preferably once his mother was gone. Opal was right impressed with Anita, though. Not once did she trying pulling anything out of Lincoln. Surely years of raising him came into play with that move. She seemed content with keeping the conversation focused safely on the furniture pieces and their upcoming projects. Like any proud mother, she lobbed compliment after compliment at him.

When Anita reluctantly declared it time for her to go, relief washed over Opal. She couldn't have asked for a more civil meeting nor could it have gone any smoother.

She should have known better.

They stood in the parking lot concluding their good-byes. Anita glanced at Opal before lowering her voice, but the sea breeze carried her words anyway. "Lincoln, I'll make your appointment with the surgeon."

"Mom—"

"We'll go with you. Just like the previous times."

"No." Lincoln cut Opal a pointed look before bringing his attention back to his mother. "Nothing's been decided on surgery yet."

"Son, you need the surgery. And like I said, your father and I'll help you."

"I don't need him!" Lincoln yanked away from his mother's outstretched hand and stumbled a few steps away from her. "Nor do I need you!"

His baleful words came out like a weapon, meant to propel the woman away. And from the hurt pinching her features, it looked like he'd met his target.

"Son, that's not fair."

"It's no fairer than how I was treated . . . how he humiliated me that day. Or how he's degraded me most of my life."

Anita's brown eyes glassed over before tears spilled down her frowning face. "And no fairer than how you carelessly reacted to that humiliation and made it a hundred times worse."

"Enough now!" Lincoln's voice roared with ample indignation to firmly shut down the conversation.

"You've been through a lot, Son, and I wish beyond

wishing that I could free you from the chains it's wrapped you in, but only you can do that." She opened her car door. Just before climbing in, she said, "Your father will forgive you if only you'd ask."

As the car slowly made its way down the road, Lincoln hung his head until the curtain of dark locks concealed his blushing face. Opal's hand itched to reach up and move the hair away, but she knew it was in her best interest to stay put. She waited for him to yell at her. To scream at the sky. Anything. Instead, he said nothing, obviously shutting down. It was a defeated stance Opal had witnessed him taking a few times since they'd met and just as each time before, it made her soul ache for him.

Lincoln got into his Jeep and peeled out of the parking lot, reminiscent of the day they had met. The only difference was that she didn't chase after him right away this go-around, knowing he needed some space to cool down. There wouldn't be any flirting and tease this time. No, it wouldn't be nearly as fun as that first game of chase they'd played.

Opal lifted up a steady stream of prayers as she closed the store, knowing she'd need any answered prayer God was inclined to grant her before coming clean about her meddling and asking for forgiveness that wasn't much probable at that point.

15

Exhausted physically and drained emotionally, Lincoln slung his cane down in the sand and eased himself onto the top porch step. After a few stuttered breaths that did nothing to settle him down, he lowered his head into his hands and allowed the pent-up hurts their freedom. Wave after wave of emotion rolled over him. He could only hope it wouldn't overtake him completely.

A good bit of time passed as Lincoln sat there. The pounding in his head matched the throb in his leg, but he couldn't bring himself to stand to go find something to ease either one. Nothing really worked anyway. There was no motivation to do anything but sit there and wallow. The pain was deserved. His penance for the mess he'd made of his life.

The puttering sound of a familiar van pulled up in front, and when he heard the popping echo of the door shutting, the breath he'd been holding came rushing out. Lincoln had known Opal would make her way there eventually, and even though he was spitting mad at her, some of the pain in his chest instantly alleviated with her arrival.

Lincoln didn't look up, but moments later her clunky sandals came into view and stopped on the second step in front of him. Her tiny hand reached out and threaded gently through his hair, smoothing it back to reveal his damp face. His eyes remained downcast, ashamed to even meet her gaze.

When she didn't speak, he cleared his throat and rasped, "I'm good and sore at you."

Opal kept working her fingers through his hair, sending goose bumps down his neck and across his shoulders. "I know."

"You had no right." His voice came out close to a strangle from holding back all that wanted to be said. Nothing good would come from laying into her for meddling, and he was pretty sure she was remorseful about it anyway.

"I know," she repeated. While one hand kept slowly weaving through his hair, Opal placed her other against his neck. "Each pulse you have is another chance. Another opportunity." She grew quiet while keeping her fingertips pressed against his neck. After a minute or so passed, she whispered, "You're a living breathing miracle. Your life is a gift from God and yet you've just wasted eighty-eight chances to appreciate that in the last minute." Her fingers tapped the side of his neck, driving home her point.

"You don't know what I did," he bit out.

"You're right. I don't. So how about finally telling me." Opal went to move away from him, but Lincoln clamped his hands on her hips to help stay grounded while searching for the words.

"I've never been good enough for my father . . . I didn't just let my country down, but I became a disgrace to him. It was so bad that my momma put August up to trying to talk me into moving here. My own parents didn't want me anymore."

Opal's hand stilled in his hair. "Oh, Linc. Surely that's not true."

"It is." He swallowed as the stinging hit his eyes again. "The pain and shame after that first surgery was too much. And each surgery and recovery following, it got worse, so I started taking heavy pain meds to combat it."

"That's understandable—"

"No, it's not. I started using them to get away from my dad and not the pain. . . . I was staying with my parents, and he made it his job to make each day a living hell. Pointing out what I did wrong, what I should have done differently, and how I needed to suck it up and get my act back together." Lincoln scoffed and shook his head. "All this from him before I was even allowed to walk yet. And once physical therapy started, he was there for every session to bark orders at me and constantly degrading me in front of my therapists, doctors, and anyone else he could."

"I'm sorry he treated you like that."

Lincoln's head snapped up and met her watery gaze. Their conversation had started out docile enough, but the look she was giving him that matched her words was enough to have it careening into hostile territory. His lip snarled back as he spat out, "Don't you dare pity me!"

"I don't! But I do find it to be a pity that you're letting your father's actions tear you and your family apart."

"Not his actions. Mine!" Lincoln slapped himself hard in the chest. "It's on me."

"I don't understand." Opal finally dropped her hands away and took a few steps back down to stand in the sand, putting some space between her and his anger.

"Before coming here I was at my lowest. For months I stayed high on pills to stay numb to the world and didn't much leave my bed. Momma begged me to go to this family reunion. She finally guilted me into going, but I was too weak to do it sober. Took so many pills I barely knew I was in the world." Lincoln used the collar of his shirt to wipe his face as he took several jagged breaths.

"So you stumbled around and embarrassed your family?" Opal guessed.

Lincoln dropped his shirt and shook his head. "No. Pills . . . they didn't really have that kind of effect on me. I wasn't sloppy and falling down. More so, I was a zombie, but it also brought out a beast of anger in me. When I was high on them, I couldn't contain all the hurt and would lash out. That day at the reunion my father took it upon himself to shame and ridicule me each chance he got."

Opal took a step forward but remained in the sand with her arms crossed. "How?"

Lincoln looked away from her and trained his eyes on the ocean waves. "All that day different kinfolk kept coming up to me. They thanked me for serving our country, wished me to get well, most feeling sorry for me. And all the while my old man was quick to shoot it all down. He gave me a dressing-down about my wrinkled clothes, my long hair, my beard . . . I was unacceptable. And then in the midst of my grandfather retelling about my first tour where I saved a few civilians from a roadside bomb, Dad interrupted it to berate me for botching my last mission. Said it served me right to have my leg ruined . . ."

Opal's arms uncrossed and reached for him, but Lincoln jerked out of her reach. She gasped but didn't make another move to touch him.

"Dad kept slinging the insults about me until I lashed out . . . one punch . . . right in front of our entire family. Broke his jaw in a few places . . . All that anger exploded out of me in just one punch . . ." Lincoln shook his head and held up his index finger, still not believing he struck his father with so much malicious force that it sent the strongest man he'd ever known to the ground. "I somehow made it home, packed a bag, and ended up here . . . The guilt's been eating me alive ever since."

"Well, I think it's time for you to soldier up and go make things right with your father."

When Lincoln said nothing one way or the other, Opal surprised him by simply leaving with no theatrics. He could hardly believe that she had nothing more to say after his confession. One sentence and she was done. Maybe seeing the truth of him and his failures was finally enough to have her hightailing it. It was for the best. He knew she deserved a better man. Didn't make the sting of her rejection any less painful, though.

● ● ●

After a fitful night's rest, Lincoln knew there was no other choice but to do as Opal had suggested. The sun had barely begun its rise by the time he had the Jeep loaded up. He took a minute to sit on the bench by the door one last time before leaving it behind.

Pulling up to Growler's Bait and Grocery to grab a soda and a pack of Nabs for the road, Lincoln's mind was on the journey ahead and didn't notice one of the last people he'd want to run into. He had one foot already out of the Jeep before spotting Josie and wondered if he could load back up without her spotting him. Giving it a go, he eased his leg back inside and was about to close the door when the tall blonde turned and caught sight of him. She had that little lady Miss Dalma with her and both were dressed in fishing attire. Well, Josie wore a T-shirt and baggy jeans, but the lady was wearing a bright-yellow fishing bib and a hat filled with fishing hooks. She started pulling Josie in his direction in a flash, seeming rather nimble for a senior citizen.

"You beat the chickens this morning, young man. You going fishing too?" Dalma smiled pleasant enough, but he wasn't feeling it.

With a quick getaway not being an option, Lincoln let out a weary sigh and climbed out. "No, ma'am. I'm heading out of town."

"What?" Josie asked, somehow managing to stutter the one word.

"I've made a mistake back home and I need to go sort it out," Lincoln muttered while rubbing the back of his neck.

"This sounds like a conversation over a cup of coffee and a donut." The old lady climbed into his Jeep before he could figure out how to deter her.

"Whoa, Miss Dalma." Josie beckoned her to get out, but Dalma buckled her seat belt in response.

"It's early enough, the donuts will still be warm at Sunset Sweets. Don't that sound good, honey?" Dalma asked Lincoln as if Josie wasn't trying to pry her out of the seat.

Nothing sounded good, but he had no idea how to get the lady out of his Jeep that didn't require force. If anything, he could ditch them as soon as she climbed out at the donut place.

Josie gave him a rueful smile and quietly said, "Sorry."

"Follow us," Lincoln ordered in a resigned tone. There wasn't enough energy or fight left in him for it at that point. His plan was to drive over and barely slow down enough to let Dalma out before hightailing it out of town.

"What have you been running from?" Dalma asked as she fiddled with his radio, settling on some Southern rock station.

Lincoln opened his mouth to refute her question, but a confession fell out before he could catch it. He poured his heart out about what had gone down in Beaufort, emphasizing his nasty habit with the pain pills and how it escalated into the fight with his father. He could hardly believe he'd just spilled all that to a stranger, but she kept nodding her head like she understood and patted his arm every so often when he'd choke up.

Lincoln parked beside the donut shop and shut off the engine. "I'm supposed to be a Cole. A good Christian soldier. Not a pill-popping lowlife who can't control his fists." Instead of exiting or kicking Dalma out, he leaned his head back and let out a shaky sigh.

"You're certainly not the first Christian to flub up, and you won't be the last. . . . David was a scoundrel. You know that, right?"

He rolled his head in her direction and squinted. "Ma'am?"

Dalma waved a hand, trying to shoo away his confusion. "Moses was a murderer, King David committed adultery with a lot of *pretty awful* following that choice, and Peter flat out denied his Maker. God allowed them a second, third, and fourth chance. And eventually those thickheaded fellers got it right."

"I'm not sure my father will be open to giving me another chance."

"I don't know your father, but I had a daughter, God rest her soul, and any time she made a mistake or defied me, the most hurtful part was when she would shut me out. I'd imagine your father is probably more disappointed about you shutting him out."

"I broke his jaw!" Lincoln threw his hands up.

"Does he love you?"

Lincoln scrubbed his palms down his face. "I think so."

"Then he'll forgive you, but you have to go show him you're sorry. Don't be too prideful."

"That's why I'm heading home to make things right with him."

"That's a great idea." Dalma opened her door. "I don't know why you're wanting to lollygag with getting donuts when you have more pressing matters to get to, young man."

"Wait. Do you . . . ?" He pushed a hand through his hair and tucked it behind his ear. When she turned to look at him, he asked hesitantly, "Do you have any advice for me before I go?"

Dalma tapped her chin with her index finger with a gaudy ruby ring on it, which was the last thing Lincoln thought went with fishing gear. "If you can't tie a knot, tie a lot."

Lincoln blinked at her retreating form. "Come again?"

"Don't pay that last part any mind," Josie spoke close to Lincoln's ear, startling him.

He angled around and found her standing by his open window. "I need to hit the road."

Josie made no move to step away from his door when he cranked the Jeep. "Please tell me Opal knows you're leaving." She looked over her shoulder to make sure Dalma made it safely inside the shop. "Have the decency to let Opal know."

Lincoln gripped the steering wheel. "It's the only way. A clean break, or I won't be able to handle walking away."

Josie redirected her attention to him and clucked her tongue. "You? What about her?"

"Opal's so much stronger than me. She was the one who set this into motion. She had to have known this would be the outcome."

Josie waved off his excuse. "I need to get in there to Miss Dalma before she orders who-knows-what. Just go fix your family and your leg. Then come back here ready to fix things with Opal."

"I can't make any promises, but I'm going to do my best."

"That's all I ask." Josie took a step back. "Now go on so you can hurry back. No hem-hawing around." She motioned for Lincoln to get on with it.

"Will do." Lincoln settled in the seat and tried settling into the path he was about to take.

Three hours later, Lincoln saw the sign for Beaufort. It welcomed folks and let them know it was a historic location that had been established in 1711. As he passed it, a sermon he'd heard several times growing up came to mind. Sure, his and his father's situation was a good bit different from the Prodigal Son and his father, but the basis was eerily similar. Both sons had left behind a ruined relationship with their fathers, and after time passed and they digressed lower and lower, they'd both had to humble themselves and come home to ask for forgiveness.

Lincoln turned off the main highway and onto a narrow two-lane road, lined with ancient oak trees dripping with silver moss. It would lead him home within six short minutes. He could only hope his father would be as forgiving as the one in the Bible.

16

Opal knew before even stepping foot inside the beach cottage that it had been deserted right along with her. After Lincoln's confession the day before, she sensed it. He'd reached his limit. The problem was not knowing which direction he'd run. She hoped his path would lead him home to his father and then back to her, but that was probably hoping for too much.

She got no further than the tiny foyer before stopping, her gaze catching on the bench wedged beside the right of the door. A small dusting of sand in two distinct piles underneath it drew her attention, evidence that a few pairs of shoes had been kept there. The vision of Lincoln sitting on the bench to put on his shoes had a sad little smile pulling at her lips. It was hard to decide whether she was disappointed or relieved that he'd left it behind. Was it because he didn't want it, or was he planning to return to it?

Opal reached over and lifted the lid. It was empty except for the powdery-white sand dollar she'd given him the night of their first back-road cruising. The wish she shared with him over the shell whispered to her.

"I wish that wherever you end up finding yourself, you'll remain intact. You're one rare find, Lincoln Cole, just the way you are."

Opal brushed her fingertip over the smooth surface of the shell and decided to leave it there, hoping it was a clue that Lincoln would eventually return for it. And her.

She glanced at the wall clock that hung behind his recliner and sighed. She loved her Sand Queens meetings but just wasn't feeling it at the moment. Pulling her phone out, the thought of texting a cop-out was mighty tempting. With another sigh, she shoved it back into her pocket and headed out.

Today's meeting was going to be held on the back deck at Driftwood Diner with a few more joining the girls. Glancing at the lonely-looking cottage one last time, Opal got into the old car she'd inherited from her great-grandmother and made the five-minute drive over to the diner. She found Josie and Dalma at the deck table with Sophia, Collin, and Ty.

"Sorry I'm late," Opal said, a little out of breath. She made her way around the table, offering quick hugs to everyone except Collin. She picked the little guy up and dotted kisses all over his sticky face. "Yum! You taste like a pancake!" She smacked her lips, sending the toddler into a fit of giggles.

"Ofal!" Before she could protest, Collin reached down and came back with a fork full of dripping pancake. She had no choice but to accept the bite and the syrup dribbling down the front of her peasant blouse.

"So good," she garbled out before sitting him back in his high chair. "You're a special little man to have Mr. Jasper make you pancakes for lunch!"

Everyone at the table laughed. Everyone, that was, but Ty. Mr. Star Athlete was too busy studying his phone. In designer sunglasses, a hat pulled low on his head, and wearing workout gear, he was still larger than life sitting out there on that deck. And from the second glances of everyone passing by, there was no doubting people knew it was none other than *the* Ty Prescott.

Collin reached over with another mushy forkful and said in toddler gibberish, "Dada. Eat."

Ty didn't even bother to look up. Just leaned out of reach and mumbled, "No can do, buddy. Wasted carbs."

The little guy took it in stride and moved the offering to his momma. She started to accept it as Ty spoke in a distracted tone. "Mommy doesn't need the wasted carbs either."

Sophia's smile wobbled as she kissed the back of Collin's pudgy hand. "You eat it, baby. Jasper made them just for you."

Opal felt they needed a conversation change before she told Ty exactly what she thought of him, so she brought her attention to the little fisherwoman in her bright-yellow fishing bib and a floppy hat covered in shiny lures. "Miss Dalma, have you been fishing today?"

Josie swatted the air. "No. Miss Dalma decided to ride her bike to Growler's this morning. They gave me a call to fetch her after she started rearranging the drink and bait coolers."

"Why were you doing that?" Sophia asked, her perfectly sculpted eyebrows pinching together.

"I figured it would be easier to have your soda pop right beside the bait. You know, one-stop shop and be on your way. But looks like I'm the only one to think so." Dalma clucked her tongue while swiping an onion ring through a mound of tartar sauce.

As Opal unwrapped the covered plate waiting for her, Josie leaned close and whispered, "I'm here if you want to talk about it."

Opal picked up a wedge of lemon and focused on

squirting it in her glass of iced tea while trying to figure out how Josie already knew. "I appreciate that, but not now."

"What was that?" Sophia asked as she handed Collin his sippy cup. Even in yoga pants and a formfitting tank top with her hair tied back in a neat ponytail, the brunette was the epitome of poised and polished.

"Nothing," Opal said and immediately took a bite of her shrimp salad sandwich.

Josie and Sophia both watched her suspiciously and seemed to be ready to pounce on her, but Dalma let out a hiccup of a burp and sent the women snickering instead. Even Collin giggled.

But not Ty. He was too enamored with his phone to notice anything else. "I need to get in a workout." He stood while tapping out a text.

Opal jumped to attention. "Sophia, why don't you go with Ty and get a workout in with him. You know . . . have some *alone* time with your hubby." She winked at Sophia. "I'll take Collin down to the beach and see if the ocean can get the sticky off of him."

Collin bounced in his high chair and clapped his pudgy hands.

Sophia shook her head. "Not today, baby." She looked over at Opal. "I had him at Doc Nelson's office before coming here. Poor baby has an ear infection, so we have to get his medicine filled and then we're heading over to my parents' house."

"Oh no . . ." Opal reached over and combed through his baby-soft curls. "I'm sorry you feel bad. We'll go another time soon."

"What did that old geezer mean when he told me, 'Ain't nobody studyin' you'?" Ty inquired in a lame attempt at a mocking Doc Nelson, showing he was at least half-listening to the conversation going on around him.

Dalma cackled, sending her glittery lures to dancing along her hat. "He was telling you—"

"Doc just meant we needed to focus on Collin. That's all," Sophia answered over Dalma.

Opal smiled to herself, loving the way Doc Nelson had chided big ole Ty Prescott about thinking he was all that and a bag of chips, and he didn't even know it.

"Did you hear Doc Nelson is retiring?" Dalma chimed in.

"Really?" Josie asked while gathering the dirty dishes. As soon as she had them piled up, a busboy came by and began carrying them away.

"Yeah. Bertie and Ethel were carrying on and on about it last week. Said Doc has some fancy-schmancy doctor from Alabama taking over the practice next year." Dalma stood and her tiny frame let out a crackling sound. "Ugh. My bones are getting rusty." She made a face at Collin, making the little boy giggle.

"I'll meet you back at your parents', babe." Without a parting kiss for his wife or even a smile for his son, Ty tossed a hundred-dollar bill on the table and walked away.

The couple might have been too distracted, but Josie let Opal know she wasn't when the tall blonde latched on to her arm and said, "Opal Gilbert, you're not getting away so easily."

"What are you talking about?" Opal stuttered as panic kicked up her heart rate. She tried to recall if she'd meddled with Josie lately but was drawing a blank. Sure, she had something brewing, but not for the next twenty minutes at least.

"Don't you want to talk about Lincoln?" Josie nodded in encouragement.

Sophia paused in gathering Collin's belongings. "What's going on with Lincoln?"

"Oh, he just had some business to attend to back in Beaufort." Opal reached over and scooped up Collin for one last hug.

Once Sophia and Collin said their goodbyes and were out of sight, Opal said, "She's got enough on her plate. No need in bothering her."

Josie scoffed. "You're always there for us when we need you, but when the tables are turned, you're just going to brush us off."

"How'd you even know about Lincoln leaving?" Opal asked, scanning the busy beach shore. People were out walking dogs, collecting shells, or simply sitting in beach chairs while admiring the ocean waves.

"Miss Dalma and I ran into him this morning at Growler's on his way out of town."

"That's one strapping young man." Dalma whistled low. "All that long hair is something else."

Both young women paused to glance at Dalma. She grinned with no shame, owning her swooning like a champ.

Josie brought her attention back to Opal. "What can I do?"

People called Opal a meddler, but Josie was a fixer and she'd just given Opal the opener she needed to do some more meddling.

Opal wiped off some sand from the rail and leaned on it. "I need a distraction. Something to get my mind off Linc leaving." She knew he had to go, but it sure didn't make her feel any better about the way he went about it.

"You have any distraction suggestions? Or do I need to come up with something?" Josie was already pulling her phone out, but Opal waved her off.

"Remember that car Great-Granny left me in her will?"

Josie nodded. "The one you've had in storage for, what, three or four years now?"

"Yes." Opal motioned for them to follow her off the deck. "I want to donate it to the Grand Strand Car Museum, but I think we need to take it for a spin first."

"Can I drive?" Dalma asked, her face bright with hope.

"Mm . . ." Opal tapped her chin. "Maybe next time." She laced her arm with Dalma's to help the lady maneuver the sand.

Once they rounded the diner, Dalma came to a sudden halt. Her teeth came close to falling out. She shoved them back in and mumbled, "*That's* the car?"

Opal waved her arm, mimicking a game show hostess. "Teal-and-white '57 Chevy Bel Air. Maybe the finest automobile ever made."

"You are correct, so why on earth would you want to give this baby away?" Dalma unraveled her arm from Opal's and walked over to give it a thorough inspection. "Can we put the top down?"

"Sure," Opal agreed, and with Josie's help, the roof was down in no time. They were about to climb in when Dalma stopped them.

"Our outfits simply won't do. Josie, dear, take us to my house. Opal, follow us." She headed for Josie's truck without waiting for a reply.

Josie sighed, already wearing her martyrdom expression, while Opal clapped her hands and somehow found a giggle hiding just past her tender heart.

One Gorton's fisherman granny, one bell-bottom-wearing hippie, and one reluctant tomboy entered Dalma's beach house and went straight to what Opal viewed as a treasure trove of various decades' fashion that Dalma kept in the guest bedroom closet.

Thirty minutes later . . .

Three women exited Dalma's beach house, looking as if they'd walked straight off the set of *Pleasantville*.

Dalma and Opal donned lollipop dresses, white gloves, and their wild hair was pinned in updos. Their sling-back heels tapped down the outdoor stairs in an enthusiastic tempo. Josie followed behind them, wearing a silky sheath dress with a hemline just this side of being too short. She tugged it down and then adjusted the oversize white sunshades.

"The sunglasses are the only thing that fit," Josie complained, her flip-flops flapping out a much-less eager rhythm.

"The scarf fits too," Dalma defended, pointing to the polka-dot scarf tied around Josie's pinned-up hair. "You look prettier than Marilyn Monroe!"

Josie plopped her hands on her bony hips. "No, I don't. Marilyn would have had curves to fill this dress out." She helped Dalma into the front seat and shut the door. She then hiked up the already-short skirt a little higher, lifted a long leg over the side of the car, and climbed in the back.

Opal snorted. "That was *so* ladylike."

"That's as lady as it's going to get today." Josie waited until Opal was in the driver's seat to lean up and say just loud enough for only her to hear, "We look ridiculous. If anyone sees us—"

Opal scoffed out a laugh, cutting off Josie's threat. "Honey, this set of flashy wheels is about to be cruising down Sunset Cove Boulevard. There's no question we will be seen."

"And with us all spiffed up, I bet we'll make the paper and maybe even the news!" Dalma chimed in.

Josie tried climbing out of the backseat, one leg slung over the side before Opal stopped her with a serving of guilt.

"What happened to you wanting to be there for me?

Declaring it even?" Opal lowered her cat-eye sunglasses and raised an eyebrow.

Josie dropped her leg and huffed.

Dalma pulled out a tube of lipstick from her purse. She flipped open the sun visor and applied fire-engine red to her wrinkly lips with precision even though it bled like tiny rivers around her mouth. She turned from the small mirror and asked Opal, "How do I look?"

"Fabulous," Opal declared as Dalma passed her the tube, but she played at waving it off just to tease the old lady. "No, I shouldn't. Oh. Okay!" She accepted the Chanel lipstick and applied a quick coat and tried to hand it to Josie.

"I'm good."

"Oh, for heaven's sake, humor an old lady and put the dang lipstick on." Dalma plucked the tube out of Opal's fingers and shoved it into Josie's hand. "We're wasting daylight. Come on now, before Ethel's ornery butt shows up and tries strong-arming me into a nap. I only have a good decade left in me. I'm certainly not wasting it napping." Dalma pointed a stern gloved finger at Josie, finishing off adding a layer of guilt to Opal's effort.

Josie barely dabbed the lipstick to her puckered lips before handing it back, but Dalma seemed satisfied with her effort enough to turn forward in her seat.

Opal glanced at Josie in the rearview mirror as she cranked the car. Worry tried nagging her that if Josie was this tetchy about playing dress-up and cruising around town, she certainly wouldn't take well to what was in store during their little joyride. Never one to back out after committing to a task, Opal accepted a fallout would probably end up being the outcome and put the car in drive anyway. She took a deep inhale of the salty air infused with a hint of the car's old leather and gently pressed her foot to the gas pedal.

As the convertible began sailing down the narrow inlet road, Opal tossed a hand in the air and yelled, "Ya-ya!"

Dalma quickly joined in, her smiling face tipped slightly toward the gloriously bright sun above them. No doubt the image would have made a perfectly retro Grand Strand postcard. Before they turned off the avenue and onto the oceanfront road, Josie dropped her sulking and was pulling up a fifties music station on her phone. Going as far as *shoo-wopping* along with the song as the Bel Air moved at a crawl's pace down the breezy road.

After one pass around town, the three women really got into the spirit of things and brought out their best beauty queen wave and offered it to any passerby they glided by as if they were in a parade. Opal kept her mask of fun in place while her eyes frantically searched for the object of this little outing. She had it on good word that a famous artist was in town for Carter's thirtieth birth-day. August Bradford needed his attention pulled away from his world of art long enough to recall the hopes of one day including Josie in his world. It's what he shared in a late-night phone call last year, so Opal felt she was simply doing them both a favor. Hopefully, in the long run, they'd view it as such. A party was under way at the moment at the Bradfords' beach house. She and Lincoln were supposed to be in attendance until he bailed on her without so much as a word of goodbye.

Her lips began to frown, so Opal brushed those thoughts to the side and made another loop around town. She completed several more loops that had them driving by the beach house until finally she hit pay dirt. As they approached, a tall figure dressed in black with a matching beanie shoved low over his head stood from where he was crouched on the driveway. Once they were a little closer, Opal could see he was drawing something on the surface with his youngest brother. Both had chalk in their hands.

Opal beeped the horn and August Bradford turned to look in their direction. Wayfarer Ray-Bans covered his eyes but there was nothing obscuring the view of his wide grin as he dusted his hand on the side of his black jeans, leaving a streak of pink, before lifting it to wave at them.

Opal and Dalma returned it with their very best beauty queen wave while Josie let out a screech in the backseat.

She leaned forward and hissed in Opal's ear, "If you stop this car, you're gonna see a wrath that'll make Hurricane Lacy look like a subtle breeze."

The hairs on the back of Opal's neck stood, but she kept waving. Josie didn't pull out that lethal tone very often, but when she did, the naturally docile woman meant business. With no other choice, Opal reluctantly pressed her foot back on the gas pedal and drove past August and little Zachary. She glanced in her rearview mirror and saw his grin fade into a questioning frown as they left him right where Josie had kept him for the better part of a decade—out of reach.

Dalma turned in the seat and clucked her tongue. "Are you blind, Josie Slater? That's the best-looking feller Sunset Cove has ever produced. Why can't we just go back and look at him for a spell?"

Josie ignored the little lady and directed her attention to the driver's seat. "I should have known you were up to no good, Opal Gilbert."

Opal shrugged a shoulder while coming to a stop at one of the three stoplights in town. "I don't know what you're talking about."

Josie growled. "You drove by his family's beach house *six* times, so you can drop the act."

"What's so wrong with that?" Dalma piped in. "Humph. August sure doesn't look like a starving artist with those broad shoulders. Don't even pretend, girlie, that you didn't see how well he's filled out in the last six years."

"Yeah, well, I've concluded there's no reason to notice things that aren't . . ." Josie cleared her throat. "Besides, he's only here for a day and will be on a flight back to New York in the morning."

Opal glanced over her shoulder just before the light turned green. "Ha! You have been keeping up with him!"

"The entire town keeps up with all things August Bradford and are mighty quick to stop in at the counter and tell me all about it." Josie's voice broke on the last part.

Opal eased her attention to the rearview mirror and caught sight of Josie batting a tear away from underneath the edge of her sunglasses. She knew how her friend felt, dreaming for one thing only to be served another choice.

The Everly Brothers began singing "All I Have to Do Is Dream" from Josie's phone. The phone was quickly switched off and the joyride grew somber.

After a few sniffles from the backseat, Opal knew she had to rectify her well-intended wrong, so she dropped the subject and kept her foot on the gas until they'd passed over the old swing bridge. Just on the other side was a drive-in diner, complete with servers zooming around on roller skates. She pulled in and parked by one of the intercom menus, knowing a round of chocolate milk shakes was exactly what the trio needed.

With the awesome set of wheels and the women's killer outfits, they fit right in with the kitschy atmosphere and were treated like royalty. By the time the milk shakes and orders of onion rings on the house were delivered, the somberness had been lessened to a manageable enough size that the women seemed content with shoving it into the Bel Air's glove box to be ignored until a later time.

The ride back across the waterway, hands were catching the breeze passing by and smiling faces tipped in the direction of the sun. Opal was impressed with her and Josie's little act even though it would undoubtedly only last until each woman returned to her rightful home. Dalma began snoring, causing Josie and Opal to crack and let out a genuine giggle and grin. Opal reached over and straightened the tiny lady's head in a better angle before returning her hand to the steering wheel.

"This isn't our entire story, Jo. It's only a season." Opal glanced in the mirror long enough to see Josie nodding. "We just have to keep navigating it for now and be patient."

Josie said nothing, so Opal let it go.

Hopefully, the two brokenhearted women would find a way through the season of wait. Opal just knew that's what both of their situations were and felt certain that God had big plans just on the horizon. They just had to keep having faith in him and in their dreams.

17

No fanfare or welcome wagon greeted Lincoln as he stepped out of the Jeep and strode up to the front door of his parents' colonial-style house with its pristine white paint job, much to his relief. It wasn't a sprawling estate like what Opal's parents owned, but it had always felt like a castle to Lincoln growing up. Being the only child with his father oftentimes stationed overseas, it tended to be a lonely castle.

The crisp American flag waved proudly from its pole beside the porch with the red Marine Corps flag doing the same just below it. He took a deep inhale, taking in the familiar murky notes of the creek that ran the back of their property, before letting himself inside. It opened straight into the living room, which was dim with nothing but the late-morning light seeping through the sheer curtains. He knew where to find his father, so with a slow gait, he walked to the back of the house and stopped at the home office that was more of a hunting and fishing game room.

The door sat ajar, giving Lincoln a view of the worktable where his father sat meticulously cleaning a pistol. The scene wasn't playing out anywhere close to the one in the Bible. Lincoln figured it was in his best interest to stay rooted by the door.

"You just gonna stand there all day?"

Lincoln jumped slightly at the booming timbre of his father's voice. Colonel Jefferson Cole was one loud man even when he whispered.

"No, sir." Lincoln took a step inside the room but remained close to the door.

"This mean you're back?" He set the cleaning rod down, eyes trained on the barrel of the gun as he inspected it.

"Yes, sir."

"Suppose we need to clear the air on some things."

"Yes, sir." Lincoln looked his father over. Relief washed through him when no visible scar could be found along Jefferson's clean-shaven jaw.

Jefferson looked up from the pistol and raised a bushy eyebrow. "You gonna say more than 'yes, sir' and 'no, sir'?"

"Yes, sir." As soon as Lincoln answered, a smile cracked the stony expression on his father's face.

"You up for a walk?" His father's smile slowly seeped away as he looked at the cane in Lincoln's hand.

"Yes, sir."

Jefferson shook his head and stood from the table. In a gray T-shirt tucked neatly into a pair of black cargo pants, the man looked ready to take on the world. Or perhaps just a rebellious son. "Maybe we should just have a seat on the porch."

"Yes, si—Okay." Lincoln nodded and let his father lead the way, not feeling worthy enough to be followed by anyone, especially the highly decorated colonel.

As the day warmed and the birds chirped, the two men cowered in their wicker chairs on opposite sides of the porch. Neither seemed to know where to begin.

Finally his father spoke first. "Heard you need another surgery."

"Yes, sir, but that's not why I'm here."

"No?"

"No, sir." Lincoln shook his head but kept his attention on the budding azalea bush in his line of vision. The entire front of the house was lined with them. Most folks had bright-pink or white ones, but the Cole family was proud to have the red variety. "I'm here to ask for your forgiveness."

A silence stretched between them, making Lincoln more and more uncomfortable. He knew he didn't deserve his father's forgiveness, but boy, did he want it.

"And I need to ask for the same thing of you."

Lincoln's head snapped up and found his father watching him. "Sir?"

"Son, I've always thought I needed to tough-love you like I did my recruits, but I was wrong. You didn't need another drill sergeant. You needed a father. I'm just sorry that all this had to happen for me to finally understand that." Jefferson motioned between them. "And for what it's worth, I'm proud of you."

Lincoln's eyes grew hot as tears pooled. Before he could try blinking them back, they escaped down his cheeks. "But you said I deserved this." He raised his left leg slightly before gingerly setting it back down. He'd just finished another round of antibiotics, but his mangled knee had remained fevered this round.

"Those words should have never been said. I certainly didn't mean them. I was angry that *my* kid was the one to get hurt that day. You were a mighty fine soldier, and I had high hopes that you'd retire with the same honors all the other Cole men have earned." Jefferson stopped to clear his throat, seemingly aware that his voice was rising a little too loudly. "It wasn't fair to you."

"It's not fair for any soldier to get hurt or killed for that matter, but that's a risk that comes with the service." Lincoln wiped the tears away with the back of his hand. "I'm sorry I let you down."

"You've not let me down—"

"But I struck you." Lincoln choked the words out on a sob, the tears a steady stream. "That was beyond disrespectful." Shoulders trembling, his head sagged to the palms of his hands. Another spell of silence took over with only his sobs disrupting it until strong hands gripped him by the shoulders. Looking up through the sheen of tears, he watched in astonishment as his father knelt before him with his own set of glassy eyes.

"Maybe I needed to be knocked down to be able to see things right."

"No, sir. Not like that and certainly not by me." Sniffing, Lincoln used the sleeve of his shirt to mop his face and watched as his father sat back on his heels with agility most twenty-year-olds didn't even possess. There was no doubting that Jefferson was in better shape than him even without the knee injury.

"Suppose I could punch you back to make us even." Jefferson's face was set in stony seriousness.

Lincoln braced himself and jutted his chin out to accept it. "Yes, sir."

Jefferson raised his hand and gave Lincoln's shoulder a manly slap while letting out a boisterous chuckle. "That's my boy. Willing to take it like a man." His laughter died down as he grew serious once again. "But, Son, let's be clear on one thing. I'd never get any satisfaction inflicting pain on you."

"Yes, sir. I understand that more than you know." The

pain in his leg was nothing compared to the regret he carried for striking his father.

Jefferson stood, stretching his six-three stature to full height. "But could I strong-arm you into taking a trip to the barbershop with me?"

Laughter wiggled free from Lincoln, and the effect of it was cleansing. "No, sir," he managed to say, wiggling a laugh from his father as well.

"How about shaving that scruff off your face at least?" Jefferson hitched up a thick eyebrow.

"No, sir. I kinda like this look." Lincoln grinned while rubbing the side of his bearded cheek.

"Then I reckon if you're up to it, you can go help me check on the catfish hooks I set out last night."

Lincoln stood and picked up his cane. "So long as you don't plan on dumping me out somewhere along the river."

"Nah. I just got you back. Think I'll try keeping you around for a while." Jefferson slapped him again on the shoulder. It was forceful enough to make a weaker man cry, but Lincoln couldn't contain the appreciative smile. His father knew he could handle it, perhaps letting him know he was stronger than he thought.

"I'd like that . . . to stick around a while, if that's okay." He followed his father around the corner to the back garage, where the boat trailer was already attached to the white King Cab. Both the boat and the truck a reminder of a childhood where when his father was home, it wasn't so lonely.

"Good, because after you get that leg squared away, I'll need your help sorting through the bait shop." Jefferson let out a sharp whistle, producing Fletcher instantly. The ten-year-old German shepherd came trotting up to Lincoln and nudged his hand resting on top of the cane.

"Hey, old man." Lincoln petted the graying war hero.

Fletcher's handler had been one of Jefferson's best buddies. Vincent managed four tours without so much as a scratch but fell dead from a heart attack not even a week into his retirement. Vincent's will had left Fletcher to Jefferson.

"He seems to be doing well," Lincoln commented as he opened the back cab door for the dog to hop in.

"Oh yeah. Spoiled rotten as ever. Your momma cooks better for him than me." Jefferson climbed in and cranked the diesel, the rumbling a welcoming sound to Lincoln.

Vincent was like an uncle to him and his death stung, but Lincoln was glad his parents finally had a dog. When he was growing up, his mother had always said it was enough to tend to him while Jefferson was overseas. She couldn't fathom adding a dog to the mix. Funny how she had now grown more attached to the dog than anyone else.

Lincoln got so caught up in his reunion with Fletcher that he'd almost forgotten about his father's comment. "What did you mean by sorting through the bait shop?"

"Paps is finally retiring. The doors aren't reopening this season."

"Well, at eighty-seven, I'd say he's earned the right to close the doors. Too bad, though. That bait shop is a piece of fishing history in these parts."

"True." Jefferson headed over a bridge and then pulled into a private landing a little ways past it. He put the truck in park and began fishing underneath his seat, coming back with a familiar dark-blue cap with the Marine Corps emblem. "At least put this on so all that hair ain't in your face."

Lincoln took the offered hat and with a wry smirk slid

it on his head backward, effectively tucking the problem behind him. "Better?"

His dad gave him a swift nod. "Yes. Now I can see those eyes you got from your momma."

Lincoln couldn't hold back the genuine smile that comment produced as he scooted out of the truck. Even at thirty-three years old, it still felt good to receive a compliment from his old man. It made him feel special and wanted.

It was like second nature to be back helping his father guide the boat into the water, and so it took no time before they were coasting along the lazy river. Fletcher sprawled in the middle of the boat and kept a watchful eye out for wayward dragonflies or any other threat that might interrupt his peaceful ride.

Jefferson slowed the boat as a small red flag came into view where it was tied to a low-lying branch near the edge of the dark water. Lincoln didn't have to be instructed on what to do. Just simply leaned over, grasped the string, and began pulling it up. From the nonexistent tension on the line, he already knew it was empty but brought it up anyway to rebait it with some chicken livers his father had in a bucket.

Jefferson moved on down the river after the hook was dropped. "You mind telling me what the holdup is with having surgery?" he asked out of the blue as Lincoln leaned over and let the river water moving by wash his hand off.

Lincoln gave it some thought before answering. "I ain't gonna lie, at first it was because of us." He moved a hand between them. "I was ashamed to come back here. But last week the doctor warned that amputation may be the only option once they get in there and see what we're dealing with."

Jefferson scoffed. "That's what they said the first, second, and third time. Why let it get to you this round?"

"For one, my leg is in worse shape than it was. And . . ." Lincoln shifted on the bench and looked over at several turtles sunbathing on a floating log. "The first round, I didn't feel like I had much to live for. Didn't even care if I woke up from the surgery or not." He braved meeting his father's eyes.

A harsh grimace set along Jefferson's face. "Lincoln Alexander Cole!"

He tossed his hands up. "It's the truth."

"Whether you cared or not, I sure am glad you woke up from each and every surgery." Jefferson guided the boat over to another red flag. "From what your momma says, you have a lot to live for now."

Lincoln glanced up and found the grimace had been replaced by a sly gleam. Shaking his head, he grabbed for the hook and found it equaled the fierce tension building inside him from the uncomfortable conversation. "We got one." He fought with the line until a fat catfish finally surfaced.

Fletcher raised his head and barked at the creature flapping around as if to tell it to take its capture like a man. After giving it a sniff, the dog moved back to his spot and resumed dozing.

Once the two men had the fish placed in the live well, Jefferson headed on down the river another piece. "You gonna tell me about Opal or am I gonna have to drag it out of you?"

Lincoln rinsed his hands again and resettled his leg to a little less painful angle. While wrestling the catfish, he'd jostled it and his knee didn't take too kindly to it. "She's the most amazing woman God ever decided to create. She's kind, giving, beyond talented, and . . . I don't think I'm good enough for her."

Jefferson seemed to give that some thought before nodding his head. "You're right. You're not good enough for her." He gave Lincoln the look that meant for him to keep his mouth shut and listen up. "I'm not good enough for your momma, but thank the good Lord she'll have me anyway."

Lincoln remained quiet and set his gaze on the rust-colored water gliding by.

"And I'm thankful you've found someone to put up with your ornery hide too."

"Me too," Lincoln mumbled, wondering if Opal would put up with him any longer after he up and ran off like he did.

At the moment, he couldn't focus there. One mission at a time, and presently it was reconciling with his father, who was much more willing than he'd ever thought possible. A shell glinted from the riverbank and the sight of it made his throat thicken.

I wish for your relationship with your family to be mended.

So stunned that it left him breathless, Lincoln realized he'd just witnessed one of Opal's prayers answered on his behalf. Thinking about all the shells in the back of the Jeep, he could only wish that they would all be granted on his behalf.

Jefferson's phone rang and he answered it with several *yes, ma'am*s and *no, ma'am*s before hanging up. "Party's over. Your momma said for us to cut our river tomfoolery and get our behinds home."

Lincoln chuckled, helping to loosen the knot in his throat. "Sounds like Momma."

"And just so you're warned, she and your grandma are already working on putting together a feast for after church tomorrow to celebrate you coming home."

Tears sprang to his eyes, but Lincoln managed to keep them at bay this time. "Okay."

"We'll need to be ready for church by nine in the morning." Jefferson lifted his brows in challenge.

"Yes, sir."

"Son, I've held you to too many obligations. For that I'm sorry. I want you there not out of obligation, but out of want."

"I want to be there." Lincoln paused, searching for how to express what was on his heart. "I've always been honored to be your son . . . I just never felt worthy enough. And so I've not felt worthy enough to be God's child either since the injury."

"Again, that's on me. Tough love was what I was raised on and that's how I thought I was supposed to raise you." Jefferson glanced out over the water and then back to Lincoln. "I've spent a good bit of time since that day you left coming to terms with where I went wrong as a parent. I wanted to go to you afterward, even drove out there a few times. But Paps said you needed space, so I'd just drive around until I got a glimpse of your Jeep before heading back here. Seeing it was enough reassurance that you were okay."

"You did that?" Lincoln's chest tightened with a new-found emotion he couldn't even describe.

"Yes."

Swallowing with a good bit of difficulty, Lincoln rasped, "That really means a lot, Dad."

Jefferson let out a stuttered breath, revealing how much their talk was affecting him too. "I've learned the hard way that I was wrong, and I'm sorry if I've been a hindrance to your faith."

"Seems we've both gotten some things wrong, but I'm willing to work on mending them if you are."

Jefferson pulled the boat back up to the dock. "We'll have plenty of mending time after the surgery and during recovery. Now tie us off so I can go get the truck."

"Yes, sir." Lincoln was grateful he had time to fix things with his father and his father seemed just as eager to do so, but the surgery remained like a thorn in his side. His entire leg for that matter. Suddenly determined, he was ready to get that appointment made, no matter the outcome.

18

Focus had always been a strong suit for Opal. Most folks only took her at face value and considered her flighty. Those folks, with their misassumptions from judging her outwardly instead of taking a more attentive look, had no clue about the business degree she'd earned online or the fact that the store's office cabinets held the secrets of her success: detailed plans, budgets, advertising schedules, project proposals, etc. She'd always found it a fun game of sorts to keep that part of Opal Gilbert to herself and allow them to think what they would.

Admittedly, when Lincoln took off, he managed to take her focus with him. Right along with her heart and creativity. Working and holding the easygoing persona in place became a chore.

Opal's thoughts remained on Lincoln as she settled inside her office and turned the computer on to attempt getting some work done. A few hours passed, and the only thing she was sure she accomplished was missing him even more.

"What's on the agenda for the day?" Josie asked, startling Opal out of her thoughts.

She blinked a few times at the computer screen in her

office before glancing over at her friend where she was leaning on the doorframe. "Hey, you."

"What are you doing with that pile of new mattresses outside?" Josie hitched a thumb over her shoulder.

"We are going to deliver them, along with those bunk bed frames I refinished, over to the homeless shelter." The mattresses had arrived anonymously the day before, but she knew who was behind the delivery.

Josie straightened. "That's so nice of you. I like the nautical colors you chose to paint them."

Opal waved the compliment off. "It's no big deal. You painted that beach mural on the wall, so I thought the soft reds and blues would tie in well with it." She shut the computer down and stood up. "Did your daddy bring over a trailer?"

"Yep. He's outside waiting on your instructions."

"Great. Let's do this." Opal followed Josie outside, welcoming the afternoon's distraction.

By the time they moved out the old cots and set up the new beds, the sun had set on the day and Opal was plumb wiped out. Sophia and Ty had pitched in and donated new bedding. Of course, Ty's agent made sure the star athlete was photographed carrying bags of pillows into the homeless shelter, much to Opal's dismay. Once the beds were made, she snapped a picture with her phone and sent it to Lincoln. He sent back a thumbs-up emoji as his reply.

As she pocketed her phone and tried not to be disappointed at the brief response, Opal's father snuck in the back with pizza and sodas for everyone. She helped serve the food and was pleased with how her father was doing it privately, after the camera crew was gone.

After everyone was served seconds, Opal grabbed a slice of pizza, stood off to the side, and proudly watched her father share a meal with several homeless residents. Senator Gilbert spent a good bit of time listening. Many were war veterans struggling to fit into society. Their nightmares sent them to dark places, and they were using whatever they could find to combat them. Opal thought of another soldier down on his luck, praying he was finding his way out of his darkness. She wished he'd let her be by his side. Just thinking about Lincoln and their last day together ruined her appetite. Unable to stomach the pizza, she discreetly dropped it in the trash.

Opal considered herself one tough cookie. She had a fairly thick skin, due to dealing with people thinking it was their place to call her out on being different, but none of that had prepared her for the hollowness in the middle of her tender chest from missing Lincoln Cole. Some days, that longing left her aching to the point that she was almost convinced she was coming down with the flu. When no fever or other symptoms would show up, she'd allow a few tears in private before bucking up and carrying on.

Blinking the tears back now, she scanned the room once more and noticed how many sets of eyes looked as defeated as Lincoln's had the last time she talked with him. Unable to hold it together any longer, she slipped out the back and made her way home.

Later that night, Opal sat on the edge of her bed praying for Lincoln like she did every night. But tonight, her prayers shifted to asking God to lead her to a way of helping more soldiers having the same sort of problems as Lincoln. Surely there was something that could be done for the brave souls who defended their country. They deserved more than being tossed to the side like used-up, defective devices. Like her furniture pieces, even if they weren't able to do one task any longer, there had to be another purpose that could be found for them. They needed someone to care enough to guide and encourage them.

● ● ●

The plump middle-aged man shoved his glasses higher on his nose and squinted at Opal. "Are you serious?"

"Mr. Randal, that word and I really don't go together. Serious *seriously* clashes with my style." She straightened the oversize felt hat on her head, emphasizing the point. It seemed to only make the man more perplexed. A better part of an hour had been wasted following Mr. Randal around the showroom, and by the looks of it, it wouldn't be concluding any time soon.

"But the price is a little steep." He picked the tag up from the bakers rack and showed it to her as if she didn't already know the amount.

"The work it took to create it was steep as well."

"What gave you the wild hair to saw a dining table in pieces to make this?"

Opal stared at the rack. "There was a burn in the middle of the table, but it still had potential." She shrugged.

"Are these shelves even sturdy?" He reached out and pushed a palm against one of them, clearly no give to the shelf in sight.

Opal let that be his answer. "Feel free to look some more."

"No. I like this one, but what if I don't want to use it as a bakers rack?" He frowned at the tag in his hand before placing it back on the whitewashed surface.

"Then don't. It can be anything you want it to be." She kept smiling even though his frown deepened. It was all she could do to suppress an eye roll, baffled by how people seemed to always want to make everything so complicated.

After Mr. Randal circled around the bakers rack and tested the shelving once more, he asked, "Will you hold it for me?"

"Sure, but only for a week."

He balked. "Only a week? You held that porch swing for over a year for me."

Opal pointed toward the corner where the swing, made from three dining chairs, still sat. "Yes, and even though I had multiple offers on it, I held it, only for you to finally tell me *last* week you'd changed your mind."

Mr. Randal crossed his arms. "Well, furniture is a big commitment."

"Yes, sir." She nodded her head at the perpetual bachelor, thinking he had commitment issues all around. "Tell ya what, I'll hold it for *two* weeks."

It took more wasted time before he agreed and finally left Opal alone. As she watched the door close behind him, her phone started ringing somewhere within the showroom.

"Oh, shoot. Where did I leave you this time?" Opal began maneuvering around the furniture pieces on a frantic search to find it. "Please don't stop ringing!" The flashing screen caught her attention on an ottoman near the back. As she rounded a hutch, her foot slammed against it and she nearly toppled over. Stumbling a few painful steps, she managed to scoop up the phone and answer it. "Hello?"

"Why are you gasping? Are you okay?" Carter asked.

"Just . . . stumped . . . my . . . toe!" Opal screeched. She plopped onto the floor, yanked the flip-flop off, and chanced a glance at her throbbing pinkie toe. "It's still there."

"That's good. Look, I'm calling to let you know that tomorrow is a go."

Toe almost forgotten, Opal's chest tightened. "Okay. I'll be there. Thanks for letting me know."

"No problem. I'll see you then."

As the phone clicked off, Opal stared at the various furniture pieces, pausing on the ones Lincoln designed. She could only hope and pray he was ready to accept himself in a new light just as he so easily did with each creation he refurbished.

19

Postsurgery was always a weird out-of-body experience. Mouth pasty and body heavily weighed down, Lincoln became aware of the familiarity of it all coming back as he regained consciousness. What wasn't familiar was the antiseptic scent tinged with a hint of honey. It took a minute, or maybe an hour for all he knew, before he could talk his eyes into opening long enough to search for his sweet-smelling pixie, but he found her nowhere. He knew it was wishful thinking, but disappointment settled into his empty stomach anyway.

"It's about time you woke up," Jefferson said from the side of Lincoln's gurney.

Lincoln had seen his dad when he glanced around, but the scowl on Jefferson's face and the frustration with not finding Opal had him wanting to play possum, so he allowed his eyes to drift back shut.

"Son, you okay?" A firm hand clamped down on Lincoln's forearm.

Without opening his eyes, Lincoln mumbled, "Depends."

"Depends on what?"

"Do I still have a leg, and if not, are we still allies?"

"Yes to both." Jefferson's voice boomed around the recovery room, startling Lincoln enough to reopen his eyes.

He licked his dry lips and tried swallowing with a good bit of difficulty. "Then what's the verdict?"

Jefferson stood a little taller and released Lincoln's arm. "How about getting my boy something to drink." He barked the order, making Lincoln aware for the first time that a nurse was on the other side of the bed.

"Mr. Cole, does a Coke sound good?" the blonde asked in a soft tone, totally opposite of his father's.

"Yes, ma'am. Thank you."

"I'll be right back with it." She scurried away.

As the curtain fluttered closed behind the nurse, Lincoln's father began, "The doctor rattled on and on, but I'll spare you all that for now and just give a briefing."

Lincoln's mind was so muddled that he wasn't confident he'd understand a brief version, but he nodded his head anyway. The room swayed a bit, so he stilled and blinked up at his father.

"So your leg had all sorts of pieces of shrapnel so embedded that they were overlooked during the other surgeries. The doctor said this is common, but what's not common is that your leg even survived with that much damage." Jefferson sounded right proud of that fact, from what Lincoln could tell. "And, well, as that went to shifting around inside your leg, it caused more damage, so they removed as much scar tissue as possible and had to do an entire knee replacement."

"Again?" Lincoln already had that done once. The nurse hurried back in with a cup. She elevated his bed and held the straw to his lips. Lincoln took a sip and relished in how refreshing the cold soda was going down his parched throat. He went to take another greedy sip, but the nurse moved it out of reach.

"You need to drink slowly or risk getting nauseated," she warned with a look of pity.

He was already nauseated but decided not to share that tidbit, worried doing so would cut him off the soda supply altogether. He watched her place the liquid gold on the side table and jot something down in the chart before checking his vitals.

"Everything looks good. We'll be moving you to your room soon." Blondie smiled and left as quickly as she appeared.

"That woman is moving around too fast," Lincoln grumbled while rubbing his bleary eyes.

Jefferson chuckled and handed him the out-of-reach cup. "Don't guzzle it."

"Yes, sir." Lincoln held the paper cup tight and took a long pull from the straw.

"I'm gonna go get your momma before she storms in here and kicks me out."

Lincoln looked around again. "You been here the whole time?"

"Since you got out from surgery, yes. Had to make sure my kid was okay." Jefferson tipped his head and vanished behind the curtain as well.

Lincoln inhaled again, wishing to find a hint of sweet honey but only finding the astringent odor. When the cup was empty, he closed his eyes and tried to doze back off into a place where he could find Opal. It had been a lonely time without her, but a tiny package he'd received the day before had given him the encouragement needed to face the surgery and long recovery.

●　●　●

Nausea pitched Lincoln's stomach and sent the room into a spin, but he managed to swallow the bile back down. No way was he letting his father get the best of him again.

He knew he was stronger this time, and he was determined to prove it to Colonel Jefferson Cole.

"Stop acting like a little girl!" Jefferson spewed the insult as he slapped the mat near Lincoln's head.

Lincoln, in turn, groaned as he managed one more one-legged push-up. His chest and arms were on fire and sweat puddled on the mat below him, but he'd be darned if he was going to let his sixty-six-year-old father show him up.

Jefferson did as promised with the dare and did two more regular push-ups to Lincoln's one. "You . . ." He grunted and his arms shook as he finished the last one. ". . . ready to give up?"

"Ain't happening, old man," Lincoln said gruffly as he positioned his good leg to take on his weight while lifting the other.

They'd formed a good-size audience at the gym as the Coles went head-to-head in the push-up challenge. It had been their norm as of late. After the therapist took care of working Lincoln's healing leg, Jefferson would take care of working out the rest of him. The last month of competitions had been quite beneficial in more than just the physical aspect. They'd developed a bond that had never existed before now, and Lincoln was certain he could lean on his father on those hard days and have the man's support 100 percent.

Evidence of this showed up the day after post-op when a blood clot had formed. Jefferson stayed by Lincoln's side steadfast and comforting. He'd always been steadfast, but the comforting side had thrown Lincoln for a loop. Nonetheless, it had proven the dark days would be just as manageable as the easy ones.

"It's all right, momma's boy. You can phone it in,"

Jefferson whisper-yelled, sending a chuckle through the group watching on.

"This is a walk in the park!" Lincoln taunted as he pushed through another push-up, determined to go for one more after that to prove his point. "You . . . seriously need to . . . up the ante on these . . . sissy challenges." His eyes blurred and his chest screamed for him to hush up.

Lincoln would never admit the training with his father was more rigorous than basic training had been, but there was no denying how much stronger his body was growing from it. Most nights, Lincoln would fall into bed out of pure exhaustion. The nightmares didn't stand a chance, due to him being so tired his mind hadn't enough energy to produce them. As a result, Lincoln woke up each morning ready to get out of bed. The quicker he did, more often than not beating the sun up, the quicker he could get on with living.

The weighted defeat had lifted for the first time since waking from that first surgery well over a year ago. In the last month, he realized no pill or person or feeling could lift it. It was turning back to God and accepting his grace that had Lincoln finally finding his healing. No, he wasn't perfect and never would be, but God was willing to take him as he was—broken and defeated—and make him new. To offer a second chance at life and to be a beacon for others to do the same.

Seashore Wishes was a foundation placed on his heart to help other soldiers after coming home from career-ending injuries. It was only a wish at the moment, but Lincoln was confident that God would see it come to fruition. He'd not gone through that dark trial in vain. There was a purpose behind the second chance, and he lifted his own wishes that God would reveal it.

As he finished one more push-up before collapsing on the sweaty mat, Lincoln recalled one of the shells Opal had given him after that one botched physical therapy session.

The woman hadn't admitted it, but he had known she was praying for his healing. At the time he assumed she was praying about his knee, but now he suspected the wise woman was wishing for his soul and he was thankful it had come true.

"I . . . could . . . do this . . . all day," Jefferson grunted out as he pushed through two more wobbly push-ups. "But we've . . . got to . . . get to the bait shop." He collapsed in the same graceless fashion as Lincoln.

After showering, Lincoln rummaged around in his closet, where he'd left behind a majority of his wardrobe last fall. It took a while, but he finally found a pair of jeans with minimal holes and a plain, clean T-shirt. He took the time to pull his hair back, knowing it was the way his parents preferred him wearing it. His mother had commented on how beautiful and full his long hair was, but that she didn't care for it hanging in his handsome face. He'd give them that out of respect, but he made it clear no scissors were coming near his head. He'd also taken to keeping his beard trimmed neatly. Forgoing the flip-flops, he shoved on a pair of worn boat shoes and met up with his father outside.

"That walk of yours is getting smoother by the day," Jefferson commented. Of course, he was wearing a pressed T-shirt and cargo pants with shiny work boots on his feet. The familiar blue hat was shoved low on his salt-and-pepper head.

"Yes, sir," Lincoln answered. Thankfully, he was off the crutches and back to just the cane.

They both loaded up into the truck, along with Fletcher, and headed over to the bait shop, making small

talk the entire way with ease. Their normal tense quietness had abated ever since Lincoln had come home. For
that he was thankful. The two men talked constantly,
catching up on years wasted. It all came to them with
such ease that an outsider would have never guessed the
father and son ever acted otherwise.

"We got a job ahead of us," Jefferson said as they both
sat in the truck staring at the old store that looked like a
weathered shed with its natural wood siding and rusted
tin roof. A simple sign hung above the screen door—Bob's
Bait Shop.

"Paps know we're here to sort through it?" Lincoln had
only seen his grandfather at the Sunday dinner a month
back before he and Gran took off on an RV road trip.

"Yeah. His direct order was to have it done by the
time he got back." Jefferson chuckled and climbed out of
the truck with Lincoln following suit.

Lincoln pushed open the front door and was met with
dust motes dancing along the sunlight seeping in through
the windows. Off to the side, the antique soda cooler box
caught his attention. For old times' sake, he reached over
and slid one of the glass tops back, wishing it was filled
with the icy cold drinks again. Feeling nostalgic, he wandered around some more until his father declared it was
time to get down to business. They rummaged around
the dusty store for a while, discussing a plan of action as
Fletcher stretched out on the small front porch.

"I'd say call around to the other stores and see if they'd
like to take some of the supplies off our hands for a rea-
sonable price," Lincoln commented while roaming down
the aisle of artificial bait and lures.

"That sounds like a good idea. Paps said for us to take
whatever we want first." Jefferson held up a fishing dip
net and nodded his head at it.

Lincoln laughed at the unspoken joke in that, knowing his father wasn't going to let him forget about losing his net to an aggressive alligator last week. "May need to swipe a few of 'em to be on the safe side." He turned, being mindful of his knee, and headed over to the live bait section. Of course they had already been cleared out, but what caught his attention was the long wooden cricket box on a metal stand. He ran his fingers over the metal mesh fronts as he opened the hinged top. A segment of rotten potato had been left behind, adding to the sharp stench of ammonia. He overlooked the smell and kept inspecting the lid, finding the hardware a little rusty but in good shape. It always reminded him of a treasure chest in a weird way, and suddenly that childhood notion gave him an idea.

"Found something over there?"

"Yes, sir . . . Hey, how do you feel about helping me out with a project?"

"What do you have in mind?" Jefferson walked over with a few dip nets tucked under his arm.

"I think this cricket box is ready to be transformed into a new purpose."

"You think so?" Jefferson quirked a bushy eyebrow up.

Lincoln smiled. "Yes, sir." He lifted the side, testing the weight and finding it manageable. "You reckon we can get this loaded in the back of your truck?"

"I don't see why not." Jefferson walked to the door and whistled for Fletcher to come over. Holding the door wide, he pointed. "Sit." The dog listened, his big body holding the door open. "Stay," he commanded before walking back over to Lincoln.

They both took a side and began maneuvering the box out.

Jefferson's nose wrinkled as he angled his face off to the side. "Phew. You have any idea on how to get that stench out?"

"Yep," Lincoln grunted, trying to keep his leg out of the way. "Opal has shared a trick or two with me."

"Let's set it down on the porch for a few." Jefferson waited until they were past Fletcher and Lincoln began lowering his side before doing the same. "You missing her yet?"

Lincoln sucked in the fresh air to cleanse away the putrid smell stuck in his nose. "I missed her before I even decided to leave," he admitted, taking a moment to pet Fletcher. The dog seemed to not care for the smell, so he wasted no time moving to the other side of the porch.

"Why not go see her then?"

Lincoln patted the top of the box. "First, I need you to help me turn this into a treasure."

"I can try, but I ain't got much confidence in that happening." Jefferson regarded the rusty, stained box, looking unconvinced. He motioned for Lincoln to pick up his end.

After nearly dropping it just once, they managed to get the cricket box loaded up with little trouble.

"You have a seat and prop that leg up while I nose around a little more." Jefferson dusted his hands off and nodded toward the porch.

"I'm okay to help." He swatted a fly away and began heading up the steps.

Jefferson pointed to two chairs. "Sit right there and work on a list of supplies you'll need for the cricket box."

Lincoln did as instructed and sat. Before he could reach over and pull the other chair over for his leg, his father was there doing it for him. He bit the inside of his cheek to contain the smile. "Thanks, Dad."

Jefferson grunted in response and hurried inside but was back in a flash with a few life vests, which he used as pillows to prop Lincoln's leg. "Now stay put or I'll have no problem ordering Fletcher to stand guard."

Feeling like he truly belonged again as a Cole, Lincoln settled in the chair with no desire to go anywhere for the time being.

20

There was nothing quite as spectacular as a beachside sunrise, kissing the ocean with rays of pink and orange. Opal normally took the time to appreciate the view, but the early morning found her on a mission. Eyes on the sand, looking for a treasure to help send a message of encouragement to Lincoln.

Encouragement. It could be executed in infinite ways, but she remained true to the tradition she began with him last fall. It was always a shell and a simple line of encouragement to let him know she wasn't giving up on him.

A clamshell with both sides still fused together drew her attention. She bent down and plucked it from the sand, knowing what addition it needed to relay the message this time. It wasn't a pearl but was just as precious in her opinion.

Kicking her flip-flops off on the back deck, Opal made her way into the kitchen and rummaged around her spice cabinet for the little bottle of mustard seeds. It only took a handful of minutes to glue one of the tiny seeds inside the shell and tuck it into a mailing envelope. She added a small square of paper after scribbling a summary of the Bible verse from Matthew 17:20 and a line of encouragement—*Faith as tiny as a mustard seed can move*

a mountain. I have faith that you are moving mountains as
we speak.

She gathered her tote and the small package and
headed out to the post office like she had every Monday
for the past month and a half.

The gray-headed woman in her official blue uniform
straightened her glasses and narrowed her eyes at Opal
with disdain. "You again."

"Don't give me that tone, Ethel." Opal placed the
package on the scale. "You'd be bored out of your little ole
mind if I didn't come in here once a week to wake you up."

Most locals waited until they had to make a trip
inland to visit the other nearby post office just to avoid
Ethel Matthews, but not Opal. No, she'd taken on the
hateful old lady just for the challenge of it.

Ethel cleared her throat and punched the few keys on
her computer to process the small package. She yanked
the labels out as quickly as the machine spit them out
and slapped them on the front of the padded envelope.
"Two seventy-five."

"Why, Ethel, what if I needed stamps or packing
tape?" Opal offered a wide-eyed innocent face, sending
the old lady's scowl to wrinkle her wrinkles even deeper.

"Well, do ya?"

Opal leaned onto the counter. "Do I what?"

"Need stamps or tape or a straitjacket?" Ethel asked
through her gritted dentures.

Opal waved her off. "Oh no, ma'am. Just the package
today, but thanks kindly for asking."

Ethel had been rooted at that front desk in the Sunset
Cove post office for entirely way too long in Opal's opinion, as well as that of most of Sunset Cove's residents.
Even though she could have retired over a decade ago, the
crabby woman seemed to be staying out of spite.

She shifted on her stool and harrumphed when Opal pulled out a jar of coins and began counting the pennies first. "You've mailed that boy a love letter every week for six weeks now and ain't one time has he sent one in return. That should tell you something."

Opal let out a played-up sigh and moved the pile of pennies back to the rest of the coins. "You made me lose my count, *Ethel*." She put a lot of stress on the old lady's name. "Besides, how do you know he's not replied?"

"I sort the mail, you nitwit."

"Aww, Ethel, you do care about me enough to riffle through my mail and keep an eye out for love notes." Opal batted her eyelashes and began counting again, but this time out loud. When she'd counted out two dollars and seventy-five cents' worth of coins, she pushed the pile over to Ethel.

The seething woman glanced around, finally producing a small, discarded box. She shoveled all the change into it and tossed it underneath the counter. From the sounds of it, she lost a few wayward coins to the floor.

"Won't you get in trouble for that? Shouldn't you count it to make sure I didn't short you and then place it properly in your till?"

Ethel's right eye twitched, but she said not a word as she handed Opal her receipt, apparently wanting their visit to be complete. Smiling, Opal placed the receipt in her tote and retrieved the small pastry bag she always brought to give Ethel. Inside was one plain glazed donut and one chocolate glazed from Sunset Sweets—the old lady's favorite. Ethel took the bag with a wink, her way of saying thank you without having to use her rusty voice. Opal winked back and left Ethel with her treat.

Mondays had always been her favorite workday, devoted to projects with no interruptions. It had recently become a haven of solitude to let her carefree persona slip away and give the turmoil of missing Lincoln its freedom. That was mostly bouts of talking to herself, blaring country music, and a good ole cry session.

Opal unlocked the back door of Bless This Mess and let herself in. The hinges creaked out a reminder that it was time to oil them again, but she ignored it. She left her smile by the door and allowed her shoulders to droop while flipping the light on. Her gaze lifted to scan the room but froze on a new piece of furniture placed underneath the painting Josie had given her. Glancing around and finding nothing else amiss, Opal set her tote on the worktable and slowly walked over to check it out.

"Wow," she whispered, taking in the mosaic panels on the front of the long wooden box that sat on top of a brushed-nickel stand. Two artistic rectangles were fashioned from broken seashells. The tans and creams of the fragmented shells stood out from the soft-green paint with a limewash finish. She ran her hand over the top and came to a halt on the brushed-nickel plate affixed in the middle. The engraving sent a shiver down her spine. *Wishing for More Wishes.*

Biting her trembling bottom lip, Opal unclasped the lid and lifted it to find one single shell inside. Her heart squeezed at finding the sand dollar surrounded by the small pieces of paper that held her words of encouragement. She looked up and watched in astonishment as Lincoln walked in from the showroom. Her body swayed from the impact of seeing him. Even though he was using his cane, it was quite noticeable how much smoother his gait was than the last time she'd seen him.

"What do you think?" Lincoln asked, his gravelly voice taking up the entire space between them.

She couldn't look away from him to where he was

pointing at the long box. "It's the most beautiful treasure chest I've ever seen. I love the color."

Lincoln held her gaze and moved closer until she felt the heat from his presence. His hair was pulled back, giving her a clear view of the bronze-red coloring his high cheekbones. "The green reminded me of your eyes."

Opal blinked, sending a trail of tears down her face. "And the shells?" She coasted her fingertips along the mosaics on the front.

He tilted his head and waited until she met his eyes. "Every wish you've given me."

She sniffed and released a small laugh. "Not all of them. I just mailed one off today."

Lincoln gathered her in his arms. "We'll get it when we go visit my parents this weekend. I can't wait for you to meet my dad."

Opal buried her face in his shirt, breathing him in and thanking God he'd finally come back to her. "Oh, I've already met him." Even though a bevy of emotions had her insides vibrating, she found the tease to her voice that had been hidden away since he left. "Quite a character, that man."

Lincoln leaned away slightly and arched a thick eyebrow. "When exactly did you meet my father?"

Opal arched an eyebrow right back at him. "You didn't seriously think I'd let you have surgery without me being there, did you?"

"Humph. I thought I smelled honey when I woke up, but I assumed it was just wishful thinking." Lincoln squeezed her playfully. "You little sneak."

"August was there too, but I ended up staying until they got the blood clot cleared up."

"You were at the hospital the entire time?" His dark eyes softened.

"Mostly, but I stayed at your parents' house some. In your room actually." The heat rose along her neck and then on to her cheeks.

A rumble moved up his chest. "Is it wrong that I really like the idea of you in my room?"

Opal giggled before growing serious. "I wish I could have stayed the entire six weeks, though. I've really missed you."

Lincoln sighed and touched his forehead to Opal's. "I'm sorry it took me so long, but I hope you understand there was a lot that needed to be fixed with my family and my leg."

"Of course I understand, Linc. It was me who pretty much pushed you into going. You needed that healing. And now I hope you're back to stay."

"I'm here to stay." Lincoln's hands tightened around her as he nuzzled the side of her neck and placed several kisses there. "You know what I thought the first time I had my arms around you?"

"That you'd just as soon choke me?" Opal offered up the joke, but Lincoln didn't laugh.

"I thought how remarkable it was that you were so much smaller than me, but you were a perfect fit in my arms." He placed his lips near her ear and whispered, "I didn't want to ever let go."

"And I didn't want you to," Opal confessed as a shiver skated along her neck.

Lincoln straightened and placed a finger under Opal's chin, guiding her to look up at him. "I still don't want to let go, if you'll have me."

"I've never let go, Linc. Been right here holding on to all the wishes I've made for us."

"What do you say we fill this treasure chest with more wishes?" He tipped his head toward it.

She glanced around the room before meeting his eyes. "There's actually one wish I've regretted holding on to. It was something I wanted to share with you, but then you left . . ."

"What is it? We'll make it happen," Lincoln declared with much conviction.

Opal shook her head. "My wish was to share with you that I love you, Lincoln Cole. I regret not telling you that sooner. Truthfully, I've loved you since that day you told me I couldn't cook."

Lincoln's face lit with a grin, his brown eyes sparkling. "I think that was when I figured out I loved you, too. I mean, I love food but was willing to put up with you not knowing how to properly cook. Surely that's true love, babe." He winked.

Opal popped him in the shoulder, making him roar with laughter.

They certainly didn't fit into the normal couple mold—Opal always thought normal was overrated, anyway—but there was no doubting what the unique couple shared was true love at its finest.

EPILOGUE

The restoration business had taught Lincoln more lessons than he could ever have imagined. An important one was that nothing was too far gone to be restored, even though its new purpose might be different from its original one. It wasn't that long ago that he had viewed his life as too far gone to ever be restored. When his career as a soldier ended, so did his purpose. But God sure showed him, with the help of one lively sprite of a woman. Since coming to terms with his personal renovation, Lincoln finally had the courage to make plans for his new life. He had such a bounty of plans that most days it took him a while to get it all prioritized.

At the moment he was mentally sorting and figuring out how to get everything done. It was a busy time but a blessed time too. Smiling to himself, one important plan floated through Lincoln's thoughts as he drove the van down the beachfront road.

"Hey? Did you hear me?" Opal's tiny fingers wove through his hair, attracting Lincoln's attention.

He released the steering wheel and captured her hand before she withdrew it and brought her palm to his lips. "You forgive me if I didn't?" Lincoln asked against her warm skin.

"Well, when you go all sweet like this, I really don't have a choice in the matter." She giggled while taking her hand back when her phone chimed an incoming text. "I asked if you minded stopping by Driftwood Diner."

Lincoln checked his watch. The morning was already zooming by with delivering furniture, and the agenda for the day was brimming with more tasks needing to be met. "I have to work on some changes for the camp bunkhouses. Can we just grab something to go?" Even though the camp bunkhouses were top priority for Bless This Mess Renovations as well as the upcoming renovation of Doc Nelson's office, his mind kept wandering back to another plan he was burning to set into motion.

"Sure . . ." Opal fired off a text and Lincoln took a peek as he came to a stop at the red light. **Good luck. You've got this. Don't let her run away!**

"Who are you meddling with now?" Lincoln moved his focus back to the road as the light changed.

"Huh?" Opal mumbled while putting her phone away.

Lincoln pulled into the diner's parking lot and put the van in park before turning to eye the little meddling pixie. Even though they were inside the van, her red and gold hair shimmered like the sun. Those big green eyes shimmered too, but with pure mischief. "Don't play that innocent act with me. What are you up to?"

"I'm going to grab us teas and shrimp burgers real fast. We ate breakfast so early, I'm already hungry for lunch." She puckered her heart-shaped lips and leaned toward him as her hand reached to open the door.

He almost leaned away and demanded she come clean with whatever she was scheming, but there was no resisting Opal Gilbert and her magic, so he accepted her kiss as the distraction she clearly intended it to be.

"Hurry up with whatever meddling you have to do."

Opal giggled. "Yes, sir, sweet thang."

He cranked his window down and watched his world skip into the diner just as a familiar figure was stepping out. Lincoln chuckled, knowing now exactly what meddling mission Opal was on. She gave the guy a hug and a quick chat, and then August Bradford lifted his eyes and connected with Lincoln. He jogged down the steps and was beside the van in a flash.

Lincoln reached out the window and gave August a manly slap on the shoulder. "No piercings and no blue hair . . . What am I going to harass you about?" Lincoln shouldn't have been so amazed by the changes in his friend, since he'd done his fair share of changing as well.

August ran a hand through his black hair. "I'm sure you'll find something to razz me about soon enough. And you saw me after your surgery like this."

"Yeah, but I thought I was still under the influence of anesthesia and was hallucinating." For as long as he'd known August, the artist had always favored color on his hair and his canvases, but never in his wardrobe. Yet here he stood with natural-color hair, wearing a bright-yellow T-shirt and blue board shorts. Lincoln blinked a few times and shook his head. "Did you send Josie running?"

August tipped his head back and released a bark of laughter. "No, but I could tell she was thinking about it."

"Well, good luck with that." Lincoln smirked, knowing August had one heck of a challenge ahead of him with that tall blonde.

"I'm going to do my best." August lifted the plastic bag in his hand. "I better get this food to my brothers. I'll catch ya later."

"All right, man." Lincoln shook his friend's hand and waited until August walked away to pull his phone out and send Opal a text. **Get out of Jo's business and come on.**

Opal sent a selfie of her sticking her tongue out as a reply but she came skipping out moments later.

Once they made it to Bless This Mess, Lincoln scarfed down his lunch while working on a set of plans. A few hours disappeared in what felt like a blink.

He dropped his mechanical pencil and rubbed his eyes.

"Have you about got it worked out?" Opal danced into the workroom and came to a halt beside his chair, taking every ounce of attention he had.

Lincoln tilted his head and puckered his lips until she got the hint and settled hers against his. Sweet and warm and so inviting. Definitely a perk of working alongside the love of his life. Opal started to move away, but he pulled her onto his lap and directed her attention to the blueprints. "I went over to the office earlier and the good news is that this isn't a load-bearing wall, so we can get the crew to take it down." He pointed to the wall that divided the lobby and the reception area where a lot of wasted space had sat untouched for decades.

Opal settled in his lap and began working her fingers through the ends of his hair as she studied the plans. "It's hard to believe Doc Nelson is retiring. The man is such a permanent fixture in the community. He was everyone's pediatrician. Even Momma's."

"So you've said a million times already." Lincoln poked her in the side.

She jerked out the way, but he didn't let her get far. "Don't make fun. It's truly an end to an era. I just hope the new doctor can live up to this town's expectations."

"It'll be fine."

Opal tapped the blueprints. "I'm not so sure. I can't get over that Dr. Sawyer hasn't even set a foot in this town yet and is making all these changes."

"With the Internet, you don't have to be in person nowadays. You know as well as I do it was time for an update. The place looks right out of a seventies sitcom with the burnt-orange Formica counters and dark wood paneling." Lincoln wrinkled his nose.

Opal scoffed. "Nah-ah. It has a retro vibe."

Lincoln shook his head. "Now you're reaching. In three short months, we're going to start the process of progressing it several decades and on into the new millennium."

"Oh, I have good news, too."

"What's that?" Lincoln placed his pen down and tightened his hold around Opal.

"Daddy has agreed to back Seashore Wishes Foundation. He's even talked several other senators into coming on board."

"That is great news. Thanks, babe, for helping me with that." Lincoln pressed his lips to her soft cheek.

"We're a team, aren't we?"

"Yes, ma'am." He smiled warmly.

"I need to go lock the front up. I'll be right back." Opal gave him a quick kiss and hurried out toward the showroom.

Lincoln decided to roll up the plans and call it done for the day as well. He was about to finish a personal plan he'd been working on when Opal darted back in with the clock box from her office. "What are you doing with that?"

"Sit back down for a moment and I'll tell ya."

Lincoln glanced at the treasure box in the corner of the room. "What if I have stuff I need to take care of?"

"It'll keep. This will only take a minute as long as you're in an agreeable mood."

For the most part he was, so Lincoln sat back down

and felt even more agreeable when Opal settled herself on his lap. He loved nothing better than having her near.

"Do you remember the first time I shared this box with you?"

"Yes. I wasn't very nice to you about it as I recall." He set his chin on her shoulder and peered down at it.

"And you weren't all that impressed by what I kept as a treasure inside it." Opal ran her hand over the clock face. "But more importantly, do you remember me telling you that God knew I needed you?"

Lincoln's chest tightened, overwhelmed by how God had such a well thought-out plan for him even when his anger and shame had him too blind to see it. "Opal, he knew I needed you."

Opal turned sideways on his lap and placed the box in his hand. "See if the treasure inside impresses you this time."

Blinking away the wave of emotion, Lincoln flipped the lid open and could hardly believe what he found.

"Marry me, Linc."

Lincoln eyed the silver ring with a rich wood inlay. "What? No!"

"No?"

Exasperated, he snapped the lid shut and handed the box back. "You're always meddling in stuff you got no business meddling in." He eased her out of his lap, stood up, and began pacing the room.

"Wanting to marry your ornery butt is my business. What's so wrong with that? Just say yes, you stubborn man!" She stamped her foot and actually growled at him.

Taken aback, he halted the pacing and leaned close to her flushed face. "No," he repeated in a terse tone. "This ain't a part of my plan."

Opal looked so livid that even her red-gold curls

vibrated with anger. After letting out another growl, she turned to hightail it, but Lincoln caught her hand and twirled her back to face him.

"Now, wait just a minute." He jabbed a finger in the direction of their treasure chest, which was already filling with shells at record speed. "Go look inside and see how your meddling threw a monkey wrench into my plans."

She heaved a few haughty breaths before doing as he instructed, but with a good bit of trepidation. As the lid opened, a gasp echoed around the room, followed by a sob.

"You know how difficult it was to track down the perfect opal? One with enough green for my woman?"

Opal sniffled but kept her focus on the ring sitting among their seashells.

Lincoln reached over her and plucked the ring out. He'd had a jeweler place the stone in a delicate platinum setting, which took longer than he'd thought it would. He would have put it on her finger the day he came back home to Sunset Cove if it'd been ready. "Customizing a ring is quite a process. It's been in the making for a while now, but your little meddling behind just couldn't sit tight, could you?" He turned her around and wiped the tears from her cheeks with his free hand.

"I know what I want and I was tired of waiting," she screeched as the tears got heavier.

"Tell you what . . ." Lincoln placed the ring on her finger. "You agree to marry me, even though I can't drop to one knee and ask properly—"

She snickered through a sob. "You know traditional isn't my style anyway."

"Clearly . . ." Lincoln shook his head and rolled his eyes. "Can't believe you proposed to me on the same day I was going to ask you . . ." Lincoln tsked.

"Tell *you* what . . ." She reached behind her and pulled the ring out of the clock box. "You agree to marry me and I'll do the same."

"Yes," Lincoln whispered without hesitation and allowed her to slide the ring onto his finger. "There's a lot more wishes I want us to see come true, and the next wish I need granted is you becoming my wife. Right away."

"Yes. That's a wish I'd be happy to grant." Opal winked one of her knowing green eyes at him as she reached up and kissed him good and proper.

Lincoln hated to but he ended the kiss to tell her, "Your daddy said as long as I put aside reading the stars, I have his permission to marry you ASAP out at the estate. Your momma and mine have already gotten the catering and florist stuff lined up." The hippie astrologist had become a running joke between Lincoln and her parents.

Opal balked. "Really?"

"Yes, ma'am. They said all we gotta do is get dressed up and be there Sunday afternoon."

Opal twisted her mouth to the side, looking thoughtful. "I suppose that's doable, but, Linc . . . I really like when you tell me what the stars say."

He grinned so big, he could feel it all the way to his soul. "Baby, if you'll agree to marry me Sunday, I'll happily read them for you the rest of our lives. It'll be our little secret."

"Deal."

Lincoln leaned down and brushed his lips against his sweet pixie's, knowing as long as he stayed close to God and had her by his side, no wish was out of reach.

Watch for the upcoming releases in the Carolina Coast series, *Driftwood Dreams* and *Sea Glass Castle*

Turn the page for a preview of *Driftwood Dreams*

Available soon in stores and online

1

Standing in the midst of the ebb and flow of her daily chaos always gave Josie Slater the same feeling as standing in the surf—it was ever-changing, yet she felt trapped in the same spot with her feet slowly sinking in the sand. She absently handed an order slip to a passing waitress while ringing up the couple sitting at the counter in front of her.

"This place is amazing." The middle-aged man handed over a couple of bills.

"Why, thank you." Josie offered a polite smile along with his change. She didn't even have to be present in the moment anymore to serve up generous portions of Southern hospitality to tourists.

"The candied pecan waffles were delicious," the wife added as her husband helped her off the stool.

The couple had been sitting there chatting Josie up for the better part of the last hour about their thirtieth wedding anniversary trip to the Grand Strand. They were both dressed in brand-new swimwear and were pasty white, except for the fresh streaks of sunburn across their noses. Even if they hadn't told her, they were broadcasting their tourist status. Josie often wondered why vacationers couldn't figure out how to properly apply sunblock.

Over the years she'd seen various red-and-white stripes, Rudolph noses, hairline sunburns, and handprints.

Even with their neon noses, Josie thought they were the cutest and wondered if such happiness was ever going to be in the cards for her. Seemed the only card she owned was the one that kept her rooted behind this counter, parroting courteous responses to customer accolades.

The man wrapped his arm around his wife's shoulder. "And just think, we were about to walk on by, but the people piling in and out of this old building made us curious enough to step inside."

"A hidden gem is what Driftwood Diner is." The wife added a generous tip to the old-fashioned milk can that served as the tip jar for counter service. "It's the best meal we've had since arriving."

Josie couldn't agree more. She was right proud of the establishment created at the hands of her parents. The time-worn, rusted shanty sat proudly, even with its arthritic lean to the left, on the sand of coastal South Carolina and had been a prominent fixture in the Sunset Cove community for nearly four decades. Its breakfast fare was legendary, and it usually took just one taste of the biscuits and gravy to have a newbie hooked for life. Josie's father replaced the traditionally used ground sausage with chopped shrimp, taking the already-decadent dish over the top.

"Y'all have a good time at the beach, and be sure to come back for lunch." She waved goodbye to the couple.

"Oh, we will. I have to try the shrimp burgers." The husband waved one last time before guiding his wife out the screen door.

Josie continued on autopilot, gathering the dirty dishes and wiping down the counter while her mind wandered toward happier thoughts of the upcoming weekend meeting with the Sand Queens.

Just as the aged shack had held its ground against passing storms over the years, so had Josie and her two closest friends, Opal Gilbert and Sophia Prescott. The Sand Queens of Sunset Cove had affectionately earned their moniker from their mothers, who practically raised them on the very sand in front of the diner. Their bond was as solid as the galvanized screws that secured the tin roof to the graying clapboard structure.

Josie had witnessed a similar bond with the motley crew of geriatric ladies who were making their way into the diner at the moment. Well . . . her dad said *ladies* was too generous a word for the Knitting Club, considering they were a thorn in many a Sunset Cove resident's side. *Busybodies* was the term most folks used for the half-dozen or so old ladies of various shapes, sizes, and races.

"Josephine, this gout is killing me. Get us to our table 'fore I fall out," Ethel grouched, limping into the dining area, carrying her walking cane like a purse strap in the crook of her arm. She was dressed in her blue uniform, so Josie knew the ole grouser would be making customers miserable at the post office later in the morning. How the woman had kept her position as head postmaster for over forty years was an unsolved mystery. She also seemed to make it her mission to call everyone by the wrong name.

Case in point, Josie's name was not Josephine, but she chose to ignore it just as she did anything that could be considered confrontational. Instead, she pointed to Ethel's arm. "The cane would be more helpful if you'd actually use it, Miss Ethel."

"Oh, hush up." Ethel plopped into her chair as several other women followed suit, each one groaning and grunting while settling in at the long wooden table.

Josie gravitated to her favorite of the bunch with her

order pad in hand. "Good morning, Miss Dalma. What can I get you?"

Dalma Jean Burgess grinned up at Josie, showing off the fact that she had forgotten her teeth. Who knew where they would turn up? Josie made a mental note to look for them later when she stopped by Dalma's house.

"I'm fine, dear. I had a bowl of cereal earlier." Dalma plucked a sugar packet out of the small mason jar on the table, tore it open, and dumped the contents into her mouth.

Josie's eyes narrowed and scanned the tiny lady who didn't even make it past five feet in height nor one hundred pounds in weight. Dalma wore a pair of worn brown corduroy overalls with a fine silk blouse in a blush shade. A straw hat sat lopsided on top of a head full of long, wavy white hair. With the eighty-nine-year-old's ever-present smile and quirky wardrobe, she reminded Josie of a friendly scarecrow one would find in the corn patch out at Pickering Farms. Except for the pink bedroom slippers on her feet, that was.

"Miss Dalma, you're out of milk," Josie stated after refocusing on the woman's comment. Milk was on the shopping list she needed to knock out after her shift. "How'd you manage eating cereal?" She reached into the back pocket of her jean shorts to make sure the list was still there.

Dalma waved off Josie's concern, the overhead lights glinting off the giant ruby ring on her index finger. "I had vanilla ice cream. Works just as good as milk." She shrugged her thin shoulder and winked one of her cloudy-blue eyes. "Tastes better than milk, as a matter of fact. Will you add another pint to the shopping list?"

Even though Dalma had retired more than ten years ago, she would always be considered the town's librarian.

Josie recalled Saturdays spent sitting on a rug in the children's room while Dalma acted out whatever book she was reading for story time. No one could tell a humorous story like Miss Dalma, and yet her own story seemed quite tragic in Josie's opinion. She'd lived long enough to bury her husband and only child, leaving her alone except for her church family and the Knitting Club. And, well, Josie too. Five years ago, Dalma's mind seemed to start slipping, so Josie stepped in and designated herself as caregiver.

Josie scribbled *two fried eggs, coffee* on the order pad before moving her attention to Bertie, who was unofficially the ringleader of what should have been named the Busybody Gossip Club.

"I heard a certain someone was back in town," Bertie drawled while keeping her eyes focused on a menu she probably had memorized. She patted down the side of her freshly teased gray hair with her free hand, going for casual but failing.

A name, followed by an image, skirted through Josie's mind regarding who that certain someone could be, but she quickly shut down those thoughts and chose not to take Bertie's bait. Besides, there was no way he would ever return to the small town of Sunset Cove when the world was his oyster.

"Would you like the Sea Traveler's Special today, Miss Bertie?" It was her usual and Josie was trying to hurry things along, but when Bertie used the menu as a fan and grinned wide, she knew there would be no hurrying along whatever was going on.

"Ah . . . traveling the world . . ." Bertie sighed. "Such a romantic idea. Don't ya think, Josie?"

Josie's chest began to burn. It was the same reaction produced each time he drifted into town for a quick visit with his family. She always made herself scarce during those times, not wanting a reminder of all the dreams that one man represented that would never be hers. It was no one's fault but life itself, and Josie would willingly lay down those dreams all over again to be there for her father. Some folks declared her too shy, while others outright claimed she was too passive. Maybe she was a little more of both than she should be, but more importantly, Josie was loyal to a fault. And sometimes that loyalty needed her to put herself aside for the betterment of others.

"Did you hear me, honey?" Bertie's question dripped with false sickly sweetness, but Josie saw past it to the pot the old lady was working on stirring.

"Excuse me, ladies." Josie waved over one of her waitresses. "Tracy, please take these ladies' orders." She shoved the pad into Tracy's hands and hurried to the counter to find something, anything, to do to tamp down her emotions. She took a minute to shoot Opal a text, asking if she was planning on stopping by. When an answer didn't come in after a few beats, she slid the phone back into her pocket and rang up a customer with a take-out order.

After a small rush of customers passed through, Josie felt somewhat settled. She scanned the Knitting Club's table and caught Dalma pouring maple syrup into her cup of coffee. She was just a wisp of a woman but had filled a giant void in Josie's life. A smile pulled at her lips as she thought about helping Dalma plant tomato bushes the week before even though the lady adamantly declared they were strawberry plants.

Josie's reverie came to a screeching halt as the screen door squeaked open and ushered in not only a briny breeze, but also a vision from her past.

With a pronounced air of confidence, August Bradford walked over to the counter and halted in front of a dazed Josie. Her heart jolted at the sight of him, something only this man could elicit. He spoke—or at least his lips moved—but she couldn't hear anything over the roar suddenly residing in her eardrums.

The Knitting Club's table kicked up in volume, sounding like a bunch of hens clucking away, but there was no focusing on what they were clucking about either. She knew the answer anyway and had a feeling their timing wasn't coincidental. All Josie could do was just stand there and stare, as if looking into his silvery-blue eyes had turned her to stone. With a hint of purple near the center, those uniquely hued eyes were made to belong to an artist such as August Bradford. The thick fringe of black eyelashes only emphasized their beauty. It was enough to spawn jealousy in Josie, her own fair lashes barely visible, but it didn't. It only tempted her to stand there and stare unabashedly. Mouth agape, that's exactly what she did.

"Are you okay?" A throaty voice penetrated the roar in her ears as a hand waved in front of her face.

Oh, my . . . that voice . . .

The words simply wouldn't come—only pitiful squeaks of breaths escaped—so Josie did the only thing to come to mind. She hightailed it into the kitchen.

As the swinging door flapped a few times before shutting behind her, she knelt behind the workstation and tried working some oxygen into her seized-up lungs. The normal comforting scents of fried seafood and sizzling breakfast meats did very little to calm her as she slowly inhaled and exhaled.

"What in the world's ailing you, Jo-Jo?" Her dad turned his back to the grill, wiped his hands on his apron, and ambled over to check on her.

She shook her head when her tongue remained frozen.

The burly man glanced out the small circular window in the door and grumbled under his breath. "We got two girls out sick today and customers lining up. Whatever this is, you need to get over it."

"I just n-n-need . . . a minute," she managed to stammer out while wiping away the sheen of perspiration that had broken out on her forehead.

With another grumble under his breath, her dad pushed through the door and then let out a guffaw boisterous enough to have Josie scooting over to the door. She cracked it open just enough to catch sight of the dark-haired man at the counter. Seeing him was so exhilarating it was nearly devastating.

"August Bradford! All the way back from New York City! How are ya, boy?" Jasper moved around and grabbed the *boy*, who was close to a foot taller than him, into a bear hug.

"Good to see you, Jasper." August returned the hug with as much exuberance while chuckling in such a deep baritone it seemed to rumble throughout the building.

"Are you just passing through?" Jasper gave August's shoulder a firm clap before moving behind the counter.

"No. I'm home to stay." August settled onto one of the stools.

"Really? I figured those hoity-toity galleries up north wouldn't give you back to us."

"Nah. I have a few of my pieces on display in a couple different galleries there, but my uncle offered me the front space in his music studio here." August shared the impressive information with as much humbleness as if he had merely said his art would be on display at the run-down flea market up the road. It was a charming characteristic Josie had always admired about him.

Dishes clanged from behind her and drowned out whatever August was saying. She glanced over her shoulder and gave the guy on dish duty a stern glare, which he returned with a confused shrug as he dropped another pan into the giant stainless steel sink. She turned back to the cracked door and leaned her head out a little farther.

"Well, ain't that great. Sure is good to have you home." Jasper nodded his head, agreeing with his own statement.

August returned the nod. "It's great to be back. I was right homesick."

"I bet that uncle is gonna have you busy with the camp, too."

August let out another throaty chuckle. "Oh yeah. The list is a mile long, but I'm pretty stoked to be helping."

"What's the name of it again?"

"Palmetto Fine Arts Camp. We're scheduled to open the second week in June."

"You boys only got two months to get it together then."

Josie watched as August's eyes shifted from the chatty man and caught her peeping out the door. He bit the corner of his lip before looking back to her dad. "The camp construction is complete. All we have to do is go in and put our stamp on the place."

The two men talked a few more minutes with Josie only catching snippets of their conversation until a few groups cleared out and were quickly replaced by new customers. She knew her reprieve was about to come to an end.

"I know you ain't in here just to see my purty mug. You want biscuits and gravy and apple-stuffed pancakes."

August grinned. "Yes, sir. I'm hanging out with my kid brothers this morning, so I'll need three orders, please."

"I better make it four, then. Those boys know how to

eat. I'll get it going." Jasper turned his head in the direction Josie thought she was hiding. "Jo-Jo, get on out here and serve August a cup of coffee."

Josie nearly jumped out of her skin at the mention of her own name, making the door bang against the side of her forehead.

"She all right?" Josie heard August ask as she worked on rubbing the sting away.

"Who knows with that girl? Probably just hormonal or something." Jasper waved off August's concern and shuffled into the kitchen.

"Kill me dead now," she mumbled to herself, mortified.

"You ain't got time to be dead." Jasper gave his daughter a stern look, leaving no room for argument as he pointed to the door. "Get out there. Now."

Embarrassed and flustered as she was, Josie somehow managed to make her way out of the kitchen and over to the coffeepot. She poured a cup and placed it on the distressed-wood countertop in front of August without spilling a drop.

"Thanks." August lifted the cup in her direction before taking a sip.

"Thank you," she replied, feeling foolish. *Thank you?* She followed it up by blurting out more idiocy. "I'm welcome." After all these years, how could August Bradford still make her so tongue-tied and rattled? She was a grown woman, for crying out loud.

August was decent enough not to call her out on her jumbled response. The only reaction he offered to her word folly and twitchy behavior was a wry smile, which he covered graciously with the coffee cup.

His free hand smoothed over one of the planks. "I've always loved these countertops."

He seemed to be waiting for her to respond, but her eyes were fastened on the planks with her mouth pressed in a tight line. Some of the boards were naturally grayed, while others had light washes of white or teal. It was one of the last projects she had completed with her mom. Of course, her dad had grumbled at first but relented when they hauled in all of the reclaimed wood and set out to renovating the entire counter space, lengthening it enough to accommodate ten mismatched wooden barstools Opal helped them find.

Josie's eyes unlatched from the counter and flickered around the dining hall, where a collection of rustic pieces of art—mostly fashioned from driftwood, seashells, and anything else that had washed up on shore—hung on the weathered shiplap walls. Several weathered signs hung precariously about as well. One of Josie's favorites stated, *Time near the coast doesn't move by the hour; it moves by the currents, plans by the tides, and follows the sun.*

The diner was a relaxed space, inviting people to come on in whether they had shoes or not, but it no longer held that comfort for Josie. Not one new piece of art had been added since that awful life storm turned her and her dad's life upside down.

Blinking the memory away as best she could before it blinded her, she managed a somber nod before moving to the other end of the counter to refill another patron's cup of coffee.

She kept busy with taking orders, ringing customers up, and checking on Dalma. At one point, from the corner of her eye, she caught August swiping a postcard from the stand beside the register. On the front of the card, intended for tourists, was a picture of the diner with blue skies and ocean waves in the background. After grabbing a stray pen from the counter, he began doodling something. As curious as Josie was, she willed herself not to look over and inspect it.

Thankfully, August's take-out order came up shortly. Before she could key it in the register, her dad interrupted.

"It's on the house."

August shook his head and fished out the wallet from the side pocket of his blue board shorts. "No, no. Let me pay."

"Nonsense. This is my welcome-home gift." Jasper made a show of pushing the bag containing the foam carryout containers into August's reluctant hands. "Don't you dare be rude like that, boy."

Admitting defeat, August put away his wallet and accepted the bag. "Yes, sir. I appreciate it."

"You hitting the surf today?" Jasper asked, wiping his hand along the grease-stained apron.

"That was the plan, but the water is like glass." August stood up from the stool. "You gotta go surfing with me sometime."

Jasper cackled at the idea and slapped the pronounced O of his belly. "It's been too many years and way too many shrimp burgers for that."

"Nah, man. It's never too *anything* to pursue what you love." August fixed Josie with a meaningful look. "It was good seeing y'all."

"You too." Jasper easily sent the polite remark back while Josie stood beside him in her mute state. She had not uttered an intelligible word directly to him the entire time. "And tell your folks I said hey."

"Will do." August spoke to Jasper but his eyes remained on Josie, like he was waiting for something. When she remained silent, he appeared to give up whatever he'd hoped for and turned to leave. The Knitting Club began calling out to him, but he was smart enough to only give them a gentlemanly nod and brief wave. Before he made it completely out the door, Opal blocked his path. The shimmering halo of blonde-tipped auburn curls floated every which way as she did her little clap-and-hop dance at the sight of August.

Josie tried not to stare as August and Opal exchanged what looked like pleasantries. The friendly pair laughed at one point with Opal patting his arm.

Opal was an artist in her own right, who took what most people considered junk and restored it into newer, more unique pieces that she sold from her downtown store, Bless This Mess. Back in their youth, Josie and Opal had taken art classes with August at school as well as a few at the community center. Opal was social enough to befriend him, and Josie had been too awkward to do anything but admire him from afar.

Evidently time hadn't changed some things.

"I'll be by sometime this week," August's deep voice rang out as he headed outside, much to Josie's relief.

Opal nodded and waved before skipping over to the counter with a sweet smile on her fairylike face. Dressed in a peasant blouse, long skirt, and thick Birkenstocks, she was the epitome of cool and calm in the middle of the stuffy restaurant.

Even with several ceiling fans rotating overhead, sweat dewed along Josie's brow. She brushed away a damp lock of blonde hair that was beginning to stick there and mumbled, "Hey."

"Isn't it wonderful August has finally made his way home?" Opal's green eyes sparkled with enthusiasm.

"Umm . . ." Josie busied herself with wiping down the already-clean counter until Opal snickered. "What?"

"You still don't know how to come to terms with your crush on that man, do you?" Opal snickered again.

"I'm too old to have a crush on anyone. And who says I ever had one on him?" Josie's cheeks lit with knowing she'd just told two fibs. By the smirk on her friend's face, she could tell Opal knew it too.

"You're twenty-five years old . . . Keep telling yourself that," Opal said as she scooted behind the counter and helped herself to a glass of sweet tea as she had been doing for as long as Josie could remember. She then moved over and settled on the stool in front of the cash register. Her first sip almost sputtered all over the clean counter as she picked up the postcard and turned it for Josie to see. "Seems you're not the only one!"

Eyes wide in shock, Josie took in the simple yet astonishingly accurate sketch of her silhouette. She was amazed that a plain ink pen was used to create such a rendering and that a fifty-cent postcard served as the canvas.

"Oh, my goodness . . ." The wild beating of her heart started up again and the oxygen to her lungs was so sparse she grew pure dizzy.

"Are you also too old for love letters?" Opal pointed to the scribbling underneath the drawing. *Untie your tongue and give me a call sometime.* Along with the simple one-line note, August included his number.

"Humph . . ." Josie paced behind the counter while Opal sat on the stool in all her coolness.

Suddenly the Sand Queens' upcoming get-together felt foreboding. Opal and Sophia would have quite a fun time at her expense. They were like sisters, which meant they were loyal but loved to rib one another.

Exasperated, Josie left her friend at the counter, marched straight outside and plunged herself into the ocean. No, not really, but she sure did consider it.

DISCUSSION
QUESTIONS

1. *Beach Haven* is not only the book's title but also the name of Opal's beach house. What haven do Lincoln and Opal find during the course of the story?

2. Hurricane Lacy wreaks havoc on the town of Sunset Cove. What role does the storm and the rebuilding in the aftermath play in the plot?

3. Opal uses her quirkiness and eccentricity as a shield from what? In what ways can you relate to this?

4. The Carolina Coast series is centered around the loyal friendships among the Sand Queens and, to a lesser extent, the Knitting Club. Compare and contrast these two groups. Do you have a close group of friends such as this?

5. The author enjoys infusing comic relief into her stories. Does any particular scene from this book come to mind?

6. Brokenness is a common theme throughout *Beach Haven*: Lincoln's injury, which left him unable to fulfill his duties as a soldier; Opal's occupation of repairing and repurposing damaged furniture; the destruction and rebuilding of Opal's store. How

do these fit together to form a new purpose for Lincoln's and Opal's lives?

7. Opal openly presents Lincoln with seashells and prayers ("wishes") on his behalf. In contrast, she presents her faith to him in more subtle ways. How can using subtlety sometimes have a bigger impact on someone than being more obvious?

8. At first glance, Lincoln is an ornery man with a harsh exterior. What are some instances that come to mind where he lets that slip away enough to reveal the tenderness and vulnerability hidden behind it?

9. Even though Lincoln's leg injury and his relationship with his father are both repaired, how did they change him? How does he finally come to appreciate these new changes to his life?

10. The next book in the series is *Driftwood Dreams*. It centers around Josie and August. From what you've learned about them in *Beach Haven*, where do you see their story heading? What do you look forward to discovering in the next book?

NOT OPAL'S
CRAB BISCUITS

Ingredients:

> 2 cups Bisquick
> ¼ cup (½ stick) unsalted butter
> ⅔ cup milk
> ¼ cup shredded cheese
> 16 ounces lump crabmeat

Topping:

> ¼ cup (½ stick) unsalted butter, melted
> ½ teaspoon garlic salt
> ¼ teaspoon Old Bay seasoning
> ½ teaspoon parsley

Preheat oven to 450°. Combine Bisquick and butter, using a knife or pastry cutter. Mix in milk and cheese, then fold in crabmeat. Drop by heaping spoonfuls onto a baking sheet. Bake 10–12 minutes until golden brown. Meanwhile, mix topping ingredients. Spoon mixture over freshly baked biscuits and enjoy!

Makes 12.

These babies are pretty tasty on their own, but they are even better when served with a rémoulade made by combining the following ingredients:

½ cup mayonnaise
¼ cup sour cream
1 tablespoon Dijon mustard
¼ cup spicy relish or a relish of your choice
1 teaspoon garlic puree
2 tablespoons chopped chives
Salt and pepper to taste

A NOTE FROM
THE AUTHOR

I have a collection of accessories, as most of you probably do. Earrings, necklaces, bracelets, rings, scarves . . . I love the collection and the options I have to complement various outfits. But I have a few pieces that complement anything, and I rarely take them off: my wedding ring and a pair of small diamond stud earrings. Both are expressions of my husband's love for me.

I view relationships in a similar light. Friends should complement your life and never take away from it. I worry that so many women don't understand this nowadays and have dressed their lives with toxic relationships. For this reason, I created the Sand Queens and the Knitting Club for the Carolina Coast series.

The Knitting Club is the older group of ladies. I had such a blast writing these zany characters, but they have a serious purpose. From six to twelve members, depending on what day of the week it is and who is available to attend their gatherings, I view this group as your wider accessory collection. Not every piece will pair well with every "outfit"—every moment in life—but when they do, watch out! Perfection! I have a similar group of friends who are always there at the right moment, no matter how much time passes between visits. We have busy lives that lead us in different directions, but when we do meet up, it's always a gift.

Then there are the Sand Queens. This tight-knit group is there through thick and thin, complementing any and every moment you find yourself in. They are my wedding band and diamond earrings, always present and highly valuable in love and loyalty. This friendship consists of only a few women who are closer than sisters. In this series, you will see how Opal, Josie, and Sophia each bring a unique quality to their friendship that complements the others.

Opal brings liveliness and provides you with courage to step out of your comfort zone. She's the one pushing you to take a chance and there to cheer you on all the way.

Josie is the shy yet tenderhearted one. Ready to hold your hand and cry with you. She is a quiet force behind the scenes.

Sophia is the voice of reason. She will talk you off the ledge and then give you a much-needed straightening out after it's all said and done. She is fiercely loyal and ready to go to bat for you.

I'm blessed with a Knitting Club and a Sand Queens group of friends, both important in their own way. I encourage you to identify your groups, seeking healthy relationships to complement your life.

Thank you for taking the time to get to know the groups in *Beach Haven*. I can't wait to share more of them with you in the next books!

BEACH HAVEN
PLAYLIST

"Bless the Broken Road"
by Rascal Flatts

"Leave the Night On"
by Sam Hunt

"Sway"
by Danielle Bradbery

"The Long Way"
by Brett Eldredge

"Hard Love"
by NEEDTOBREATHE

"In Case You Didn't Know"
by Brett Young

"Prodigal"
by Sidewalk Prophets

"A Country Boy Can Survive"
by Hank Williams Jr.

"Boy"
by Lee Brice

"Simple Man"
by Lynyrd Skynyrd

"Stars"
by Skillet

"Small Town Boy"
by Dustin Lynch

ACKNOWLEDGMENTS

I'm sure you've heard the saying "It takes a village to raise a child." I've come to understand that it takes the village of Tyndale House Publishers to guide this author in the traditional publishing world. I know I am in good hands. I'm so thankful for Karen Watson, Jan Stob, Amanda Woods, Elizabeth Jackson, Andrea Garcia, Maria Eriksen, and the entire Tyndale family.

So . . . there's one village member I must address all on her own. Quite frankly, this woman struck fear in me with her vision for this book series. My editor, Kathy Olson, came to me with the suggestion of changing the order of the books after I'd written them. First reaction: Oh no, ma'am! But I'm glad I took a breath before responding and chose to take her up on this challenge, because the stories have become so much more as a result, and I'm beyond proud of their messages. Thank you, Kathy, for challenging me to approach the process of writing differently and to keep an open mind.

I love, love to write, but so much more goes into it behind the scenes. I am grateful to my wonderful agent, Danielle Egan-Miller, for handling the business part of creating stories so that I can enjoy the fun part. You have no idea how great a burden you have lifted off my shoulders, Danielle. I truly appreciate your tenacity and enthusiasm for my dream and guiding it to become my reality.

My family has to put up with me, and that is one monstrous task when I am engrossed in my creative world. I am thankful that Bernie, Nathan, and Lydia have never complained about my absentmindedness or distraction during writing bouts. Support and encouragement is what they've offered. I'm blessed to be on Team Lowe. Love y'all.

Teresa Moise, you probably know this story better than I do by this point. Thank you for listening to me hash out scenes and ideas on our three-mile morning runs.

My Sand Queens—you know who you are—thank you for complementing my life.

Christina Coryell, we've come a long way. I am honored to be your friend and author-sister.

God has granted me this wish to write and share stories. He has also blessed me with reading friends who are as passionate about my stories as I am. Thank you.

ABOUT THE AUTHOR

TONYA "T. I." LOWE is a native of coastal South Carolina. She attended Coastal Carolina University and the University of Tennessee at Chattanooga, where she majored in psychology but excelled in creative writing. Go figure. Writing was always a dream, and she finally took a leap of faith in 2014 and independently published her first novel, *Lulu's Café*, which quickly became a bestseller. Now the author of ten published novels with hundreds of thousands of copies sold, she knows she's just getting started and has many more stories to tell. A wife and mother who's active in her church community, she resides near Myrtle Beach, South Carolina, with her family.

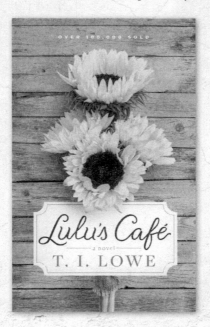